Happy
With Nothing

By W. Brunson Snipes

For

Grandmother Dot

Thursday, November 2

1

Paul Self stood at his bathroom mirror with a tie draped over his neck, both ends hanging down to the belt loops of his pants. He looked in the mirror one more time. Leaning in to examine the hair on his face he wondered if, in retrospect, he should have shaved before his shower and putting on his shirt. It was the nicest shirt he owned. Button up, button down collar, no stains. He had only worn the shirt one other time that he could remember, to a cousin's wedding two years before. The shirt hung in his closet ever since, unwashed and not ironed, but like his face and the hairs there, he had examined the wrinkles and decided they were not too bad.

Paul was not alone in his bathroom. His tabby cat, Daisy was laying on the floor behind him, sprawled out on the cool linoleum, uninterested in anything but a small spider walking along the crevice between floor and wall. Every swat of Daisy's paw was unsuccessful as the spider was too small and Daisy's paw too big to hit him. The spider was direct in its intention, scared no doubt at this furry monster attacking him but focused on the closet door of the bathroom where the towels were, knowing if he could just make it back to his home he would be safe.

"Daisy, this is the day. The day I change my life

forever." On a constant pursuit to make himself better, Paul had read countless self-help books or maybe only the first chapters of many. Sometimes only the back of the book and the first page held his attention. But nonetheless, he was always striving to improve and find the secret that would make him happy. Whether it was how to make more money, how to have more charisma, how to be more confident, he wanted to know. Truth be told, to Paul's understanding, all topics were stepping stones on the same path to the same destination--How to get the girl.

And finally the day had arrived when everything would change for Paul. The beginning of his plan was to be put into action. "Can you imagine Holly's face when I drive up this afternoon in that car?" Paul had begun fumbling with the tie at this point, putting one side on top of the other and twisting it, and pulling the end through. "This is the last time I'll be leaving to go get in that old junk car out there. Women love sports cars, Daisy. She won't be able to resist me." He said it in a half mocking way, doubting if deep down a girl like Holly would ever want a guy like him.

He pulled the tie apart and once again each end was hanging independently of the other four inches above his belt loop. He took a deep breath and stared at his face in the mirror as if concentration would help him recall how to knot his tie. One more attempt that went awry. He gave up and pulled the tie from his neck.

"You know what Daisy, I don't think I'll need this after all. It looks too pretentious, don't you think? The people at the bank probably hate customers coming in all dressed up to get a loan. I bet it's a red flag somehow." Still Daisy was more interested in the spider than in anything Paul had to say. One more jab with his furry paw was to no avail as the spider slipped under the closet door.

Paul tucked his shirt into his pants and made a quick smile into the mirror, practicing the impression he hoped to make on whomever it was that would make the decision. Impression is the first key to success. He looked good, he thought. "Yeah Daisy, I'm ready. This bank won't know what hit them." He realized how threatening that sounded and smiled as he imagined some outlaw saying the same thing in their bathroom before putting a gun in their holster and heading out the door with a completely different intention in mind. But he liked the feeling. It gave him a sense of strength that motivated him even if it was fleeting.

"Okay Daisy, I'm off to sign the papers. When I come home I'll be a new man." Looking at the clock beside the bed of his tiny studio apartment Paul saw that it was already 8:55. His plan of being at the bank when it opened was abandoned. He was mad at himself for not waking up earlier. He pulled on his coat that was draped over a chair at the clutter covered kitchen table. Papers and pocket change and dishes had set up permanent residence on the table. He rushed to the door and pulled it open. The November morning air had a bite to it. He pulled his shoulders up to his ears for the little bit of additional protection that would give him as he closed the door behind him.

Daisy, happy to finally be alone and with no one talking to her, walked from the bathroom.   Not bothered any more by the victorious spider who had made it to safety, she jumped on the bed and would begin her second nap of the morning. She was startled when the door opened again.

"I forgot my pills, Daisy." Paul rushed by her. His cheeks were already red from the wind. "I can't leave those. I'd hate to get to the bank and start feeling anxious and nervous and not have my pills to calm me down." He was upset with himself for almost leaving without them. "Preparation is, after all," he said aloud to the dozing cat, "the second key to success."

He walked directly to his dresser and picked up the pill bottle and put it in his pocket. The clock now said 8:58. He stopped next to his bed, paralyzed by the decision. He was already going to be late. What was one more minute? "Maybe I'll go to the bathroom one more time."

2

"Dammit!" Oliver Gartrell was on his knees looking under Holly Adam's bed. "It has to be here." He pushed a shoe box out of the way but could see nothing else under the bed besides dust and spider webs. He sat up on his knees. Pressing the tips of his thumbs together with his forefingers extended he talked to himself as if it would help. "It's a little black book. I have to find that book."

Holly was standing over him in only her underwear and bra. She looked out of the front window of her apartment waiting for the man in the suit and tie to stand up. The dresser beside her was covered in vases filled with dead or dying flowers. She reached over and flipped one of the petals with her forefinger and watched as the petal dropped to the dusty wood below it. "Ollie, I don't think it's here." She was exasperated at his exasperation. "I would have seen it."

Oliver stood up and pushed his thick, graying hair out of his face. He had a full healthy head of hair for a middle aged man. "It has to be here. I've looked everywhere else. It's not in my car. It's not in my office. It has to be here."

Holly walked around the ottoman that was between them and put her arms around his waist, pushing her exposed cleavage into his dress shirt. "Ollie, relax. You seem so tense."

He pushed himself away from her and lifted a stack of magazines on the table beside the recliner. "It has to be here. And don't call me that name. You know I hate that name."

Holly walked behind him and put her hands on his shoulders. Her thumbs dug into his neck. "Relax. Relax. You know I'm happy to see you. I'm always happy to see you."

For a second Oliver closed his eyes and turned his head in a clockwise motion getting lost in the deep muscle massage. Then, in an instant, he snapped back to reality. He threw his hands up with an impetuous movement to free himself of her advances. "No, no, I have to find that book."

Oliver turned to face her and she stepped again into his body, her perfect breasts once more pushed into his dress shirt. She looked up at his chin. "What's wrong, Ollie? Do you have a busy day or something? A big meeting with a bunch of important people? We have a few minutes, don't we?" And with that she touched his belt buckle with both hands and started to unfasten it.

Oliver took another step backwards and moved around the ottoman so that it would be between them. He looked around the room again wondering where a little black book could be. Then he focused on the almost naked woman in the room and said aloud what he had been thinking for the previous two days. "We have to stop doing this."

"Doing what?" Holly asked as she moved around the ottoman to touch him again.

He was angry now and knew he would have to be more forceful to get his point across. "We need to stop all of it. And I don't mean today, not just this." He moved his hands back and forth between them. "We need to stop everything." He threw his hands into the air as if making a snow angel while standing. "Me coming over here in the morning, the phone calls, the notes on my car, all of it. It's just too much right now with the election coming up."

Holly was not willing to give up so easily. She walked around the ottoman again and stood on her toes to put her lips close to his neck and whispered, "Are you afraid she's going to find out?"

"Who? Sheryl? I'd appreciate it if you wouldn't bring her into this." He withdrew again turning his back to her and walked to the dresser with the dead flowers in dusty vases and looked around them, still searching. "But yes, yes I'm afraid she'll find out and that would ruin me on Tuesday. I need good news leading up to Tuesday, not anything like that."

"But you said yourself she'll never find out and that you wouldn't care if she did. You said, 'She's in her own little world.'" Holly was defensive now and worried. She sensed Oliver was serious and the thought of him not coming by to see her was too much for her to bear. She felt anxiety when she repeated what he had said to her in the past to contradict his current demeanor. She knew those derogatory things Oliver had said about his wife were said to her in the heat of passion, usually when neither of them had on pants but she refused to accept the fact that words spoken while naked had no meaning when clothed. She believed Oliver's wife to truly be an awful person and not just presented that way by Oliver for his benefit.

"Maybe she's had a change of heart. Nothing would make her happier than seeing me lose this election now that her friend from la la land is running against me." Oliver walked the circumference of the room, looking at the base boards and pausing to look in corners.

"I can't believe she'd be like that. Your own wife. She should support you and do everything it takes to make you happy. Like I do." She approached him and again put her arms around his waist while he looked around the room biting his lip. She was eager to rectify the discord growing between them. "Come on," again her hands went to his belt buckle, "Let me give you your birthday present."

"No, stop it. Stop it. My birthday was three days ago and I would rather forget about it. I'm going to be late as it is." He looked at his watch to emphasize that he was in a hurry and also to place his forearm between himself and her advances. "I have to go but," he turned in a circle looking at her apartment, "I have to find that book."

Holly remained close to him. Oliver put his hands on her shoulders and moved her to one side out of the line between him and her apartment door. He treated her in the way a person would handle a child. He picked up his coat laying on the bed and began putting it on still more interested in the whereabouts of the black book he had misplaced than the almost naked woman standing in front of him. "It has got to be around here somewhere. It's got to be."

In a last attempt at gaining his attention, and since he was putting on clothes rather than taking any off, Holly decided to join his mission. "Okay, let's look for it. I'll look under the bed and the dresser." She turned her back to him and dropped to her knees. She leaned under the bed exposing her body to him fully aware of the submissive position it put her in. It was one last attempt to seduce him. Her effort was ignored and she had no choice but to stand up. "Why do you need the book so badly anyway? What is in it?"

"It's got a number, a phone number. I need to talk to a guy about something."

"You're good at numbers, Ollie. You can remember it, I'm sure. You don't have the number in your phone?"

Oliver's hand was turning the doorknob. "No, a number like this can't go in my phone. If anyone knew I had it that would be bad news for me. Very bad news. Listen, I have to go. I'm going to be late. If you find it call me." He reconsidered. "No, don't contact me. I'll come by later today." But that was not a good idea either. His confusion and stress was about to get the best of him. "I don't know what I'll do. Just find it. I have to have it." And with that he opened the door and stuck his head out into the cold November air. He pulled is head back into the apartment and closed the door. "Hey, come here."

Holly moved excitedly across the room for her goodbye kiss. It was not the interaction that she had anticipated when he knocked on her door that morning but kissing him at least would put her mind at ease. When she reached him Oliver stepped away from the door and let her pass. "Look outside and make sure nobody's out walking around."

Hurt and feeling anger boil inside her Holly quickly put on her bathrobe and put him on the spot one more time. "When is your wife going out of town so you can take me to your house and I won't have to do this? You've talked about it for so long and it's never happened. I'm ready to see where you live."

Oliver's impatience was visible, again looking as if he was dealing with a child but not his own, somebody else's. "That's not going to happen. You're not going to see my house. That would be too risky. There's no way." He switched back to the issue at hand, leaving her apartment unseen. "Is it all clear?"

Holly pulled the bathrobe closed and took her time tying the sashes no longer caring for Oliver's harsh tone. She stepped outside on to the cold concrete breezeway in front of her apartment and quickly looked up and down the parking lot. Her hands came up to her shoulders to show her boyfriend that she was cold and to make him understand the sacrifice she made. She stepped back into the apartment and told him, "All clear."

He walked out of the door and Holly knew she would not get the long passionate kiss he had given her in the past but waited for him to turn around and at least kiss her quickly before leaving. He did not turn around but walked out on the breezeway and quickly looked to his right and left. The only thing Holly heard him say was, "I'm going to be so late."

Clutching the lapels of his coat and bringing them together, Oliver ran flat footed to his car. With his chin to his chest and looking to his sides to make sure no car was coming, he never looked back to the woman in the doorway of her apartment. He unlocked the car and in one fluid motion disappeared from Holly's view. She was hurt and worried that the man she loved may not be as open to loving her back as he once was. Her concentration on the Mercedes backing out of the parking space was interrupted by a voice calling her name.

"Hi Holly. How are you today?"

She looked to her left to see her next door neighbor walking by. She thought his name was Paul but did not say it fearing it may be Peter or John. "I'm fine. How are you?" Her mother had taught her to be polite.

"I'm great." Paul replied. Enthusiasm is the third key to success. "Nice weather today, huh?" She smiled meekly and nodded in agreement. "Have a great day, Holly"

Paul Self walked to his beat up car and fumbled for his keys. He looked up one more time, hoping to catch another glimpse of the most beautiful woman he had ever known. He looked in her direction just as her door latched and she was gone.

3

As Paul approached the thick glass doors of Weatherton Community Bank he told himself to breathe. Deep breaths calmed him in difficult situations when he was out of his element. He saw his reflection in the door just before opening it and realized his shirt tail now was hanging out on one side from below his jacket. He regretted not having worn a tie.

He stopped himself from that line of thinking and spoke sternly to his reflection in the door. "No, Paul. Stop it. Stop being negative. You don't need a tie. You look fine."

He quickly shoved his hand into the top of his pants pushing his shirt down with it. He focused on the reasons to be positive. This day could already be considered a successful one as he had interacted with Holly. Any day he saw her was a good one. Any day they exchanged pleasantries made it even better. With him taking action toward his goal of a new car, one that would no doubt impress her, he felt a sense of confidence growing in him. An excitement ran through his body as he opened the door of the bank and walked inside.

Three days earlier Paul had been in the bank and met with a Mr. Farr. Mr. Farr had nodded many times in their brief meeting. He gave Paul a few short forms to fill out as 'a matter of formality' and told Paul to come back on Thursday and finalize the loan. Paul had been 'pleased with the process and felt it could not have gone any better'. Already he was considering what he would leave as a review of the service he had received.

"Can I help you?" The woman was sitting at the desk immediately inside the door.

"Um, yes, I came in the other day to apply for a car loan. I spoke to a Mr. Farr. Is he available?"

The lady at the desk leaned over and picked up the phone. As she brought it to her ear she paused, as if reconsidering her actions. "Is he expecting you today, Mr.....?"

Paul was looking around the bank and wiped his palms on the back of his pants. Despite the cold air outside his hands were moist. He was preoccupied with his thoughts. Nervous in what he felt was a portentous moment, he did not realize she was asking him a question.

"Who can I tell him you are?"

An awkward question but Paul came to attention. "Oh, Paul, Paul Self. Yes, I spoke to him the other day." He realized his nerves were showing. He put his hand in his pocket and felt the small bottle of pills and clinched his fingers around it. He was angry he had not had the foresight to take one before leaving his car.

The lady at the desk punched a button on her phone. "Yes, Mr. Farr, a gentleman is here to see you. He says he came by the other day. A Mr. Self. He is interested in a car loan." She smiled at Paul and he began to relax. She quickly swiveled in her chair so that her back was to him. Paul would never have been so forward with her looking at him but while her back was turned he reached out and took a sucker from the glass bowl in front of him. As he put the sucker in his pocket the woman said into the phone, "Well, can you come talk to him, please?"

She hung up the phone. "He will be right with you."

Paul looked at the chair in front of the desk but decided to stand. He took a few steps back to the door and was looking at framed documents the bank posted to tell about their business. He jumped slightly when the booming voice of Mr. Farr called his name. "Mr. Self. So good to see you again." The man's large hand was coming at him and Paul reached out and shook it. "Come on back."

Paul followed the well-dressed man back to his office. Again he regretted not having put on a tie before leaving his apartment. Down the hallway Mr. Farr stopped at his office door.

"Mr. Self, thank you so much for coming back by. I am in the middle of a very important conference call at the moment but let me give your information to Alison here and she can help you. Will that be alright?"

Paul had no choice but to agree as Mr. Farr had already walked into the office across the hall from his.

"Alice, this is Mr. Paul Self, the customer we spoke about a few minutes ago. Here is his information, credit and app. Could you spend a few minutes with him explaining our process? Thank you, Alison. I really need to get back on this call." He handed her a thin file and briefly turned his attention back to Paul. "Thank you for coming in today." With that he gave Paul a quick pat on the shoulder and walked back to his office and closed the door.

"Hello, Mr. Self." Alice stood and extended her hand to him. In a red business suit she looked about his age. Likely a recent college graduate he thought and with the exact look the bank wanted. "How are you?"

"Fine. I guess."

"It has gotten cold outside, hasn't it?" Paul smiled knowing she was only being pleasant with a generic comment. He did not think it was particularly cold for early November. "Please have a seat and let me look over your information."

Paul sat down and waited again while she opened the file on her desk.

Paul looked at the corner of her office, up near the ceiling. He noticed a small brown stain, water damage of some kind on the ceiling tile. As he waited he wondered how many other people had been in her office and noticed the same thing. Not many he imagined. The lady who sat there every day had probably not noticed it. But he had. He was observant that way. His eyes went down the wall to the credenza beside her desk. He smiled to himself imagining her unpacking a box labeled 'First Office Starter Kit'. He noted the awards on the shelves, a few business related books that he imagined had never been opened, a few pictures of this lady, standing with friends outside a sorority house. Beside that was a large, framed portrait of her standing behind a handsome man with her hand on his shoulder showing an engagement ring. A small glass figurine of an elephant sat on a shelf alone. Odd. He noted all of the things in her office while he waited and again wiped both his hands on the knees of his pants.

He had an overwhelming urge to leave. A sense of panic overcame him. It was often he felt that way. He became aware of his breathing and questioned if it was labored or not. He reached to his pocket and felt the pill bottle there. He knew he could not take the bottle out at that moment but he would need to as soon as possible. Perhaps he could excuse himself but that would seem odd and the woman across from him would think less of him. A deep breath. "Calm down, Paul. Calm down." He closed his eyes for what was in essence a very long blink.

He began thinking about his work rather than the situation immediately in front of him. Paul had an unsettling feeling about his job. He should have told his boss, Fletcher, he was going to be late that morning. Deep breath. Paul knew that Fletcher would be out of the office that morning. "But what if he's not? What if he's looking for me right now?" Deep breath. The woman was taking too long looking over the little information Paul had given to Mr. Farr a few days before. Something was wrong. Again his mind jumped from the lady in front of him to his boss. His mind never stopped moving. Fletcher's absence had worked out in Paul's favor but what if Fletcher had someone watching his employees to make sure they got to work on time? Paul had not mentioned his trip to the bank at work in the off chance this process went smoothly and quickly. He would have caused aggravation from his boss and stress for himself for no reason. Paul knew Fletcher would be livid if he found out his employee had been late. All Paul could hope for was understanding. His boss would understand his motivation. A quest to impress a girl. Fletcher had been in love before. He had done crazy things, Paul was sure of it.

Alice was silent as she flipped through the pages of the file. She looked up quickly from her desk and with a stern expression looked at the door. She flipped to the next page and the next. "Okay, I see." She closed the file and pushed her chair back from her desk. "If you'll excuse me just one minute. I'll be right back." With the file in her hand she walked out of the room.

This gave Paul a chance to stand and reach into his pocket. Quickly he pulled out the small bottle of pills and twisted the cap. He got as much saliva in his mouth as he could and quickly popped a pill onto his tongue and swallowed with as much force as possible. He sat back down and turned in his seat. He could see

Alice and Mr. Farr in the office across the hall. The door was open and he listened closely to what was being said. Alice was rather loud.

"You can't keep doing this to me, Hugh. You keep dumping this stuff on me and make me deal with it. It is not fair. It's not. This is the last time I'm doing this for you. This is it." She still held the file and pointed it at Mr. Farr like it was a weapon and she was threatening to hit him with it.

Paul could not hear what Mr. Farr said but Alice responded. "No, I'm not going to calm down. This is the last time."

A second later Alice walked back into her office. Now she paused to close the door behind her and straightened her red skirt. With her very athletic build, Paul imagined she was likely a runner or gymnast. She smiled again and sat down.

She looked at Paul with kind eyes. "Mr. Self, first I want to thank you for choosing First Quality Bank. We appreciate so much you taking the time to complete the application and inquiring about the car loan. Unfortunately,"

With that word Paul's heart sank.

"We won't be able to provide the loan you have applied for. Yes, I'm sorry. We currently are very stringent with our loan policies. I'm sorry but your credit score was not quite where we need it to be to approve the loan. If you work on getting that up a little bit come back to see us, okay."

Paul did not know why Alice had even taken the

time to sit down if that was all she was going to say before standing back up. From his chair he looked up at her. Her hand was extended to him. The engagement ring was indeed very large just as the picture showed. "Thank you again for applying with us. Can I get you anything to drink on your way out?"

He was being invited to leave. Paul had no choice but to stand up and shake her hand. "So I'm not getting the loan?" Why he wanted to hear her say it again he was not sure.

"No sir. I'm sorry." Sir? They were likely the same age. He felt she was patronizing him in an effort to appease him. He walked to the door in front of Alice. He turned to ask a question but could not think of anything to say. He saw Alice look through Mr. Farr's office window with an expression that could kill him through the glass. She put her hand on Paul's shoulder. "Thank you for coming in. Have a good day, okay."

Paul found himself back at the desk where he had first come in. The lady there picked up the phone and said 'Hello' as he approached though the phone had not rung. Paul had no choice but to walk to the glass door and out into the chilly November air. He saw his reflection and he could only shake his head. He said aloud to his apparition in the glass, "I should have worn a tie." He walked to his car slowly, ignoring the frigid air that stung his ears. He felt the all too common resulting sting of defeat which always left him wondering, regardless of the cause, why he had even tried for the thing in the first place.

4

The parking space was the closest one to the building. Oliver pulled his Mercedes in quickly with his back right tire on the line. Parking etiquette was of no concern to him at the moment. He got out of his car and walked quickly to the building and pulled the door handle. It fought against him and he pulled harder. The electronic door did not want to budge. He walked back to the post he had just passed and punched the handicap button and the door swung open. His urge to put his foot on the small metal post and bend it over was strong but he refrained knowing someone would see him. Aggravated he walked inside.

In the hallway people stepped aside to let him pass. That was only in part because of his pace and long strides. Most of these people in City Hall had been berated by him in the past. Some publicly ridiculed had made a point to never interact with the man again. A few people, either brave and confident or ignorant and somewhat impressed by his title, said, 'Hi Mr. Mayor,' as he walked by but to each he only halfway glanced and nodded quickly. Just a few days before an election he should have been nicer, more accommodating but he was in a panicked state and did not have time to please his constituents.

Oliver got to the door that had the words 'Mayor's Office' printed on the glass. For four years he had wanted someone in the maintenance department to come add his name below the title but still it had not been done. Now with an election looming it may have been a cost saving measure that the maintenance department had never gotten around to doing it. The thought made him more aggravated not because of the disrespect shown to him but the feeling in the pit of his stomach that it may prove true.

Lane Oglesby sat behind her desk flipping the pages of a magazine. The pages would snap with each flick of her wrist. With her back to the door she did not see Oliver before he saw her. She put the magazine down quickly, dropping it at her feet under her desk while sitting up in her chair. She waited to be reprimanded for her laziness but knew that Oliver would not be serious and would only do it as a matter of duty. She did not fear him. She disliked his stern voice and commands sometime but she knew that the indiscretions she had witnessed sitting in that office provided her with job security until the day she did not want to be there anymore.

Oliver did not break his stride moving toward his office door. He said while looking straight ahead, "Lane, hold my calls for thirty minutes or so. I have to check on a project and can't be disturbed."

Oliver walked to his large, leather office chair. He pulled out the top desk drawer and rambled through the junk that had accumulated there. He did the same with the drawer on the other side. He had looked through both drawers no less than twenty times before and he knew there was no need to spend any more time looking. He put his elbows on the desk and hung his head. He looked out of his window on the sixth floor of City Hall. Taking a deep breath, he spun around and snatched the phone from its cradle and dialed a number.

"Sergeant Michaels please." He waited and scratched his head. "Hello, Sergeant Michaels? This is Mayor Gartrell. I need you to drive by my house and check on things like yesterday." He tapped his fingers on the desk with an impatient demeanor, waiting to overcome the objection that was coming from the other end of the line. "Let me deal with Chief Mullins. I need you to go by my house and call me if that car is in the driveway again. I don't know who it is. That's why I'm asking you to go. My wife is up to something and I want to know about it. I know it's none of your business, Michaels. Go by the house and report back to me. Fired? You're not going to get fired. No, it's not. In November? Now think about that Michaels. Why would a pool cleaner be needed in November? Honestly. Aren't you trying to make Lieutenant over there? Come on. Listen, I told you to let me deal with Chief Mullins. I'll tell him you're on a special assignment. Don't worry about that. Just go out there."

After he put the phone back in the cradle Oliver stood up and looked out of the window. The cord on his blinds was crooked. He swatted at it with his hand to make it hang straight. The strings seemed to get more tangled. He was being challenged. He grabbed the strings and began weaving one through the other to make them even and apart. Still they were twisted. He began to get angry. Now this was a mission. He was determined to fix those blinds. He was concentrating and did not hear Lane open his office door.

"Mr. Gartrell, Albert King is here to see you. He said it is urgent but I told him you were in a meeting. He refuses to leave."

The cord to his mini blinds was forgotten. Oliver had no choice but to straighten his coat, pull his hands down his cheeks and face the man he did not want to see. "Okay, send him in." Oliver's hand went to his forehead and he pushed his hair and patted his head as if about to have a picture taken. He wiped his hands on his dress pants and then made two tight fists and released them in an attempt to relax.

In a second an older man walked in the room and nodded at Lane as she left them there and closed the door behind her. The man stood leaning on a cane. He was a feeble looking man of eighty with a back that bent over in an unfortunate way that appeared painful. He could not stand up straight but had to look at Oliver by turning his head to one side. As pitiful as the man appeared, Oliver feared him. He knew saying one wrong word to the man could cost him dearly.

Albert King paced back and forth in front of Oliver's desk with his hat in his hand. He had gone back and forth three, maybe four times before he spoke. He was a man of few words but intimidated Oliver like no other person in his life.

Finally he stopped and turned his torso to the desk so he was looking at Oliver from one side. "I want out."

Oliver waited for the old man to continue and realized that was all he intended to say. Oliver needed clarification and wanted desperately to be told he had misunderstood to put his mind at ease.

"Out? You don't want out. We're almost done with the whole thing." Oliver tried to maintain a calm, strong tone to convey confidence but he was afraid there was a slight crack in his voice.

"I don't think we are almost there, Oliver. That's not what I'm hearing. I'm hearing that you're blowing it."

"Blowing it?" Oliver tried to sound incredulous. "No, no, I'm not blowing it. Everything is going according to plan. We are right where we need to be. The steps are falling into place."

Albert paced some more. "The steps are falling into place? What steps? Step one is you winning this election. That is step one and frankly, from what I've heard around town that may not happen."

Oliver laughed but the nervousness could not be hidden. "No, trust me, I've got it all under control. I do. My numbers are good. Better than ever." Oliver had walked around to the front of the desk now. He would reach a hand out and place it on Albert's shoulder if needed. Albert only shook his head at

Oliver's confidence. "Listen, once the election is over and I'm starting my next term it's all going to fall into place. The River Mill development will come back up in front of the commissioners and we'll get the votes. It's a sure thing."

Albert hung his cane on the front of Oliver's desk and put his hands out to his sides as if dropping a box on the floor at his feet. "But what if you don't win the election? What if that woman wins? What happens then?"

Oliver took that opportunity to put his hand on Albert's shoulder and get a look at him. He looked at him in the eyes and waited a couple of beats to appear confused and taken aback. "What woman? Is it Myers? Is that who you're worried about? Listen, there is no way that woman is going to win. No way. I'm as good as re-elected. Count on it. Wednesday I'll be right back here planning my next term. You've got nothing to worry about."

Oliver walked to a small desk in the corner of his office and pulled out the bottom drawer. A bottle of scotch was presented to Albert with a glass. "Would you like a drink?" Albert King raised his hand blocking the offer. Oliver persisted. "Come on. You need to relax. Have a drink."

Albert shook his head. "It's nine thirty in the morning for God's sake, Oliver. No, I don't want a drink."

Oliver shrugged but that did not stop him from setting the glass down on the table and pouring a shot of bourbon into it. Albert could only shake his head. Disgusted. Oliver threw his head back and swallowed hard.

"The woman cutting my hair was talking about Melanie Myers an awful lot yesterday. Everybody in there was talking about her and it just seems like she's gaining support. She's gaining momentum. If you don't win…" His words trailed off giving Oliver the opening to reassure him.

"No, Mr. King, when I win. Listen, she has no idea what she is doing and frankly is in way over her head. Now sure there may be those people out there talking about her like she has all the answers but those are the people who don't know the questions. Am I right? Of course I'm right. Her so called supporters won't even show up to the polls. Probably aren't even registered to vote. There is nothing to worry about. Vote for me on Tuesday and relax. Everything is going as planned. Okay? It's a sure thing." His garrulous nature could turn the average person but he knew Albert King was too intelligent for that. He forced himself to stop talking.

Oliver put his hand in the middle of Albert's back and guided him towards the door. Oliver remembered the cane and went back to his desk to retrieve it hoping Albert would not fall over in the meantime. Albert maintained his balance and held his hat in front of him with both hands. He stopped before exiting, refusing to be treated like a cow ushered through a gate. "I've invested too much in this, Gartrell. You understand? Too much. I've padded pockets. I've done what I needed to do. But I'm hearing rumors that my candidate is in trouble. I don't like hearing that and you can see why. That makes me nervous. And when I get nervous I do things I shouldn't do. Don't make me nervous."

"I've got everything under control, Mr. King. A week from now everything will have fallen into place just like we talked about. Guaranteed. The River Mill project will be back on the agenda and magically there will be money there to fund it."

Albert shook his finger in the air at Oliver. "Not magic. Results. I don't believe in magic. But I can make someone disappear." He seemed proud of his line as he walked from Oliver's office to the door. He repeated it, still holding his hand in the air. "I can make someone disappear." Oliver chuckled at the fragile man's tough demeanor but was nervous nonetheless.

"There is nothing to worry about Mr. King. I assure you." As he opened the door to his office, Oliver leaned back and looked at Albert's head. "And I don't know who this woman was that cut your hair, but it's a little uneven back here in the back. If she thinks Myers is going to win she may know as little about politics as she does cutting hair." Oliver exaggerated the criticism but wanted to shift Albert's anger to someone else.

Lane looked at Oliver with a strange expression on her face inviting her boss to explain just what that meant. Oliver was in no mood. Once Oliver had ushered Mr. King through the frosted glass door into the hallway he closed the door behind him. He put his hand on his now aching stomach and said to Lane, "Tell anyone else that I can't be interrupted." He closed the door to his office and collapsed into his chair wondering what he had done to find himself in this predicament. The phone rang and Oliver looked at it with disgust but lunged for it when he saw the name of the caller.

"Hello, Michaels? Did you go by the house? Again!? The same car? Are you still at my house? It's not the pool cleaner, Michaels." Oliver was angry and yelled the words into the phone. "Park around the corner and walk to the backyard. See if anybody is back there…. Of course you can, you're a police officer and this is official police business. Do it….. Because I'm the mayor and I command you to do it, that's why. Michaels?"

Oliver hung up the phone and felt like he could throw up. That nagging pain in his stomach he had felt for the past two weeks had returned. "This is unbelievable." He put both of his elbows on his desk and rubbed his face. "Just unbelievable."

5

Paul parked his car behind City Hall and ran to the door marked 'Maintenance' behind the wall of decorative bricks which hid from the public trashcans and soiled mops and drying Welcome Mats draped over a low brick wall. Paul pulled the door and found it to be locked. Puzzled, he pulled again. He realized he had no choice but to walk around the building and climb the fifteen steps from the sidewalk to the front door of City Hall. He would have to enter as everyone else did. At least he was dressed nicely after his trip to the bank and would fit in with the other people coming and going.

Paul approached the door and from around the corner a very well-dressed black woman in a red suit passed him. With a cell phone to her ear she did not acknowledge anyone around her. Paul could not help but admire her slim, athletic physique. Paul quickened his pace. He skipped every other stair as he ascended the intimidating concrete in order to open the door for the woman. "Good morning." Paul said it in a jovial tone. The beautiful woman stared straight ahead and did not acknowledge Paul's presence or kind gesture. He shrugged knowing that she was an important lady and if he were in her position, he would not have time to acknowledge someone like himself either.

As Paul entered the building his anxiety turned to despair. There in the middle of the marble floor, under the atrium that allowed a person to look up to the sixth floor of the building was Archibald Fletcher. His corpulent body stood at attention, his short cropped afro shined under the light. He stood with a scowl on his face. His short sleeves barely covered his massive arms.

Fletcher was a former military guy. Marine, Army, Navy, Air Force, Paul was not sure. He had never asked him fearing that the conversation would only turn into a negative one with Paul's lack of knowledge about anything to do with the Armed Services. Fletcher took pride in himself and in that way was the antithesis of his employees, namely Paul. He was always five minutes early to anything. He expected the building to shine. Paul often felt his boss put too great of an importance on how a particular sink or bathroom floor looked. Fletcher was a talker, very articulate and knowledgeable. Paul respected his boss but did not emulate him which was a difficult position to be in. Fletcher was often expounding on what was wrong with the younger generation in this country and what he would do to fix all of its problems. Paul knew those conversations were directed squarely at him as one of those members of the younger generation Fletcher despised so much. Arriving thirty five minutes late to work would only give him more reason to reprimand his employee.

It was when he got closer that Paul realized what Fletcher had in his hand. Held like a rifle by his side was a once white toilet brush now turned gray by so much use. As he walked toward his boss, Paul thought about the remark Fletcher had made the day before about likely not being at work. Paul was dismayed to see that whatever the reason it had not come to fruition to keep his boss away. Now his day was immediately even worse with the denial by the bank and the presence of his boss.

"Hi Fletcher. I did not realize you were going to be here today."

Fletcher's voice was deep and stern. The anger on his face was noticeable. "Obviously."

"Didn't you have some place to be? Something about a friend needing something out of town or...something." Paul was rambling and nervous. He wanted to steer the subject from his tardiness to something Fletcher could talk about without making Paul the subject of the conversation. But Paul knew, based on Fletcher's still solemn expression that would be unlikely.

"I was supposed to go to a funeral today but the whole thing depressed me so much that I skipped it. I decided coming to work and scrubbing toilets would cheer me up, put me in a better mood, but then I saw that I have an employee taking advantage of my loss and it has depressed me all over again."

Paul's only choice was to answer apologetically but

directly. "Oh yeah, I'm sorry about that. I had an appointment this morning."

"A job interview I hope."

There was no smile on his face when he said it and this alarmed Paul. Paul had come to know Fletcher as a witty man but was guilty of the trait Paul found the least becoming. He laughed more at his own jokes than anyone else. In this case he did not laugh. "No, no, I love my job. I meant to tell you about my appointment on Tuesday but didn't get a chance. I had to go to the bank this morning and talk to a lady."

Fletcher did not care. "It must have been like all of your lunch breaks and taken a lot longer than you thought. I'm not happy with you, Self. I get here to work and you're nowhere to be found. I look out in the courtyard and there is trash everywhere."

"I'm sorry Fletcher. I didn't get a chance to clean that up last night before I left but I'll go out there first thing, after I change, and get on that."

Fletcher looked down the hallway and called out to Paul's coworker standing at the elevator.

"Hey Sullivan, get over here."

Paul groaned when he saw Mike Sullivan walking towards them. Sullivan was a tall, lanky guy from New England who had moved to Georgia years before when he had impregnated his girlfriend and needed 'a change' as he called it. He left his girlfriend and kid in New Jersey or wherever it was and had moved to Weatherton, Georgia. In his own elevated opinion of himself Sullivan was smarter, better looking, stronger, than anybody else. Paul was not a competitive person by many means but Sullivan was the one person who could ignite that fire in him.

Adding to his animosity towards his coworker, Paul felt that Fletcher seemed to love the guy despite their different backgrounds. Fletcher was a disciplined and tough black man, with a high school football coach's demeanor. He could snap somebody in two if he felt disrespected. Sullivan was all talk. Small in stature but always talking a big game with his slicked back hair and cigarettes in the pocket of his pants, Paul thought Sullivan would be just the kind of guy Fletcher despised. Without being blatantly racist Sullivan often said things that Paul had to ignore to not be angered by it and hoped one day Fletcher would turn a corner just as Sullivan was saying something stupid. But it was often that Paul would see them in the hall together, laughing and talking about their weekend plans. Paul did not desire to be Fletcher's best friend nor cared how he would spend his weekend but knowing that Sullivan had that connection with him made him resent the guy even more.

As Sullivan approached, Fletcher turned back to Paul. "You know what, I'm going to put Sullivan outside today. He could use some fresh air. You're going to need some fresh air when this month is over with, Self. Take this brush up to the sixth floor and get to work on the men's room and then go over to the lady's."

Sullivan was now beside their boss with his arms

folded across his chest in a smug way, a toothpick was in the corner of his mouth. With a vacuous mind and an overcharged libido, Sullivan would often just stand in the hallway with a blank look on his face watching women walk by.

Fletcher cut his eyes at Sullivan. "Sully, how do you feel about being outside today? Get some fresh air and sunshine while Paul here takes over toilet duty. Does that sound good to you?" He did not wait for Sullivan to answer but decided to get one final dig in at Paul. "And Paul, I expect that porcelain to shine like never before because the more I think about you taking advantage of me the more depressed I'm getting."

Sullivan was in on it now. "And make sure you get real good up under the edge, those toilets can be tricky. Hey boss," Sullivan had an idea and hit Fletcher on this bicep to make his point, "you know what you should do. You should make him eat cereal out of one of them toilets. My cousin, Freddy, did that one time to his nephew. It was hilarious." His cackle of laughter echoed in the hallway.

Fletcher stepped away from Sullivan, making distance between him and the stupidity of his comment. "And Paul, I don't want any complaints out of you. The thought of you cleaning toilets is the only thing putting a smile on my face. You're lucky I don't fire you."

Paul could not show his despondency but fought hard against it. The bank had proven his inadequacy as

41

a human and his punishment of spending a day cleaning bathrooms made it that much worse. "I'll go change clothes and then get to work on it."

Fletcher looked at Sullivan and felt a sense of power over his two employees. "There is no time to change. You'll go like that. If anyone sees you they'll just think you're a concerned citizen who wants the Mayor's crapper to be clean."

With that Fletcher handed the brush to Paul and turned and walked down the hallway leaving Sullivan and Paul alone in the rotunda of the building. Sullivan could not help himself. "It's a great day, ain't it? You cleaning my toilets and me out in the sunshine and fresh air watching all the women walk by." He held his hand in the air waiting for Paul to extend his to give him five. Paul turned and walked away.

Sullivan snapped his fingers and called out to him. "So Paul, did you get that car you told me about? Can I go outside and look at it when I'm on break?"

Paul regretted ever having mentioned the car or anything else in his life to Sullivan. He turned and looked over his shoulder at the greasy man child. "I'm still thinking about it."

Sullivan laughed loudly not caring if passersby were startled. He called out, "Thinking or hoping? You ain't gonna get that car and you know it. Look at you. Look at where you are man. People wearing jumpsuits with their names on their pocket don't drive cars like that unless it's at the car wash and you're moving it for a customer. Hey maybe that's what you should do. Get a job at a car wash. You may get the chance to sit in one, huh? You can drool over it from the inside." Paul had stopped and looked at him only in an attempt to get his coworker to lower his voice. It had not worked.

Paul turned and walked to the stairs still holding the toilet brush. He ignored Sullivan's laughter echoing off the marble floors and high ceilings behind him.

6

It was just days before the biggest election of Oliver Gartrell's life. His quest for a second term as Mayor of Weatherton was more monumental than being elected for his first. The first election had been the most exciting time in his life. He loved the competition. He loved the debates. He loved making his points that would highlight the faults in his opponent's arguments leaving them speechless at a podium. He loved, more than anything, watching his opponents sink to the bottom of the voting pool never to be heard from again. He had always been victorious in any endeavor he put his mind to. 'Win at all costs' had become his mantra and he never regretted anything he did to win. To this point in his life he never had to feel the cold hand of defeat. His election to Mayor four years before had been the culmination of all of the lessons he had learned in life. But this time, this election he knew could be different. He was no fool. This Melanie Myer's woman had come from nowhere. The common person's candidate, the one making her own points putting Oliver and his platform on the defensive, was gaining momentum at the worst possible time. He knew that campaigning lasted for months but the election itself only took three seconds, the three seconds a person needed to pull a lever or fill in a bubble with a pen. If Melanie Myers could win those three seconds his previous five months would have all been for nothing. For once Oliver felt like his platform was not made of steel. It did not seem to be an ironclad ship but seemed more and more like just an inflatable toy raft in the middle of the ocean.

Albert King was worried and Oliver had eased his mind for now but he knew deep down everything Mr. King had said was the truth and he shared the same concern. What bothered Oliver most about Melanie Myers was not her points, or her growing contingency, or even her fresh look at the issues in their growing city. What concerned Oliver was how much this woman running for Mayor reminded him of himself. She shared the win at all costs mentality. That was the cause of the sleepless nights and upset stomachs, the anger in his voice and the painful headaches.

He sat in his office with his feet on his desk looking out of the window lost in deep thought. His concern over the outcome of the election he fully understood. Losing the election would have very ugly consequences for him and the people close to him for reasons he now regretted. But now he had an additional concern and one that he himself was shocked to discover bothered him more than the election itself. The thought of his wife's infidelity was forefront in his mind and would not yield to the election, or Melanie Myers, or even Albert King. The election caused him concern and yes even panic at what may happen but this latest news outside of politics caused him sadness.

His wife's reasons were obvious if he chose to look at them. He knew his commitment to her over the past years had been paper thin and nothing more than a farce. He had found himself in places he should not have been, doing things that no happily married man would ever do. They had no intimacy. They merely passed each other in the hallway of their house, their laconic relationship a burden to them both. But the thought of her committing those sins against him was something he could not accept without emotion. These thoughts ran through his head as he stared out of the window behind his desk. For what reason was the unknown car at his house each of the past three days? Who was the man driving it? What service was this mysterious man providing? So deep in thought Oliver did not hear the door open behind him. And for the second time that morning he was caught off guard by a visitor to his office.

"You certainly look busy this morning. The hardest working mayor in the state. You get my vote."

Ann Strickland had become a force in the town. Smarter than most, better looking than most, she had become a powerful person in the financial office of the city but when she wore that red business suit, when she knew men were distracted, she felt more powerful than ever being admired and feared in the same instant.

"Oh Ms. Strickland, thank you for barging in and saving my secretary from getting up and letting me know you were here. I wish everyone was so courteous." Oliver was trying to dispel her strength with apathy but she noticed how quickly his feet were taken from his desk and put on the floor.

"I did not see your secretary at her desk. I assumed she was out running an errand for you, burying a body perhaps."

With that she swung her briefcase on to the desk in front of Oliver. The loud thud was intended and the papers on the desk now covered by the briefcase were ignored. Their importance nullified. "You may be aware I had some questions for you about a few expense reports that have been filed recently."

"Yes, I do believe I have gotten all eight of your voicemails, a mailbox full of emails but you know, Ms. Strickland, right now is not a good time for me." Oliver was always trying to establish himself as the dominant force in any room but Ann Strickland was one person who, while in her presence, he would have no chance of that.

Ann raised her eyebrows. "Oh, would you like to get back to what you were doing when I walked in?" Smirk.

Oliver turned to the window, unable to maintain the eye contact that she refused to break. "I actually do have an appointment."

"Oh Mr. Mayor, I was joking. I know you have time to talk to me now. What else could possibly be more important to you than not being incarcerated? Hmmm?"

Her sing song voice and first grade teacher like demeanor had Oliver sweating. The contrast of her dark skin and white teeth, the red business suit, the strong shoulders, he could not focus on anything she was saying. He realized how tight the neck of his dress shirt was. He could feel moisture on his lower back, that wetness he despised. This was one thing he had no time for. For the fiscal department of his city to anatomize his business dealings could lead to ruin for him. But he had no choice but to nod and accept the challenge.

Oliver shrugged and smiled. "Sure, since you're here, now will be as good of time as any I suppose. I apologize for not getting back to you sooner. But I am the mayor. I am a busy man. Things come up."

Ann smirked again. "Yes, so I've heard."

"What is that supposed to mean?" Oliver was on the defensive now. He thought of Holly's apartment and how careful he was when going to it or leaving but now felt as if he had likely been caught and Ann knew the truth. His paranoia had grown by the day in the past week. He expected her to pull pictures from her briefcase of him and Holly. He was sweating but still he would deny it as long as he could.

"Whatever you want it to Mr. Mayor. Now, these expense reports." She sat in the chair facing his desk and unsnapped her briefcase. Oliver sat down in his chair and felt his back stick to the leather.

Oliver knew it was important to show his disgust and impatience with the conversation. "So what do you want to discuss? Did somebody not put the latest roll of toilet paper on an expense report? Is somebody using too many sheets when they go to the bathroom? You let me know because this outrageous abuse of the system will not be tolerated."

Oliver had spent his life trying to diffuse stressful situations with humor. If he could make the other person feel stupid or make them think their point was trivial he knew he had won. His now moist shirt and tight collar was a result of the realization such tactics would not work on the person from the finance department determined to bring him down.

Ann took out a stack of documents and dropped them on the desk. Oliver was at least relieved to see no pictures among the stack of papers. Again, a loud thud. "Balance sheets Mr. Gartrell. I assume you are aware that they are supposed to balance. Do you know what happens when they don't?"

Oliver's palms were moist. "They fall off the table?" He tapped the stack with his index finger pushing them toward the edge of his desk.

"No, when they don't balance I leave eight voicemails for you to set up an appointment until finally I show up unannounced."

Oliver leaned back in his leather chair and crossed his hands on his stomach, intertwining his fingers. Still he was trying to give the appearance of holding the alpha status in the room. "Well, isn't it your job to make it balance?"

Ann laughed, showing her teeth, as if Oliver was a

cute first grader who had just made an adorable comment. She went back to her sing song voice that did not put him at ease but emphasized her lack of respect for the man in front of her. "For me to get these to balance I would have to be a much more creative person. That is not one of my strengths Mr. Gartrell, fabricating stories, but you certainly appear to be quite good at it."

Oliver's hands went back up to the desk. He was being challenged and his complacent attitude left him. Ann flipped through some of the pages in front of her. "Ah, here it is. Fifteen hundred dollars for public service party hats. What is this, Mr. Gartrell?"

Oliver stood up and leaned over the desk appearing at first to be interested but Ann understood it to be the action of a caged animal wanting out. Oliver pointed at the stack of paper and lied. "I can explain everything in that file, each page, each entry."

Now it was Ann who leaned back in her seat in complete control. "Okay. Let's do it. Because frankly Mr. Gartrell even though the questionable items in here are not large expenses, they are all under the threshold that would cause extra scrutiny at the time of entry, when aggregated together they amount to a very large, considerable expenditure."

Oliver made one final attempt to get out of the cage and prove he was the one with the whip. "Wow, Ann, such big words. Somebody must be trying to get a promotion over there in finance, huh?"

Ann's eyes narrowed, looking like a cat. She was

tired of the conversation and decided to just put out there what her whole point was when she walked in the door. "I think you're up to something, Mr. Gartrell. I can't quite put my finger on it but I smell something and I don't like it."

Oliver was smug. "The party hats were for last year's New Year's Eve party in the civil service division. I approved it because I feel it's important to show the employees of this city that..."

"Oh save it Mr. Mayor. You're hiding something. I know it. I haven't found it yet but I will." She looked as though she had just stumbled on something, as if a realization had just occurred to her. Oliver was more nervous. He fell back in his chair and his shirt made a soppy sound against the leather, like a wet towel being thrown on the bathroom floor. He hoped his nemesis had not heard it.

Before he could respond Ann's cell phone began to ring. She leaned down to the bag at her feet and pulled out her phone. "Hello, Ann speaking."

Oliver turned back to the window praying that this woman would have to leave his office. The sweat on his back now felt like he had been swimming with his shirt on. His arm pits were stained he was sure. The stress was building in him. His stomach caused him pain. He listened to Ann behind him.

"I thought that had been resolved. He did what? He does not have the authority to do that. Only I or Mr. Henderson can approve that kind of entry. Okay, fine, fine, I'll be right there." She hung up her phone and put the papers from Oliver's desk back into her briefcase. She stood up holding her bag.

Oliver took one last shot at his nemesis. "Oh no, are you needed back at the castle? Did one of your flying monkeys make a mess on the floor?"

Ann showed her teeth again. "Mr. Gartrell, if you're trying to flatter me with the intention of making me go easier on you it won't work. You have been granted a reprieve. It appears that we won't be able to go through the files today."

Oliver shrugged with accommodating charm. "If you leave all of the files with me I'll go through them and get back to you."

She laughed again. "Good try, Mayor. You get all of your records together. Every receipt, every purchase order, every party hat, everything. And this time I expect to see you in my office on Monday morning to go over it."

Oliver shook his head. "Oh, yeah, that's no good for me. I don't know if you've heard but there is an election coming up on Tuesday that I have a little bit of a stake in. How about we make it Wednesday? You can come back here then and congratulate me on my victory."

Ann stood in the doorway of his office. "I hope you haven't spent too much money on campaign signs Mr. Mayor or party hats for that matter. I don't think you'll be needing them."

"Ah Ann, thank you. You think I'm a sure thing, huh?"

She laughed once more. "See, I told you that you were creative. This election should be the furthest thing from your mind, Mr. Mayor. Have a good day." And with that she closed the door behind her.

Oliver smiled until he was sure Ann Strickland had made it through the frosted glass door of the reception area and into the hallway. He stood up from his chair and went to the door and locked it. Turning back to his desk he put his hands over his face and his shoulders slumped over. His life had been complicated for quite some time but now he felt, in the course of only a few hours his life was unraveling around him. He was trapped and he desperately needed to figure out how to escape.

7

The Weatherton County City Hall and Courthouse is an odd place. They are actually two buildings side by side connected by a courtyard. Paul worked only in City Hall and rarely did he cross the courtyard to work in the courthouse. The main floor of City Hall is beautiful and extravagant with marble floors and high ceilings and expensive chandeliers illuminating the hallways in both directions. The floors above the first are vastly different in appearance and one would be justified in believing the City had run out of money after decorating the first floor.

The first floor has the grandeur to match the lobby of any five star hotel. The floors above the first however, have more an appearance of a cheap hotel with long, narrow, dark hallways. But rather than dingy hotel rooms City Hall had dingy offices. It is on the sixth floor though, when stepping off the elevator a person is back on the marble that matches the first floor and chandeliers once again hang in gaudy illumination. It is as if the four floors between the first and sixth were squeezed in between the two stories of a beautiful two story building.

When Paul wanted to escape his job and any duties associated with it he had found that the sixth floor provided sanctuary that none of the other floors offered. For that reason he did not mind being sent to the sixth floor for his punishment. He knew he would not be watched and could waste time without fear of being caught.

Paul stepped off of the elevator onto the marble of the sixth floor with prominent members of the community passing in the hallway and talking business and politics. Still dressed in his best button up shirt and nicest pants he imagined he could be mistaken for someone of some importance. He could very well pass as a young attorney coming to talk to the DA maybe or a real estate investor wanting a deed or to find some property in a book of plats. The toilet brush in his hand though probably unraveled any thread of appearing important that he could muster.

He did not want to clean any porcelain be it sink, floor or toilet. His work ethic was an intermittent one at best when his task involved those things he did not mind doing, tending to the courtyard or mopping a floor but when told to clean toilets or sinks he would rather spend the day hiding and take his chances of Fletcher's reprimand. Due to his tardiness and the anger Fletcher had expressed Paul felt obligated to at least walk in the bathrooms to see the condition they were in. To Paul's delight the bathrooms appeared clean. There was no mess on the floor. The counter top appeared to be wiped down. The toilets held no unwelcomed surprise that would need his attention. He put the toilet brush in the back corner of the last stall and walked back out into the hallway.

Beside the bathroom was a short corridor with a window at the far end. Beside the window was a slight enclave that was large enough for a person to stand in without being seen but not enough room to lay down or even sit without remaining visible to a passerby who would see two feet sticking out into the floor. Out of sight from anyone walking down the hall was a shelf. On the shelf Paul kept a notebook. It was only a normal three ring college ruled notebook that could be purchased for a dollar at any grocery store. But it was very important to Paul. He often would take his trip to the sixth floor and draw pictures and write stories. The notebook helped him pass time until he could go home.

Paul had an affinity for art and literature. He had been told during his school years that he was quite good at writing and drawing though those courses of study had never been pursued. This notebook at work was the only time he ever took to work on his craft. He had begun drawing a picture each day or writing a one page story that had begun to percolate on his drive to work.

The notebook stayed there on the shelf and he would put it back each day. Paul trusted that Fletcher would not find it, his body was too big to fit down the narrow corridor. He knew Sullivan would never find it. He rarely went to the sixth floor and likely did not have any reason to hide. He would be lazy in front of Fletcher. It did not matter to him.

The sixth floor had an additional architectural adornment that the other floors did not which made it the perfect place to seek refuge and peace and quiet and work on his art. What the sixth floor had that the others did not was a ledge. Climbing out of the window at the far end of the corridor provided the perfect hiding place for anyone so inclined. The six floors between him and the courtyard below could have been intimidating to some, maybe to most people, but Paul was not bothered by it.

The maintenance men kept the marble floors and the brass door handles shining. The walls were always painted and the windows were always clean. But years of wear had taken a toll on the old building in small ways. Some doors did not close as tightly as they should and some locks on windows were broken. That was the case for the window on the sixth floor at the end of the narrow corridor. Paul did not break it but had found it that way in his year and a half of employment at City Hall, while always looking for a hiding place. He placed both hands on the base of the window and slowly lifted it from the sill. With a quick motion lifting his leg while ducking his head, he was out on the ledge of the building without being seen by anyone.

About two feet wide the ledge was enough to stand on and be comfortable. Walking about ten feet to the left once on the ledge there was another enclave that offset the one inside. Here a person could sit down with their back to the building and their feet pointing to the ledge that went around the building. With only the soles of one's shoes visible from the ground Paul had found it to be the nicest and most secure hiding place in the entire building. The morning sun shined directly on the ledge so even cold November mornings could be tolerated while in his secret place.

He had recently brought with him a bucket that Fletcher had discarded in the maintenance room in the basement of the building. Knowing it would not be missed Paul had brought it to this hiding place to be turned over and used as a short chair. It was there on the bucket that he could easily spend twenty minutes in relative silence sketching or writing whatever he was working on at the time or beginning a new picture or story that had come to him.

On this day still in his nice clothes Paul made himself comfortable and closed his eyes with his head leaning against the brick building. He knew thoughts would come to him once he was out there and he would want the notebook to jot down anything so as to keep it from escaping his mind and being lost forever. He leaned against the wall for a few minutes with the notebook resting on the concrete slab beside him. He closed his eyes and forgot about any failure from that morning or toilet that needed scrubbing. He was alone and free. The humiliation and disappointment he had felt at the bank was a distant memory. Fletcher's reprimand was forgotten.

His watch was set for twenty minutes. That was the maximum amount of time he felt he could be gone without being questioned by Fletcher or reported on by Sullivan. He had every intention of enjoying a nice nap of solitude. He remembered the bank and the one good thing that had come from that experience. From his breast pocket he withdrew a sucker he had taken from the mean woman's desk. Grape. He removed the wrapper and put it in his mouth. "Sullivan's cleaning the courtyard huh?" He tossed the wrapper over the edge and watched it fall between his feet toward earth. A slight breeze blew its way into the enclave and Paul was at peace.

The peace was soon interrupted however when he heard a noise.

Paul's first inclination was that he had been discovered. He expected to see Fletcher come shimming along the ledge to find him there relaxing and he knew if that was the case he would be fired. His termination would not be devastating he imagined but to be caught in this way would be embarrassing if nothing else. He waited. No one came. Deciding the noise was a bird or only his imagination he closed his eyes again and relaxed but then it was there again. Heavy breathing. He heard someone say, "Oh no."

Paul's alarm turned to curiosity. He stood up from the bucket and took the two steps to the ledge but still saw nothing. He heard another noise. It was the grunting of a person in trouble. He walked back to his bucket and picked his notebook up from the ledge. With no other option he pulled out the back of his khaki pants and slid the notebook between his belt and back with half of the notebook left exposed. Having been in the shadow of the enclave the bright sun caused him to hold his hand in front of his face to see what the origin of the noise could be. To his left, the way he had come, he saw nothing. But to his right he saw the source of the grunting.

A man dressed in a suit was standing on the ledge with his back toward Paul. His legs were shaking and his chest was pinned to the brick wall as if an invisible force was holding him to it. The man kept his head away from the wall and appeared to be staring at a spot about two feet above him. He said over and over, "Oh God, Oh God."

Paul did not want to frighten the man. It was obvious he was terrified enough as it was. But the man obviously was in need of help. Why he was on the ledge was still open for debate but Paul assumed the worst. The man's fright was proof he was not out there for relaxation or to hide from anyone.

Paul said in a calm, monotone voice, "Hey, um, excuse me, can I help you with something?" A stupid question Paul knew but it was all he could think to say at the time.

The man tensed even more at the sound of another person's voice. He had to tilt his head back to have enough clearance to turn his head in Paul's direction to see who was speaking to him. His chin just barely scraped the bricks in front of him.

Paul recognized the man. He had dusted the man's picture that hung in the lobby for the year and a half he worked there. "Oh, it's you."

Oliver, though still scared and shaking became immediately disgusted on top of it. "Oh, I don't believe this. Do you people follow me twenty four hours a day just waiting for me to lose my mind? Well, good job, it looks like it's happening right now. Who told you to follow me? Was it Melanie Myers? Did she send you? Or was it King?"

Paul felt for a minute like he must be the subject of some bizarre joke. He questioned if he was still sitting on his bucket and this was a hallucination if nothing else. The scene was so out there, so strange and for the man to be asking him questions as if he knew what was going on when Paul was only trying to escape from work made it that much more surreal.

"I'm not following you. I'm just," Paul was stuck. What explanation could he give anyone as to why he was on the ledge in the first place? He saw his favorite hiding place slipping away from him. "I'm just out here to....you know." And he moved his hand in an arcing motion towards the ledge, his arm and hand shaped to mimic a swan.

Oliver seemed puzzled and confused and with doubt in his voice said, "Oh, you were going to jump?"

Paul shrugged. "I guess great minds think alike."

Oliver snorted. "Troubled minds." Still he clung to the side of the building, his knuckles white from gripping the window sill to his left, his right hand only holding bricks. Paul thought if he would just relax he would be much less likely to fall.

The contrast between the two men's demeanor, one perfectly at ease on the ledge six stories in the air and the other panicked and scared gave Paul confidence. He was in control. "I know who you are. You're that mayor guy. Gartrell. Right?"

Oliver turned his face away from him, again having to look up to move his chin past the bricks in his face. "Just leave me alone, okay. Go back around the corner and forget I'm out here."

"Oh no, mister. I can't do that. If you're thinking about jumping and you do it and I'm thinking about jumping and don't do it, there is going to be a mighty big mess for me to clean up down there in that courtyard. That would ruin my day. Pigeon crap is one thing to scrape off those pavers but a mayor stain would be much worse I would imagine. Now come on. Why are you out here?"

Oliver's face turned back toward him. "I don't know why I'm out here. Things are building up around me, making me crazy. I don't even know how I got out here but," he exhaled, "it's just," he paused again and glanced down and realizing it was a bad idea, looked back to the sky, "I've got people all over this city coming down on me."

The sucker in Paul's mouth was now gone and he was left with the stick. "Oh I see, so you want to come down on them for once. When they walk out the door." For emphasis and to mess with the well-dressed panicked man Paul tossed the sucker stick over the edge.

62

"Hey, you shouldn't litter." Oliver seemed overly offended in light of the situation.

"Relax, I'll pick it up when I go down there."

Oliver looked at his feet then quickly his eyes turned back to the sky. "Are you the janitor?"

"I'm the maintenance guy." Paul laughed to himself. "That's kind of odd when you think about it. I'm the maintenance guy scrubbing toilets, picking up trash. I have all kinds of reasons to be out here, thinking about, you know...." Again he made the arc with his fingers. "But you're the mayor of the city. You've got people kissing up to you all day and I'm sure you get anything you want, but here you are on the ledge right beside me. Wanting to end it all. That's kind of ironic when you think about it." Paul noticed Oliver's leg shaking, his pants going back and forth. The man was terrified. Paul decided that keeping the man engaged in conversation would be the best course of action to prevent him from making any rash decision that would result in more than one cracked paver in the court yard and a lot of questions from Fletcher. "Hey, can I ask you a question?"

Oliver still clung to the bricks. He closed his eyes tightly and put his forehead against the building. Paul took his silence as a 'Yes'.

"What kind of car do you drive?"

Oliver opened his eyes at the stupidity of the question. "What do I drive? What does that have to do with anything?" Oliver was getting annoyed and forgetting about his predicament though his grip on the building had not relaxed and his legs still shook.

"Well, see, that's just it, today I go to the bank to get a car loan right, I drive an old rusted out junk car. But can I do better than that thing? Apparently not according to the bank. The lady I talked to just shook her head, looked at me with this pitiful look on her face, like my dog had died or something, and said, 'Sorry'. That was it. Just 'sorry'."

Oliver was now coming back to his usual form. "Oh well pardon me, you drive an old car. By all means, you can go first. You go ahead and jump and I'll watch."

Oliver's irritation had the same effect on Paul. He began thinking about the bank again and was getting more upset. "You know what. I would trade places with you in a heartbeat. You and all of your rich friends, living it up on easy street."

Oliver took his hand off of the window sill for a second but quickly put it back. "Ha, easy street. That's the misconception you people have. All of you think it's some easy job, cheating the public, getting away with everything, doing crooked deals but it's not."

Paul cut him off. "Oh, is it harder than it looks?"

"You couldn't begin to understand the pressure I have on me every day. I've got investors wanting to back out of deals, accountants breathing down my neck, the most important election of my life coming up, and now just five minutes ago I find out my wife," he stopped and looked away. "I can't even say it."

"What? Is she leaving you?" Oliver did not answer

but Paul was intrigued by the direction of the conversation. "Oh, is she cheating? Now what makes you think that? Did you catch her in bed with somebody?"

"Not quite, but finding out some strange man has been going to my house every morning for the last week while I'm at work has kind of gotten me a little upset."

Paul shrugged. "Maybe it's just somebody doing work on your house. Like a pool guy."

"It's not the pool guy." Oliver yelled it at him but quickly regained his composure and fear. "Listen, I don't want to talk about this. My desire to jump was fading but now it's coming back."

"I think you should just ask her point blank. 'Honey, are you humping some other dude?' Get it all out in the open."

Oliver looked disgusted now. "Thank you Freud. But we're way past that now."

Paul could sense that Oliver's desire to jump was waning but wanted to get him back inside. He needed to force Oliver to look on the bright side. "At least you're married. I've got nobody. I mean there is this one girl I'm interested in but she doesn't know who I am. But look at you. You're the mayor. Money, power, prestige. You've got this huge advantage. And me? I've got nothing. No money, no nice car, no way to impress her. I think sometimes, 'What am I even doing, chasing a girl like that?' She's probably got some rich boyfriend."

Oliver saw his chance to be the dominant male. "See, that's your problem. You see something you want you've got to go after it. Take it. Don't sit back hoping." For a second he forgot where he was. "Forget about her boyfriend. Who cares? You want her you have to go for it. You have to tell yourself you're better than that guy and you deserve it more than he does."

Now Paul looked away but unlike Oliver he did not mind looking over the ledge to the ground. "Yeah, I don't buy that. I mean it may work for some people but I come to work and put on a jumpsuit with my name on the pocket. Not exactly Mr. Powerful, you know."

"But that doesn't have to be who you are for life. Get better, grow, change. You clean the building I'm in charge of. See the contrast here? You know the difference between us? I'm never satisfied. I'm happy with nothing. Nothing. I always want more and more. And I get it. But you are content to just get your minimum wage, whatever it is. Come to work. Go home. Drink beer. Sleep. And come back and do it all over again the next day. You can't be that way."

Oliver was on a roll now. "You've got to have a fire in your belly. Without that, without something driving you and getting you up in the morning you're no better than," the man stammered to think of something when he saw the only other being on the ledge with them, "than that pigeon. That is what separates us from the birds and dogs and...mice. Ambition. You

66

have to want something, anything, and go after it."

Oliver was in his element now telling somebody how to be. Paul continued looking over the edge, between his toes at the ground. "Yeah but see, I'm happy with nothing too though. But just in a different way. Right now, even though I've got no woman, a junkie car, a horrible dead end job, I'm for the most part happy."

"Nope, there's no way you're happy. You just tell yourself you are. You're disgusted with who you are and rightfully so. Look where you are, buddy?" Oliver saw Paul's reaction. A look of disgust spread across the maintenance man's face. "No offense. Don't take that personally. You should hate where you are and do anything to change it. Find a need and fill it. The rich people in this world are the ones who can give other people the prospect of more health, more money, or more sex. That's it. Think about it. Every wealthy person in this country, in this world, does one of those three things."

Paul shook his head and looked down. "Eh, I don't buy it. You've got to have connections. Start out rich to get richer. And I've got nothing."

The pigeon that had just been insulted squawked behind Oliver and startled him. His grip came off the window sill for a split second before he reattached himself firmly to the wall. He saw the stupidity of where he was. He had calmed down. "Listen, guy, I'm getting off this ledge. I've had enough of this."

Paul thought he would have a little more fun at the

mayor's expense. "Alright. Are you going the safe way or the short way?" And he moved his hand in the arc motion again.

Oliver turned his head again past the building this time his nose scraping slightly across the bricks in front of his face. "You go whichever way you want. I'm going back through my window." He started shimming on the ledge again to position himself in front of his window. Paul could see his shaking legs and his inability to take his hands from the bricks and place them on the window. He was afraid the man would lose his balance and fall backwards.

Paul found confidence and felt the need to take control of the situation. "Hey, let me go in first and that way I can pull you through the window when you let go." Paul was able to get to the window and stood shoulder to shoulder with Oliver. That calmed the mayor and the drama and place he had found himself struck him deeply for the first time. Before Paul could go through the window Oliver stood looking at his reflection in the window to his office.

"You know my birthday was a few days ago."

Paul was taken aback slightly by the casual comment. "Happy birthday."

Oliver continued. "Yeah, whatever. I'm 54 years old. Can you believe that? You know, I haven't told anybody this, but my dad," his voice trailed off considering whether it was even worth saying and swallowing hard. Paul could sense the man was getting emotional. Oliver gathered his thoughts and adjusted his grip on the window sill. "My dad was 54 when he died. He seemed so old back then and now, now that's me. That's been on my mind a lot these last few days with everything going on."

Paul passed him and dropped down onto the floor of Oliver's office but Oliver, lost now in his thoughts kept talking. "He was at work when it happened. He was always at work. He worked eighty hours a week. He was President of Weatherton Savings and Loan back in their hay days. His secretary called my mom while I was eating dinner one night. I can remember so clearly. My mom picked up the phone, said, 'Hello?' and then screamed. She dropped the phone and it landed on the kitchen floor right at her feet. BAM. And it broke into a thousand pieces. He had a heart attack sitting right there at his desk."

"That's terrible. So you never got to say 'bye' to him?"

"Ahh, goodbyes are overrated. I never told him I loved him, why should 'goodbye' be any different? My mom was devastated by that phone call and never really got over it. And you know something, all I remember thinking at the time was, 'Looks like we're going to need a new phone.' I've never told anybody that before."

Oliver snapped out of his trance and leaned over to come through the window. Paul grabbed his shirt and pulled him inside the office. They both fell backwards with the mayor landing on top of the maintenance man.

Oliver was back on stable ground, with the floor of his office beneath him and in the presence of someone who was also. As his emotions swung so abruptly from delight to despair and back to delight he was now on the top of the pendulum's swing. Oliver felt good, relieved. Adrenaline pumped through his veins. He was more in control because Albert King, Ann Strickland, and whoever the man was screwing his wife were forgotten in that instant and the only person he was thinking about was this lowly, hourly employee who worked in his building.

Oliver ran his hand through his hair and took a deep breath. He appreciated what Paul had done for him but could not just come right out and tell him. Instead he did the next best thing in his mind.

"Hey Buddy, you want a drink?" Oliver made his way over to the brandy on the small desk in the corner of his office. He opened a cabinet above it and withdrew two glasses. Paul watched him now from behind and had a chance to study this man. The mayor of the city. His thick, graying hair stood up on his head in different directions as if it was wet and he shook his head. The man's suit, Paul assumed, was more expensive than his junk car. The mayor had broad shoulders but a protruding stomach and Paul imagined he was an athlete of yesteryear, his corpulent body having seen better days.

Paul lifted his hand defending himself from the invitation. "No, no thank you. I don't drink."

Oliver held the brandy in one hand poised above the

awaiting glass on the desk and looked at Paul. "What? You don't drink?" He said it as if asking why a person would not bathe. "It's no wonder you went out on that ledge. No woman and no whiskey? I tell you what, without this stuff I'd have been over the edge a long time ago."

Oliver raised his glass to his new friend. "Cheers." The ice clinked the sides of the glass. His higher spirits were noticeable to Paul.

Paul smiled meekly and looked at the door. "I guess I better get back to work."

Oliver lifted his hand while looking down intently at the floor. "Sh sh sh." He cocked his head to one side like a retriever. "Do you hear that? What's going on out there?" He walked cautiously to the door and put his hand on the door knob. He nodded his head positive he was hearing something. He set his glass of brandy down on the credenza to his right and opened the door. An elderly lady, wearing a skirt and white blouse was standing in the doorway as if she had been waiting to come in.

"Ms. Connors? What is going on out here? What is this commotion?" Oliver was confused. It was as if a party was taking place in the reception area of his office and he was appalled and hurt that he knew nothing about it.

Ms. Connors' face had the look of relief and joy. "Oh thank goodness you're okay." She turned to the group of people behind her. "He's okay, everybody." She flung herself at him and she wrapped both of her

71

arms around his neck.

Oliver was still baffled by the scene. "Who are these people and what are they doing here?"

Ms. Connors let go of him and stepped back. She adjusted her blouse and appeared embarrassed to be overcome with emotion and relief. Paul could sense her eagerness from his vantage point in the office behind Oliver. "We saw you on the ledge and wanted to know what was going on and to make sure you are okay."

Oliver seemed perturbed by the explanation and his demeanor changed from curiosity to annoyance. "Oh, well tell them to leave." He took a step back from the door to have clearance to close it but Ms. Connors in a bold move put her hand on the door to stop it.

"They saw you save that man from jumping. There's a reporter here who wants to talk with you."

Oliver's head again turned to one side in an attempt to understand what was happening and to think a few moves ahead. Paul watched him wipe his face with his hands. He shook his head as if a bee was in his hair. He inhaled a large full breath and then in a second he was transformed. With a big smile on his face and a song in his voice he stepped from the threshold of his office to the reception area and said, "Good morning everyone. How are you today?"

Paul stepped up to the doorway and heard someone say, "There he is. There's the crazy person."

Oliver turned to Paul and said, "Give me just one second and I'll be right back." With that Oliver pulled the door closed leaving Paul in the mayor's office alone.   On the other side of the door Oliver had questions lobbed to him from the people.

"Mr. Mayor, are you okay?"

Oliver smiled but looked pained in some way, "Oh, yes, yes, I am fine. Thank you."

Another person asked, "Were you afraid? Going out on a ledge like that to save somebody. I would have been terrified."

"Oh no, I was not afraid."

Two questions came at him at once. "Did you know the man whose life you saved?" and "Do you feel like a hero?"

"A hero?"   And then the full realization came to Oliver of just what was happening.   "Oh no, I'm no hero. I was just," he paused and turned quickly to the door behind him verifying it was closed, "trying to help a guy out."

Janice McCurley, from the newspaper, stepped out of the crowd and had a notepad in her hand. "Do you have any training doing that? Talking people down from a ledge? What did you say to him? How long were you two out there before you convinced him to come in?"

Oliver took his time to respond.   He wanted to weigh each word carefully, to make sure he got the full benefit of this gift that had been given to him. Before he could say anything there was a loud shriek behind the mob of people in the reception area. The cameras and the faces in front of Oliver all turned to the door with the frosted glass that led into the hallway of City Hall. Holly ran through the reception area of Oliver's office.

"Oh my God, oh my God. You're okay. Oh thank God. I was so worried."

From the other side of the door Paul heard the voice and opened the door. A flash from a camera snapped just as he became visible again to the crowd. He could only hear Oliver say, "Come in to my office, ma'am." Paul was pushed back by the door and Oliver led Holly into the room and closed the door behind him.

Oliver looked at Holly. "You have got to calm down."

Paul was in shock that there in the same room with him was Holly, his next door neighbor. "Holly, I was just telling the mayor about you."

Oliver looked at Paul with a look of confusion. "You were?"

Holly was more confused than Oliver. "You were telling him about me?" She looked at Oliver for an explanation. With none forthcoming she turned back to Paul. "Who are you again?"

In his excitement Paul kept talking. "I was just telling the mayor about you and he told me I should tell you how I feel about you and how much I like you and he said that I should stand up and fight for you if you're the woman I want and that's what I'm going to do." Paul looked at Oliver. "Thank you for telling me that."

Oliver rolled his eyes still not quite sure of what was

happening. "Don't mention it. Really."

Holly could do nothing but go back and forth looking at both men in front of her. To Paul, "Who are you again?" and then to Oliver, "Did you really tell him that?"

Her confusion made Paul confused. Why would Holly be standing there if she did not know who he was? "I'm your next door neighbor, Paul Self."

Holly wanted desperately to understand what was going on but Oliver stood again at his desk in the corner pouring himself a drink.

"Did Oliver really save your life?"

Paul was confused by the question. "Well, no, that's not really what happened. I was," and Oliver stepped in to intercept the question.

"Young lady, I'm not sure who you are or how you know Paul but he has had a hard day. In fact, I think he may need to lie down for a while. Come here Paul, lie down on my sofa." And then to Holly while opening the door, "Please have a lovely day and we thank you for your concern."

Oliver guided Holly to the door by placing his hand on the small of her back as he did with many unwanted visitors to his office. Holly resisted slightly but his firmness told her to keep walking. She whispered to him, "What the hell is going on?" Oliver opened the door to see the group of people there still waiting for him and asking questions. As Holly was pushed through the crowd Oliver addressed the people. "The man I saved has had a terrifying experience and a rough day. If all of you would please leave us alone for a little while we would both very much appreciate it. If you would like to return in about an hour I should be able to answer any questions for your news story tomorrow. Thank you." Oliver looked at Holly. "It was very nice meeting you."

With that Oliver closed the door and once again only he and Paul were in his office. Before beginning his negotiation with the janitor, Oliver made an effort to connect with Paul in a friendly way. He shook his head as if confused by the events and the reason so many had come to his office. He said, "Unbelievable. Right?"

Paul was ready to leave the office. His twenty minute break had parlayed into something much more and he knew Fletcher would be on the prowl for him. The fact he was in the mayor's office was the only reason Paul felt he would be able to avoid reprimand from his boss as he knew his job at this point was shaky at best.

Oliver walked behind him and again pulled another glass out of the cabinet above the small desk that held his alcohol. Paul thought of his great aunt Edna who would leave burning cigarettes in different rooms of her house, setting one down and lighting a new one without remembering the other three she had lit before.

"So what is going on out there, huh?" Oliver was trying to be his friend. That always made Paul suspicious.

"It seems they think that you came out there and saved me from jumping off the building. Which is not true. Especially since you were the one who,"

Oliver held up his hand holding the glass with a finger of brandy in it. "Okay listen, I know you've had a rough day. Thank goodness I was out there, right? I mean, after all, you came back in through my window." He was trying to convince himself as much as Paul.

Paul turned away from the bookshelf and looked at the door behind Oliver. His escape was so close and he felt the sooner he left the less detrimental it would be. But still he could not leave allowing the mayor to believe, and worse, promote a fallacy. "That's true but still you were the one with an issue."

Oliver took a step closer to him. "Listen, Paul?" It was a question and he waited for a response. Paul nodded his head to affirm that was indeed his name. "Paul, you know people are going to believe what they believe, right?   And right now I need this more than you do. Being a hero or whatever, that could save me from a lot of grief and disaster. If you would go along with this that would really, really help me out. What do you say? I'll owe you."

Paul walked past Oliver to the door and turned. He was that much closer now to freeing himself from whatever conniving plans this politician was recruiting him for.

"You want me to tell everybody that I was out there on the ledge about to jump?" He waited for Oliver's response and the mayor only held out his hands as if to hug him. Paul saw a splash of brandy hit the floor. "No. No way. What would people think? What would Holly think? No, I don't think so. I'm not interested."

Oliver took another step to him with his arms out. He set the drink down on the credenza next to the glass he had a few minutes before. "People already believe it. You heard the reporter. They thought you needed help. And hey, isn't that what you told me when we were out there? Remember?" Oliver moved his hand in the arc that Paul had done on the ledge. "Come on. Do this for me. People would start seeing you as a person with feelings. This could help you as much as me. What do you say?"

"Oh I don't know," Paul was shaking his head. "No, I don't think so." He pinched his lip as if considering his options. Then he shook his head. Convinced. "No, I'm not interested."

Oliver walked back to his desk and sat down in his chair. This was where he did his negotiating. He had made big deals while sitting in that chair. Some of those deals helped the city he served but all, invariably, were made to help him.

Leaning back Oliver said, "Okay, what is the one thing in life you want more than any other. I'll help you get it. What did you say you went to the bank for? A car?" Oliver opened the top desk drawer and placed his hand on a checkbook but did not reveal it to Paul. It was too soon.

Paul stood there now interested in the negotiations and not wanting to make a dumb move. Though Oliver was in his element, Paul was like a game show contestant being put on the spot in front of millions of people, being asked to make a decision.

"Wow, if I had that car things would start changing in my life for sure."

Oliver was now the game show host, moving things along before the commercial break. "Okay then, so you want the car?"

Still biting his lip Paul said, "Yeah. If I had that car she would notice me."

"Who would notice you? Holly?"

Hearing her name made him excited. "Yeah, that's the girl. That's the girl I was telling you about. I can't believe she came down here."

Oliver now had Paul exactly where he wanted him. Oliver smiled to himself knowing the checkbook would not be needed. Quietly and inconspicuously he slid the desk drawer closed. Paul's desire had been identified and Oliver knew he could manipulate this to his advantage. But he had to let it go a little longer, grow a little stronger. "And I can see why you like her. She's a cute girl." Trying to relate to Paul in a locker room kind of way, Oliver held his hands out in front of his chest and raised his eyebrows as a further comment on Holly's looks. Paul showed his disgust at the gesture and Oliver made a note of that. "So really it's not the car you want more than anything. It's this Holly person? Is that right?"

"Yeah, she's so beautiful and," Paul was getting lost now in his thoughts, "perfect."

79

Oliver stood up with his hand to his chin as if he was thinking. "I tell you what. If I could get you and this....Holly, was it? out to dinner together for one night, I'll pay for dinner, would you be willing to go along with what everybody is saying, me being the hero or whatever and saving your life and all that?"

Paul smiled, unable to control his excitement. "Dinner with Holly? Like in a nice restaurant and everything? That would be a dream come true."

Oliver held his hands out beside him like a magician in front of a mesmerized audience. "Done." He held his finger up. "Now I can't guarantee what would happen after that. That's up to you two." He knew he was being a horrible person but that comment, one caveat that he felt would protect Holly's dignity, justified the offer and made right the wrong he was committing. "So, a nice dinner. A chance to get to know her, to woo her with your charm. How's that sound? Is it a deal?"

Paul tried to be logical though his emotions had already determined what his answer would be. "And how long do I have to pretend that you saved my life?"

Oliver swatted his hand in the air, discarding the comment. "Oh you know how these stories are. People will talk about it for a day or two and then they'll forget all about it. Something else will happen that will get everybody talking."

Paul sat down on the couch and looked at the floor between his feet. Thinking. Oliver looked out the window but kept one eye on the janitor in his office trying to read him. Paul slapped his hands on his knees and stood up. "Okay, for a dinner with Holly I'll do it. But how will you know how to contact her?"

Oliver smiled. "Give me your number and I'll see what I can do."

8

Dusk came to Weatherton after a strange day. When the sun was setting, when it was not quite dark but everyone else had gone home to their other life outside of work that was Oliver's favorite time of the day. He liked the evening breezes that blew through the town and the promise of what the night may bring. The chill of a crisp November night gave Oliver his second wind after ten o'clock. He relished those days when he had a mission, a task at hand that needed to be completed before he went to bed. Often it was a civic club's dinner that he would speak to or he would find himself as the Master of Ceremonies at a charitable event in town. He wanted to be seen. He wanted to be the man up on the stage holding a microphone while holding everyone else's attention.

On this day, a day that had brought so many unusual events and circumstances he had a more direct mission. He knew because it involved only one person that needed to be convinced of something it would be far more difficult than convincing the masses of anything. With a group Oliver found he only had to speak to a small number of about ten percent of the people present. They had to realize that what he was talking about made somewhat good sense. It was unnecessary to convince the small majority that it was the best plan or the most logical, only that it may be the best. And once those ten percent were willing to listen, once they began nodding their heads slightly, Oliver knew he had them. Begin talking to only those ten percent, he had learned a long time ago, make that handful of people feel smarter than everyone else in the room and then watch, like lambs to the trough, all of the other people begin to follow. And the amazing thing he had come to understand was that those few people who had bought in ten percent would then be outpaced by the others who were willing to buy in sixty percent and then Oliver could sit back and watch the lambs convince each other of what he was saying. He loved that moment. He could always identify that second when the room changed and came over to his side. It was moments like that he lived for.

But this night was different. It was late, almost midnight. He would not get to see one group goad another along the pathway to his way of thinking. For Oliver to accomplish his mission it would be completely up to him convincing a single person to go along with his plan.

He sat on the corner of Holly's bed with his hands clasped in front of him fully aware it would appear to an onlooker that he was praying. He needed her to do this and he would not be above begging for it.

Holly pushed a strand of hair behind her ear. She wore only a pair of red panties and a blue bra. She had changed minutes before when Oliver called and said he was on his way over. He had once told her that this combination, the red and the blue, he liked more than anything else she wore. He had gone on to say he liked it as much as her naked body. That comment stung her and almost nullified his previous compliment. Holly was a smart girl and she recognized this was Oliver's way of doing things. Any compliment he gave her would make her respond with delight and increase her confidence but she had learned to expect, within five minutes of being lifted up, that he would say something else to send her crashing down. Other men in her life treated Holly like a queen but Oliver Gartrell was the one person in her life who made sure she knew he was the king. She found that appealing, the fact she was not in control. She used the ability she had to make a man do anything she asked and basked in the desperate smiles men gave her. Oliver was the one exception to that rule and it was for that reason he had the tightest grip on her. She was under his control when they were together. She craved his compliments because they were so rare and never freely given.

"I don't know, Ollie. All of this sounds so strange."

Oliver clasped his hands together more firmly. "Come on Holly. You have to do this for me. I offered him a car, money, anything I could think of and all he said was, 'No, a nice dinner with Holly is all I want.' And I told him I would see what I could do."

Holly looked at herself in the mirror. She was looking exceptional in that patriotic combination of the red and blue, Oliver was right about that and so she was a little dismayed he had not yet made a move on her but instead was talking about this janitor from work. "He turned down a car?"

84

"That's right. Flat out turned it down."

Holly turned to him and considered sitting on his knee but remained strong wanting him to make the move that would initiate something more. "But Ollie, I'm a stripper not a prostitute. And I don't know, this sounds a little bit like prostitute territory, you pimping me out to some weirdo."

"He's not a weirdo." Holly was repulsed that he objected to the wrong thing. "He's a nice, reasonably normal guy."

"Who went out on a sixth story ledge this afternoon to kill himself. Yeah he sounds real stable. Why do you even have to help him at all? If you saved his life, you saved his life. Is he not satisfied with that?"

Oliver stood up and Holly took a breath and held it, waiting for him to touch her. "It's a long story. But I'm trying to help the guy out."

Holly exhaled. "Since when did you become all charitable? Is this because of the election? Is this to get his vote? Because if you expect me to go out to dinner with everyone who is undecided you can forget it."

Oliver turned his back to Holly to keep her from seeing his eyes roll. "No, just Paul. You'll do it this one time, right?"

Holly walked to him and reached out and held both of his hands in hers. She pulled him closer to him. Because Oliver had left his final plea in front of them he did not object. She was skilled at manipulation just like him.

"Ollie," she had used that name repeatedly, the one he hated, just to see if he would correct her and to this point he had not, "I'll have to think about it. This morning when we were talking I felt like things were changing between us, we were growing apart and that hurt me. And now not even fifteen hours later you're standing here in my apartment begging me to go on a date with some other guy. It's strange Ollie, you've got to admit that." She walked to the linoleum floor beside her stove to see if he would follow her.

Oliver made the decision to follow but knew he would have to remain strong. He pulled her close to him and hugged her. Her chest pushed against his. "I know things have been strange between us but it's this election. It's making me crazy. Do you know that woman bought up every billboard in town? Her ads are on the radio every time I get in my car. Where did she get the money? I can't figure it out."

He hugged her tighter, trying to squeeze sympathy from her so she would do what he asked. Her silence bothered him. He had not yet overcome her objection. He closed his eyes and shook his head slightly. He would have to do it but did not want to. "You know I love you, right? This is just for one night. One dinner. What do you say? It will help him. It will help us."

Holly stepped back to look him in the eye. Her expression was stern and serious. "You love me? You've never said that before, Oliver. At least not in my kitchen, with both of your feet on the floor." Her hands came together in front of her face. She covered her mouth and nose. Her eyes were moist. Oliver hated himself in that moment. "I love you too, Oliver." Her smile was like none he had ever seen on her. "Okay, I'll do it. I'll go to dinner with him but on just one condition."

Oliver turned his back again. He clinched his fists and gritted his teeth, angry with himself for taking such an unnecessary step. He felt he was slipping to have conceded something so cheap to expedite the outcome of his visit. His shame may have had a little to do with her emotional response and the pain she may endure in the future because of it but mainly the shame he felt was for playing such an easy card. He would say anything he decided to manipulate another person. What did this woman want? She could not be satisfied. He tried to hide the annoyance in his voice. "What? What is it?"

Holly had that look in her eye. An excitement, a daring, a cunning. It was the look he remembered from the first night he met her and they ended up in a hotel room together in Atlanta. The look had excited him that night and made him consider innumerable possibilities. Now that look made him worry. "Well, I don't know him at all. I'm not sure I want to go to a restaurant with him and be all by myself. So what about," she paused to add to the excitement. Oliver realized how much his stomach was hurting. "Dinner at your house? Just you and me and him."

Oliver shook his head not even knowing where to begin in objecting to her request. Holly could see the withdrawal on his face. She had to keep the momentum in her favor. "I think that is the only way I'll do it. I'll eat dinner with the guy but only if it's at your house and you're there."

Oliver could not believe the predicament he had found himself in. Driving to her apartment thirty minutes before he knew this would be a challenge but ultimately he had expected to leave her apartment with exactly what he wanted and all on his terms. This was a twist to the deal that he had not anticipated and he felt weak at that moment and questioned his skill of negotiation. Was he losing an edge? Convincing Holly to do what he wanted had always been his fall back when he began feeling weak and started questioning his influence over others. He placed his hands on his hips, thinking. He turned his back to her and scratched the back of his head. She had made a brilliant move. He was put in check and had no choice but to move his king. He did not like her terms but was trapped.

"If we do it Sunday night Sheryl won't be there. She's got some kind of ladies club she goes to. Some charity to save the pygmies in the rain forest or something. Okay, dinner at my house Sunday night. A quick dinner." He held his finger in front of his nose as if admonishing a child.

Holly was smiling widely now not offended by the finger in her face. She felt they had compromised and both were getting exactly what they wanted. She decided to push it one more time. "There's just one more thing."

Oliver was beyond annoyed and had to bite the inside of his cheek to calm himself down. "What?"

"Say it again. Say, 'I love you, sugar plum'."

"I love you."

"Sugar plum." Holly was asking for it all.

"Sugar plum."

Holly squealed with delight and jumped up and down. Oliver could not help but watch her breasts move. They were pretty much perfection in a blue bra. She threw her arms around his neck. "I love you too, Ollie. I really do. Why don't you stay?"

He put his hands on her shoulders and glanced down at her breasts. They were fantastic, he could not deny that but unlike the past many months he could deny himself the opportunity to see them. "I can't. I have to go. There are some things I need to check on." He pulled himself away from her and walked to the apartment door. If Oliver took the time to consider what he had just done, turning Holly down, he perhaps could have found it worrisome. Never in his life had he ever refused that which was being offered to him when the person was as beautiful as Holly. Now, in less than twenty four hours he had done it twice. But he put that out of his mind. He knew it was only stress. All he could think about was Ann Strickland and Albert King and Melanie Myers. That would be enough to kill any man's drive he decided. He turned to the door without giving it another thought.

Holly poked out her bottom lip to express her sadness at him leaving. In the past she had used the pouty look to get what she wanted but this time Oliver did not even notice. Then she smiled and said, "Oh, Ollie, I've got something for you." She trotted to the dresser next to her bed again hoping he would follow her but he stayed at the door, his hand never leaving the knob. She picked up his black book and trotted back to him. "I found this earlier today after you left. It was between the sofa cushions. It must have fallen out of your pocket the last time we," she fondled the lapel of his jacket and let him answer the question in his mind. "Why don't you stay a little longer? For me."

Oliver put the book in the pocket of his coat before buttoning it. "No, I have to be somewhere. I told you."

Holly felt hurt and cold. "This late at night?"

Oliver looked out of the window next to her front door as if expecting someone to be looking back in. "I've got some….things. Can you?" He pointed at the door without finishing his sentence.

Holly made one last attempt. She walked to him and put her body against his. "Maybe if the crazy guy goes home early on Sunday night you and I can hang around your house for a little while." She touched his collar. "You can give me a tour of the master suite and we could…."

Oliver was annoyed now and snapped at her. "No, Holly. This is strictly business. I've got a lot going on right now. Too much to worry about….this." He moved his hand back and forth between them. "Okay?

So, can you look outside for me?" He had been cruel and was aware of that. He added, "Please."

Holly put on her bathrobe that was hanging on the chair next to the door. She pulled it closed abruptly to make Oliver realize she was taking her offer from the table. He did not pick up on that. She opened the door and looked out quickly. She stepped back inside and out of the way. She looked at the wall next to her when she said, "All clear." As usual her high from Oliver had led to an immediate low.

"Thanks." Oliver said it while walking out on to the dark breezeway. "I'll be in touch." Quickly he ran to his car and got inside. Once inside he pulled his cell phone from his pocket along with the black book Holly had just given him. He tossed the book onto the passenger seat without a second thought. What seemed like the most important thing in the world that morning was now the furthest thing from his mind. His day had brought new problems and opportunities that the number in that black book could not solve. He pulled a piece of paper from between the seats of his car and dialed the number he had written down earlier in the day.

"Hello, Paul? This is Mayor Gartrell. It's all set up. Seven o'clock on Sunday. And I was thinking, since we've gotten to be friends today, let's just do it at my house. Holly? Oh yeah, she's excited. She practically planned the whole thing. Okay, yes, yes, I'll see you tomorrow, yes at City Hall." Oliver hung up the phone and tossed it to the passenger seat. The thought did not occur to him that the person he had been talking to was less than fifty feet away from him, in the apartment next door to Holly's. He turned around in his car to back out and could only shake his head as he muttered the word that had somehow come to describe his life. "Unbelievable."

Friday, November 3

9

Paul woke up in the best of spirits. Things were looking up for him. There was a hope now for his future that had not existed before. Just twenty four hours before he had intended to go to the bank, get a loan, and win Holly's favor by driving a new sports car. Although he felt defeated at the bank, feeling as though he had hit some kind of bottom, he now understood that was the universe speaking to him, communicating to him on a serendipitous level. He did not need a fancy sports car. Everything else had fallen in to place.

He spent extra time in the bathroom, combing his hair, brushing his teeth, trimming his nails. Perhaps what Oliver told him was true. Holly had wanted him as much as he had wanted her. This new development made him want to look his absolute best. He shook his head at the amount of wasted time that he doubted her attraction to him.

He knew he could not be late for work that morning but he wished to see Holly outside the apartment, to have a quick discussion with her, if only to say 'hi'. He opened the door to his apartment and stepped outside. Leaving the door open he walked back in, telling himself he had forgotten something but knowing he had not. He walked outside again, this time aware he had to get in his car at that moment to make it to work on time. Slowly, reluctantly he locked his apartment door. He took small steps to his car, keeping an eye on Holly's door while doing so. He got in his car and sat there. Her door could be seen in his rearview mirror. He waited. He looked at his cell phone as if there could be an important message on it, but still kept an eye on the rearview mirror. Nothing. He was disappointed and embarrassed in equal measure. He cranked his car and drove slowly from the parking lot, still hoping that maybe she would open her door.

Paul arrived at work and was pleased to see he had five minutes to spare. As Paul walked through the hallways after entering through the maintenance door in the back he noticed more than one person he passed was looking at him, not just as a passerby but as if they wanted to say something to him but did not have the courage. One man, Paul was certain, even pointed at him while talking to a woman in the hallway. Paul at first decided the attention he was receiving had to do with his physical appearance in some way. Were his pants torn? Did he have shaving cream on his ear? His hand went to the zipper of his pants more than once to be sure it was up. He did not know the reason but the stares made him self-conscious. It was when he saw Fletcher he began to gain more understanding as to why he was the object of people's attention.

Fletcher was at the end of the hallway. Paul saw him

pacing back and forth from one wall to the other, appearing nervous and worried. As Paul studied him, Fletcher sensed that he was being watched and looked up to see his employee looking at him. It was then his boss surprised him by doing the most unusual thing. He stretched out his arms still more than thirty feet away and came walking toward his employee. Paul looked behind him as Fletcher got closer. He panicked as he was trying to figure out what his boss may do to him.

Without a word Fletcher reached his employee and embraced him in a bear hug. His huge biceps pinned Paul's arms to his side. Fletcher even leaned back and Paul felt his feet rise slightly from the floor.

Fletcher set his employee down and stepped back but left his hands on Paul's shoulders. "Oh my God. Oh my God. Paul, you're here. I was afraid you weren't going to show up today."

Paul was trying to process what was going on and in his confusion asked, "Are you this happy that I'm early?"

"No, I'm just happy that you're alive." He reached behind him and pulled a folded newspaper out of his back pocket. That was odd to Paul because he knew his boss hated newspapers. He hated cleaning up discarded paper left on benches in the building and on the floor and sticking out of trash cans. "Look, you're in the paper." He handed it to Paul.

"I had no idea you were going through such tough times. I was afraid you had gone home and done something irrational without anyone there to save you. I could imagine you putting your head in the oven or drinking ant poison or something."

Paul looked down at the paper in his hand. He was going to ask what page to turn to when he saw his picture on the front page. "What is this?"

Never a garrulous person, Fletcher was talking more than Paul had ever seen him. "You know I had no idea all the problems you had. The family stuff. The insecurities. I didn't know you were depressed. I just knew you were lazy. I'm really, really sorry." Again he put his hands on Paul's shoulders trying to coax him to look him in the eye and sense his heartfelt apology.

Paul was trying to concentrate on the paper. "I'm not really depressed so much as," he trailed off still trying to read the article.

"Now Paul, let's not do that. There is no need to be in denial. Not after going out on a ledge to do what you were going to do." Fletcher made the same arc with his hand that Paul had done for the mayor the day before. "The whole denying stage is done, don't you think? I've been hard on you and I'm so, so sorry."

Paul was growing more annoyed at the interruption and held his hand up to show he was reading. Fletcher continued. "Like yesterday, when I told you I was depressed about the funeral." Suddenly Fletcher took a step back from Paul and put his hand over his mouth. He had a look of horror in his eyes. "Is that what made you snap? It's because of me, isn't it? I can't believe this. Come here."

Fletcher reached out his two huge arms toward Paul to hug him again but this time Paul stepped back and held up his hand. "That's okay, really. I don't remember you even saying that."

Fletcher got very serious and began to whisper for emphasis on what he was saying. "Have you thought about professional help? Like a shrink or somebody? How can I help you?"

Paul was looking down at the paper wanting to be left alone. Fletcher snapped his fingers at a brilliant idea. "I know. The courtyard. Do you want me to move you back out there on a permanent basis?"

Paul heard the question and put down the paper considering the offer. "Okay, yeah, that would be nice."

"Consider it done." Paul looked down at the paper again trying to read when Fletcher stood up straight and came to attention immediately. With his chest out and his feet together, Paul looked up to see him saluting. "Hello, Mr. Mayor."

Paul looked to his right to see Oliver Gartrell walking up beside him. Oliver put a hand on Paul's shoulder. Paul did not like being touched and already it had happened too much for him that morning. "How are you today, young man? You had me real scared there yesterday for a little while. I'm glad everything worked out the way it did."

A flash bulb made Paul look up. A man was standing in front of him taking a picture of Oliver who still had his hand on Paul's shoulder. Oliver smiled at Paul as a flash was thrown at them. Then Oliver turned to the camera and smiled. Paul did not reciprocate. Another flash.

Fletcher was still fully engaged in the conversation. "Yes sir, Mr. Mayor. I saw the whole story. You're a hero, huh? You are so brave."

Oliver shrugged his shoulders. Paul thought the man would have blushed if he was capable. "I am always trying to help people. As the mayor of this fine city that is my number one concern. Yesterday I just happened to help someone in more trouble than usual."

Oliver held a brown paper bag in his hand. He reached into it and pulled out two campaign buttons that said simply, "Oliver" on it. He handed both to Fletcher. "Here take a button and give one to your wife or girlfriend. And don't forget to vote this coming Tuesday. Next week. Tell your friends."

Fletcher gladly took the button. "Oh you can count on me, Mr. Mayor. After saving Paul's life here, you should win in a landslide for sure, Mr. Mayor."

Oliver smiled and then turned his attention back to Paul. Paul rolled his eyes wishing his boss would stop saying, "Mr. Mayor," with every sentence.

Oliver looked Paul in the eye with an intensity that Paul could not deny by looking away. Another flashbulb. "And you take care now. I don't want to look out of my window today and see your bloody spot on the sidewalk below me."

Fletcher laughed nervously at the comment while

Oliver walked down the hallway repeatedly reaching into the brown paper sack and pulling out buttons to give to each person he passed.

"Paul, you get to work but don't push yourself too hard. If you need anything you let me know." Fletcher put his huge arm on Paul's shoulder one more time and squeezed him as a dad would to a son on a baseball field. "Be safe, Paul." And with that, Fletcher turned and opened the door to the stairwell. Paul could hear him whistling as the door closed behind him. Paul was left there in the rotunda with a campaign button in one hand and a newspaper with his face on the front page in the other. He looked up and down the hallway still in a fog of confusion. He could not help but wonder just what was going on.

10

Paul stood outside the door looking at the frosted glass with the words "Mayor's Office" printed across it. He had been tricked into something the day before that he now regretted and he felt going into the office again was only opening himself up for more manipulation and regret. He had become well-accustomed to dealing with short tempered people in his life, messy people, rude, even a maniac or two but to deal with a person as dissolute as Oliver Gartrell was something he was unaccustomed to. He did not want to go see the mayor but still, what he had read in the newspaper needed to be discussed. He had made a deal with the mayor the day before but this was beyond anything he had imagined. He had been tricked, duped, conned.

Paul took a deep breath, not really knowing if what he felt was anger. It was not his nature to get angry but usually chose instead to forgive and forget or more accurately avoid and ignore. His magnanimous spirit was one that he felt was a positive quality he possessed though he knew it often was a weakness more than anything else. This latest misstep had gotten his name in the paper and a label he did not like. Paul could be hard on himself and see himself in a poor light most of the time but this public embarrassment would influence other people's opinion of him. This was much more serious.

With his courage intact he opened the door determined to be strong. He would demand to speak to the mayor. In front of him was an empty desk and still yet another door he must pass through, this one of solid oak. Should he barge in on the mayor or wait for Oliver to walk out? He had waited three minutes or more when a woman walked down the hall and could see his silhouette through the frosted glass of the door. The door opened and he was confronted by a vaguely familiar face. The woman he had seen the day before, the woman who had been so relieved to see Oliver alive, stood before him with her head cocked to one side.

"Can I help you?" The woman was being cold and distant in her helpfulness but then realized who Paul was. "Oh it's you? The person from the...the mayor's new friend." And then with the softness of a kindergarten teacher to a crying child, "Are you feeling better today?"

Paul was annoyed by the question and the demeanor in which she was talking to him. He decided to be blunt. "I was never feeling bad."

Badly. He meant to say badly and now felt he may have looked less intelligent to this woman.

"You gave us quite a scare yesterday, didn't you? Going out on that ledge. I mean, it's a good thing Mr. Gartrell was there to save you."

Paul now knew what he was. He was angry and would defend his honor. "I was not on the ledge to jump off. He was out there," but his clarification was interrupted by the oak door opening behind him. Oliver was on his way to the copy machine holding a copy of the newspaper in his hand when he saw Ms. Connors and Paul in the reception area.

"Oh hello. Where is Lane?"

Ms. Connor rolled her eyes. "Is Lane ever here? I could walk in this office ten times and see her once if lucky. You need a new secretary, Mr. Mayor."

Oliver ignored the suggestion. He was too preoccupied to care. "Perhaps." He turned his attention to Paul. "And how are you? Are we feeling better?"

Paul decided not to finish his story of what actually happened in front of Ms. Connors. He would show Oliver more respect than he had been shown. "Can I talk to you in your office for a minute?"

Oliver was very animated and put his hand on Paul's shoulder to display his empathy for Ms. Connors' benefit. "Absolutely. I definitely have a few minutes to give to my new buddy. Come on in here." He directed Paul to his office and turned toward Ms. Connors and shook his head as if his honorable work was never complete.

Paul stood in front of Oliver's desk. Oliver came in and closed the door behind him. His attitude changed completely now that he was alone with the only other person who knew the truth. He walked to his desk held up the rolled newspaper in his hand. Paul for a second thought Oliver was going to swat him with it.

"How great is this? Huh? How great? Front page.

It's like we're famous."

Paul did not share the mayor's enthusiasm and said only, "Yeah," in the most monotone voice he could.

Oliver sat down at his desk. "What's wrong? You're on the front page of the paper. Everyone is talking about you. Life doesn't get any better than that, does it?"

Paul's voice began to rise. "When you're portrayed as Superman it must be pretty good but it makes me out to be some kind of lunatic."

Oliver had an incredulous, disbelieving look on his face. "Lunatic? Where does it say that?" He began flipping through the paper in an exaggerated way to settle Paul down.

Paul filled in the blanks for him. "Horrible childhood, disconnected father, maybe drugs. If my mother sees this she'll kill me."

Oliver nodded with understanding and sympathy. "Oh, so it was an abusive childhood too. That's too bad."

Paul was tired of having words put in his mouth and yelled out, "No! It was a perfect childhood. I can't believe this. I can't."

"Relax, relax. Sit down." He waited for Paul to take a seat never wanting to look up at anybody but especially not this guy. "You didn't kill anybody. You were just the guy having a bad day and I saved you."

Paul looked away. "According to the paper."

Oliver took a more stern voice, expressing his

dominant alpha tendencies, knowing he could not let this janitor have any more control than what he allowed. "No, that's what happened. The paper just wrote about it. We have a deal. Remember? Holly?" Oliver held his hands out in front of his chest in an implication of Holly's large breasts as he had done the day before. He hoped the visual aid would bring Paul back in line with their agreement and remind him of his reward in the deal. Paul had never been one to participate in locker room talk as Oliver had. Girls were never the butt of jokes behind closed doors. In that way he was as much out of his element as if discussing Caribbean Islands or choices of wine.

He shook his head but could not help but smile thinking of Holly. "I don't know. This isn't exactly the way I envisioned all of this happening."

Oliver stood up from his desk to look down at Paul. "All of what happening? Meeting Holly? Getting to know her? Of course this is not the way you envisioned it. You never envisioned it. You may have wished for it but without me it never would have happened."

Paul looked away again. "That's true but..."

Oliver cut him off. "That's absolutely true. Look, you're getting what you want, a dinner with Holly and I'm getting what I want, to look good in the community. It's a win-win situation."

Paul objected. "Well, I want to look good to Holly. What is she thinking when she reads this? She's gonna think I'm nuts. Crazy. Hide the steak knife kind of thing. The paper makes me out to be a wild animal or something that you came along and tamed."

Oliver shrugged and made his point again. "I did bring you in off the ledge."

Paul's voice rose as he put his hand on the desk but did not pound on it. "No, I brought you in off the ledge."

Oliver put his hands in front of him. "Hey, hey, keep it down. Look you came in through my window."

Just the mention of Holly's name had heightened Paul's sensitivity to what had happened and the new perception people had of him. Now granted, he would be the first to admit that no one had any perception of him before the ledge incident but he felt no perception was better than a negative one. Though he felt Oliver may disagree with that.

Oliver made one final push to persuade Paul to stick with the plan that would serve him well. "Look, Holly told me she is excited about the opportunity to have dinner with you. She is looking forward to it. Now you don't want to mess that up. You have good taste in women. She was giddy when I told her. Giddy. Now get to work, calm down and get ready for Sunday night. I have some important work to do and hey, those toilets aren't going to scrub themselves, am I right?"

Oliver walked around his desk to the office door and placed his hand on the door knob. "I'll see you at my house. Sunday night. Seven thirty. It's going to be fun."

Paul found himself in a position where he could not object. The door was open. Oliver had work to do. Paul walked out of the office and turned around to make one final plea. "But I just…"

Oliver held up his hand. "Really, Paul. I'm swamped. We'll talk later."

Paul walked through the reception area and noticed that still no one was at the desk. He opened the door with the frosted glass and walked back into the hallway. He was in no mood to think about his job and what duties he would have that day but knew he had no other choice.

Oliver stood inside his office with his back to the oak door. "Unbelievable."

11

Oliver walked back to his desk and spent several minutes doing nothing but staring out of the window. A knock came on his door. Annoyed at the interruption and making up his mind if it was Paul again he would not be so kind or patient, Oliver walked to the door. Before he could open it the door was pushed into him. Offended by the rudeness, Oliver cussed but under his breath rather than out loud when he saw who it was.

"Oh Mr. Mayor. I'm so glad to have caught you while you were on a break. What was the chance of that?" Ann Strickland made her way into the room. "How are you today, Mr. Mayor? I hope you're doing well." Sarcasm.

"I am doing lovely today, Ms. Strickland. How are you?"

Ann walked to his desk and saw the newspaper was the only thing on it. "I see you made the front page of the newspaper, Mr. Mayor. Very impressive. And you know what the crazy thing is, I knew you were going to make the front page pretty soon, I would have bet on it but this is not the story I expected to see. In this picture you're smiling."

Oliver tried to suppress his discomfort and anger with humor. "Oh Ann, did you read the story or just look at the pictures? Go ahead, read it. I'm a hero and you know how the public is, they love a hero."

"More than they love a crook, Mr. Gartrell? Which will you be known as?"

"Crook? Who's a crook? Look, I've just done my best the last years to take care of the citizens of this city. If that's a crime then I guess you can lock me up."

"Ahh," Ann smiled, "you being locked up, that brings me to why I am here. I came by to get those numbers from you that we've talked about."

Oliver walked back to his chair putting the desk between them for protection. "Ms. Strickland, you know what, I've been so busy in the last twenty four hours saving people's lives and whatnot, that I haven't had a chance to get them for you."

Ann's laughed matched his. "Now why am I not surprised that you let me down? Living in this city I should be use to that by now."

That was a low blow and the politician in Oliver reared its head. He leaned forward and put his elbows on his desk, relinquishing the laid back attitude he had first taken with her. "The people in this city are wealthier, healthier and happier than they when I took office, Ann. Surely you can see that."

Ann stopped laughing and matched his serious tone. "Oh please, don't give me all that. This is not some campaign speech."

Oliver picked up the paper. "I don't need a

campaign speech. I've got this. When these voters see they've got a hero in charge of their city there's no way I can lose."

Ann shook her head at Oliver with a facial expression that conveyed complete disdain. "Pretty soon all of the headlines in the world won't help you. This is not a game, Mr. Gartrell. This is serious. It is not another fairy tale that you perpetuate to the public. Monday morning. We're going to get to the bottom of this little charade you're running."

Oliver scratched his head like he was thinking. "Oh Ann, I would love to, I really would but as I told you yesterday there is this little election thing I'm dealing with. Monday won't be good for me either. In fact I have a debate scheduled with Ms. Myers right downstairs, so Monday won't work."

"Oh that's right, the debate. That should certainly answer a lot of questions everyone has as to whether their current mayor is a competent, literate human being."

Oliver laughed. "Oh Ann, I can read. See, I'll prove it." He picked up the paper again and held it so she could see it. "Hero. It says it right there. See?" He pointed to the headline. "Oliver Gartrell- Hero."

Ann stood up and straightened her skirt with an air of austerity in contrast to the man child before her. Oliver could not help but notice her toned arms and slim waist. As much as he disliked her he could not deny that she was a beautiful woman and he often wished their relationship was more amicable. But he knew that was an impossibility.

"Monday morning I hope you will be ready to answer all of my questions regarding the allocation of City funds and numerous missing expense reports. And as a bonus it sounds like we'll have an audience on top of it. The whole city can watch you sweat rather than just me." She walked to the door and opened it. "Oh," as if she just thought of something, "Mr. Mayor, that guy you saved yesterday, the one who must have come to the conclusion that life was not worth living, which one was he?"

The sweat comment had made him self-conscious. Oliver wiped his forehead with a handkerchief and snapped back, "Which one what?"

Ann's back was to him and she looked over her shoulder, "Was he the wealthy, healthy, or happy one in our fair city?"

Oliver called out to her as she walked through the reception area, "Thanks to me he's not dead." He walked to the door happy with his comeback to her. Ann was opening the door to the hallway and Oliver stepped out of his office. Lane was now back at her desk. "Oh Ann, hold on a second." He turned to Lane who was fully engaged with her computer looking closely at her monitor. Oliver could see pictures of shoes. "Lane? Could you make sure Ms. Strickland here gets a campaign button? I don't want her to feel left out."

Lane reached for the brown paper sack on the corner of her desk. Ms. Strickland shook her head and showed her teeth as if in pain rather than smiling. "That won't be necessary." She stepped into the hallway and closed the door behind her.

12

"Oh look, it's crazy."

Paul was rolling a bucket of water down the third floor hallway with one hand on the bucket's arm and the other on the mop sticking out of it. The three wheels on the bottom wanted to spin and pull the bucket to the left. Paul hated cleaning toilets. He hated spraying and wiping windows, but for some reason mopping floors, soaking up spills and leaks and the occasional pile of vomit did not bother him. Someone had left a trail of coffee down the center of the hallway and the prospect of using the mop to follow that line and pull it all up off of the linoleum was something Paul looked forward to doing. He hated that Sullivan, following behind him was there to interrupt him.

"Not now Sullivan. I've got some work to do."

Sullivan reached him and circled in front of the bucket to stop Paul in the hallway. "Oh I bet you do." Paul thought of the bully scenes in movies when the tough guy does his best to intimidate someone else. The one exception to this scene was that Sullivan weighed about one hundred and ten pounds and was not intimidating in the least. "What are you working on today? Figuring out a way to get the love from your mom that she never gave you?"

Paul rolled the bucket around Sullivan and

continued on his way. Sullivan followed behind him. "I've read the paper. I knew you were dysfunctional but I didn't know your whole family was."

Paul stopped the bucket and looked his coworker in the eye. He was annoyed to the point of being direct. "Sullivan, why are you bothering me?"

"Fletch told me the news. So you're back outside and I'm back to the toilets, huh?"

Paul rolled his eyes refusing to have the ridiculous conversation. "I don't have time for this. I've got a lot on my mind."

"Obviously. You're crazy. I can't imagine all of the mess you've got going on in your mind. Just don't go near the elevators. Fletch told me to keep an eye on you. He said, 'Don't let Crazy near the elevators.' He doesn't want you riding up to the sixth floor again. I told him not to worry about it. You never finish any job you set out to do so why should the whole jumping thing be different."

Paul stopped again. "He did not tell you that."

Sullivan nodded. "Yeah he did. That's why he put you back in the courtyard. He figures there's no way you could hurt yourself out there. I told him you could throw yourself on a garden spade but he didn't think you would do that. Why don't you prove him wrong? Since you've got nothing to live for."

Paul had been consumed all day with the bad news in the paper. He had felt victimized by the arrangement he and Oliver had come up with but now he had the opportunity to focus on the positive side of it. "I do have something to live for. I have everything to live for. In fact, Sunday night I'll be at dinner with the most beautiful woman in the whole city. So while you're at home heating up your noodles or whatever, I'll be eating a steak and gazing into her eyes."

Sullivan took a step towards Paul as if Paul had questioned his manhood. "Oh, is that right? And who is this so called woman you're talking about? You and your momma got a big date?"

Paul rolled his eyes at the juvenile comment. "Her name is Holly. She's the woman who came to see me yesterday at work."

Sullivan swatted his hand in the air. "I saw that broad, the one with the big cans," he held his hands out in front of his chest and Paul saw the similarities between his coworker and the mayor of the city. "There is no way that woman is going out with you. No way. You got a junk car, you've barely got a job, you've got no friends. You've got no reason to live obviously. I tell you, Paul, you and your mouth, always talking about 'you're going to do this' or 'you're going to do that' but what do you ever actually do? Nothing."

Sullivan was mad. Paul could sense that but he stood up for himself. "Not this time. It's for real. It's our first date. I'll tell you all about it Monday morning." And then to take a jab at Sullivan he added, "If I make it to work."

"If you make it to work," Sullivan practically spit the words back at him as if it was the stupidest comment he had ever heard. "Are you going to jump off a bridge this weekend since all the tall buildings will be closed?"

Paul had watched Oliver and the way he carried himself and talked down to others. Paul hated it but decided he would try to emulate it, if only to his fellow co-worker. "Don't be jealous, Sullivan. Things might start looking up for you someday too."

Sullivan became defensive. Paul was amazed at how his tough guy statement worked. "I've got so much going on you wouldn't understand. You'll never catch me out on a ledge that's for sure."

Still Paul felt like Oliver. He put his hand on Sullivan's shoulder. "Let's hope not. Now, I've got to get back to work. I've got some things to finish before I leave for the weekend."

Paul continued pushing his bucket and mop down the hallway careful to not look back but to make Sullivan aware that he had better things to think about and their conversation had been instantly forgotten.

Sunday, November 5

13

Paul drove slowly through the neighborhood. More than once he almost hit a mailbox as he looked to his left at a house he had passed and turned to get a better look. These were not houses, Paul thought, these were hotels. The neighborhood consisted of mansions with countless windows on the front of each and huge white columns framing huge front doors. Green carpeted yards and perfectly pruned hedges accompanied each house and Paul felt as if he was driving on a movie set in the dusk of the setting sun. Paul allowed himself to dream. He imagined himself driving through this particular neighborhood each day going to work in the morning and coming home in the evening. His problem was he always fantasized about his house but never about the imaginary job he was going to and from.

Social class, economic success, the daily lives of the rich and powerful, these were topics that constantly swirled in Paul's head. How does a person go from nothing to a mansion with a lake in their front yard? What is the key? Paul had spent countless hours of his seemingly wasted life looking for that key, that answer, the secret that would open the door and invite him into that world. But it was to no avail. He instead watched others walk through the door while he could only wonder what that secret was.

The immaculate neighborhood of the other people

in life made the negative thoughts begin to creep up in Paul's mind. He could feel like a failure so often in his life. He did not belong in this neighborhood. He was out of his element and considered turning his car around and driving home. He could pretend this night, this chance to have dinner with Holly in a mansion owned by the mayor was a dream. To retreat and abandon his mission would mean nothing to anyone.

He did not turn around but continued to drive slowly, looking at the number on each mailbox. Even the mailboxes were immaculate. Some were encased in brick. Some were huge metal structures that welcomed a visitor to the huge house behind it. And there it was--the mailbox he was looking for, a golden brick color, with the number 1053 on it. The name 'Gartrell' in a cursive script was below the number displayed in black, rod iron letters that stood out impressively in contrast to the gold behind it.

There was no gate across the driveway as some houses had and Paul was thankful he could drive from the road to the house unencumbered. He parked his beat up car on the pea gravel drive that circled a fountain in front of the house. He stood and looked up at the roofline of the house which seemed two hundred feet above him. This house was one of golden brick, excess of which had been used to make the mailbox he surmised, and had the familiar two white columns in front of it reaching two stories into the air to hold the roof of the porch which in turn held a huge, dangling chandelier.

Paul wiped his hands on the same pants he had worn to the bank the week before. The pair of pants had not been washed in the meantime. As he put them on an hour before he wondered if maybe there was an odor that would be noticed by Holly. He regretted in that second not having washed them but knew then it was too late.

He took a deep breath, his shoulders rising up to his ears. He held the breath and then released blowing out with force trying to rid his body of any nervous energy and anxiety. He touched the pill bottle in the pocket of his jacket. Had he forgotten to bring those he would have given up on this night. But maybe, with his medicine he would be okay. He considered taking a pill before ringing the doorbell but decided against it. He noticed his finger was shaking slightly as he reached out and pushed the doorbell.

He had to pee. He realized it while he waited there on the front porch of this mansion. Would Holly be the one to open the door? He had to pee. Would they have a romantic candlelit dinner? Would she laugh at his jokes? He had to pee. Those were the thoughts going through his mind as he waited.

He heard the deadbolt turn in the door and the curtain covering the window beside it fell back into place. The big door opened and there before him was an attractive, middle aged woman occupied with inserting an earring into her ear.

"Listen young man, in this neighborhood solicitation is completely prohibited. So take your daily newspaper subscription or church flier or whatever it is you're passing out and please leave us all alone." She stepped back and with her foot began to push the door closed.

Paul stepped forward to stop her. "No, I'm not here to sell you anything. I'm here for dinner." The puzzled look on the woman's face told him to clarify what he was talking about. "With Mayor Gartrell."

The woman opened the door a little wider. "Dinner? What kind of dinner?" She said the word 'dinner' in a way that made Paul think the word may mean something different. The word was thrown at him as if she was threatening him with it.

Paul was more nervous than he realized he would be. His hand inconspicuously went to his jacket pocket where his fingers once again curled around his small bottle of pills. Just feeling them on his possession helped calm him somewhat. He swallowed hard before answering the woman. "We kind of got to know each other at work last week and we were talking and he invited me to dinner at his house. This is Mr. Gartrell's house, isn't it? Did I go to the wrong house? I'm sorry."

The woman seemed amused and extended her hand. Her suspicious demeanor turned to one of welcoming and hospitality. "I am Sheryl Gartrell, Oliver's wife." She snapped her fingers after shaking his moist hand. "Wait a second. You're the crazy man from the ledge, aren't you?" Paul was offended by the use of the word 'crazy'. "I saw your picture in the

121

paper just before I threw it out. I vaguely remember all of that nonsense. Please, come in."

As impressed as Paul had been at the exterior of the house he was more taken aback at the interior as he stepped into the foyer. The ceiling seemed to be one hundred feet high, the hardwood floor seemed to extend for one hundred yards to the back of the house, the stairs to his left seemed to be made of gold to continue the theme of the brick and mailbox.

"I knew Mr. Gartrell drove a nice car and I expected his house to be nice but this is unbelievable." He did not know if Sheryl heard him or if he was merely talking to himself at that point. He followed her down the corridor of hardwood until they reached a huge open living room. The floor in the middle was two steps below where he stood, giving the room a small concert venue type of feel. Sheryl walked down the two steps and sat in the recliner to the far left. Paul, unsure of himself, walked down the two steps and sat on the couch opposite her.

Sheryl put a foot underneath her on the recliner despite wearing what appeared to be very nice pants and a sophisticated blouse. Paul thought she looked dressed for church. "So tell me more about this dinner tonight."

Paul was nervous to be sitting down close to her. He was fully aware of himself, how he was sitting, how he held his hands, indecisive about leaning back on the couch or leaning forward with his elbows on his knees. "Well, uh, I, after he saved me and everything, we started talking and he asked if I'd like to come to dinner." Paul looked behind him to break the direct eye contact with the lady. "Is he here?"

"No, he's not here. But surely he won't be long. So, what was your name again?"

"Oh, I'm Paul. Paul Self. I work at City Hall."

"You're a janitor right? That must be a challenging job."

Paul hated the word but was surprised, in this context, to hear himself express his disdain for the title. "I'm a maintenance man. It is hard work. You have to know a lot of things. Long hours and all but for me it's just a temporary thing. I don't plan to be there forever or anything." He was self-conscious of having said the word 'thing' so many times and knew that the lady must think he was a fool.

Sheryl leaned over and picked up a glass from the table and raised it to her lips. "Of course, you have dreams of bigger and better things. Maybe one day you'll be mayor yourself or something." She raised her eyebrows and sipped the drink. Paul knew he was not imagining the emphasis she placed on the word 'thing' as she said it each time. She was mocking him and he felt his face turn red.

Paul made an attempt to win her affection through self-deprecation, as was his usual style. "Oh, I don't know if I could ever do something like that."

She held the drink in one hand at her lap and swatted her hand in the air at him disregarding the notion. "Ahh, a monkey could do it."

123

Paul felt he was being tested but was thankful to talk about someone else other than himself. "It seems like a very difficult job. Mr. Gartrell seemed to be under a lot of stress when we met last week. I don't know, it seemed almost unbearable."

Sheryl shook her head refusing to give her husband any respect. "It's an honorary thing if even that. Don't let him fool you. He doesn't know what he's doing. Shake a few hands, make a talk at the Rotary Club every now and then. Really, it's nothing."

Now Paul had to know for sure whether he was being tested. "You don't seem very impressed by your husband's accomplishments. But you fell in love with him, you married him, you have this house."

Sheryl laughed in an odd way, tilting her head back and showing her teeth. "Two of those I can't deny." She leaned over and placed the drink back on the table. Her low cut blouse fell open and Paul could see her cleavage but looked away quickly. "Now, tell me how you met Oliver. Out on a ledge, wasn't it?"

Paul hated the story and the negative connotations people drew about him but in this instance he welcomed the chance to recount it. He would have the chance to put it in his words and felt this would be a good opportunity to rehearse the story before he would undoubtedly have to recount it to Holly.

"First of all, Thursday did not start out all that great. I was having a bad day and when I got to work it seemed to get even worse. So I was up on the sixth floor with a toilet brush in my hand walking down the hall and..."

Sheryl cut him off. She seemed enraptured by what he was saying, like he was speaking a foreign language but she desperately needed to understand each word. "Wait, a toilet brush? Ohhhh, because you're a janitor. Okay, got it."

Paul corrected her again. "A maintenance man. Yes. So I'm walking down the hall and I see this open office and the next thing I know, I'm standing out on this ledge thinking I may jump."

Sheryl was staring at him, not moving her eyes to any other distraction. "And why didn't you jump?"

Paul rubbed his hands on his knees to rid them of the moisture building. He had not been asked that question. "Oh, the mayor came out and everything."

Sheryl nodded. "Interesting. And the window you came out of, was it near Oliver's office?"

Paul did not like the questions. He felt he was being tested. This was a rehearsal of some kind. "No, um I was around the corner from it. This is a nice house." Paul began looking around and wanted desperately to stand up and remove himself from the interrogation.

"Yes, you said that already."

Sheryl slid the leg she was sitting on out from underneath her allowing her to lean forward. Again, the neck of her blouse fell free from her chest and Paul looked quickly but then looked away. He could not help but think in her awkward position on the couch that this was actually an invitation from her to look. He denied himself the urge and let his curiosity go unfilled. He had seen her husband's ability to manipulate people. This, he imagined, was hers. "So how did Oliver know you were out there if you were around the corner? How did both of you end up back at his office window? Why did he have to get on the ledge to begin with?"

The questions were too much. Paul stood up and looked at various pictures framed and resting on the shelves of the bookcase beside the sofa. "I'm not real sure. It all happened so fast and everything. I guess that um,"

Sheryl stood up. "Okay, you can stop now. I don't know what happened on that ledge but I definitely know what didn't happen. I know Oliver Gartrell did not go out on that ledge to save you. Of that there is no doubt in my mind."

Paul turned to her feeling this was the true test of his conviction and how well he could pull this off. "No, uh, yes, yes he did. He saw me out there and brought me in. He saved my life." He hated that last sentence and could not believe he said it out loud but this woman had him rattled.

"He'd watch his own mother fall off that ledge before he would go out on it. Oliver can't stand on a ladder to change a light bulb he is so afraid of heights."

Paul was getting defensive. "He did go out there. People saw him."

Sheryl turned her back to Paul. "Yes, I know. That's what puzzles me."

Paul could not decide if he should say anything

more to convince her or if his first thought was true, that he was merely being tested to see just how invested in the story he was. That theory had begun to fade as Sheryl spoke. Her tone of voice, her facial expressions told him otherwise. He began to doubt if this was a test as he picked up on the very strong, sincere thought that Sheryl hated her husband and truly knew nothing of their arrangement.

Paul was trying to decide what to say next standing in the uncomfortable silence when there was a noise at the end of the long, hardwood corridor. The front door had opened and Paul was relieved to know that soon Oliver would be joining them. He wanted to see Oliver now more than Holly as he needed some kind of buffer between himself and Ms. Gartrell. He knew if Holly arrived first the two of them would find themselves in Ms. Gartrell's crossfire and he did not want Holly to be subjected to the interrogation. His worry was that he would need to deny his instability to Holly while acknowledging it with Sheryl. That would put him in a difficult situation.

Paul looked at the door to the large living room and was dismayed to not see Oliver walk in but instead a teenage boy. He was wearing all black and his hair had a purple hue to it as if an attempt to color it had gone awry. The boy had several earrings in the one ear Paul could see. Paul could not help to wonder what in the boy's life had gone wrong. Paul decided whatever it was the purple hair was no doubt to draw attention away from some other issue which made the boy feel shame. Paul asked questions and pontificated on things like that all the time, trying to understand people's emotions and motives, why they made certain decisions and whether they were happy.

Sheryl watched the boy walk through the living room and go to the kitchen. The boy did not look at either of them but kept his eyes on the floor to avoid any interaction. A minute later he walked from the kitchen back through the living room and Paul could hear his footsteps on the staircase. Sheryl had not said anything and remained still while the boy walked through the room, as if a funeral procession had gone by.

Paul wanted to break the silence and move the topic of conversation from himself. He asked, "Who was that?"

"That used to be my son, Derrick. Now I don't know what he is. Some kind of freak. My friend Nancy's son is the same way. She says they've given their souls to the Church of Weirdo's."

She tossed her hand toward the front door, dismissing him but obviously bothered by the fact her son looked the way he did.

Paul said, "He looks familiar to me. I know I've seen him before somewhere but I can't place it."

Sheryl laughed, but in a wicked way, "A traveling circus maybe. If you'll excuse me, I need to make a phone call." She pushed herself up from the recliner and walked past him.

After she walked into the kitchen Paul found himself

alone in the living room. He had nothing to do but look at the bookshelves and the pictures there along with the little knickknacks collected over time by the Gartrell family. Someone obviously was fond of lions as he saw more than five little figurines on the various shelves in front of him. He thought of being at the bank and the elephant the mean woman had on her desk there.

Again feelings of inferiority overcame him. That seemed to happen to him often. Moments of excitement, such as being in this mansion about to have dinner with the woman of his dreams could instantly flip to a feeling of despair. He felt small in that minute. Maybe it was the pictures of Paris with Oliver and Sheryl in front of the Eiffel Tower. He had never been there and it was very likely he never would be. He could dream about it, as he often did but reality would counteract that sentiment and leave him blue. Trips to the Eiffel Tower are made by a certain kind of person, a kind of person that is born that way and he knew he was not and likely never would be that kind of person. Irrational and misguided as they were, the thoughts began to pull him down.

He tried to snap out of it. He was going to be with Holly in just a matter of minutes. He would have his chance to impress her, to court her, to seduce her with his charm. But what was the point really? Sullivan was right. How could a girl like Holly ever be attracted to him?

Paul held the largest lion figurine and flipped it over

in his hand. "Made In India" was printed across the belly. He laughed to himself as he could imagine Oliver claiming to have gone to India and picking out the statue himself. He heard the front door open and hurriedly he put the figurine back on the shelf. It turned over as he did so and caused what he assumed to be a loud bang that everyone in the house could hear. No one came running to him, so once the lion was back on its feet he stepped away from the bookshelf quickly to not be associated with the noise.

Oliver walked into the living room and set down a briefcase in the doorway. "Oh, you're already here. How did you get in?"

Paul pointed to the kitchen. "Your wife let me in."

"My wife?" Oliver said it loudly as if he had no wife and was puzzled.

Paul could see Sheryl walk up behind him without making a sound. Paul assumed she was doing that intentionally to startle him as her feet would have made at least some noise on the hardwoods had she not walked softly to prevent it.

"Hello Dear. So, we're having a dinner party tonight, I understand."

Oliver was noticeably nervous. Paul was reminded of his demeanor clutching the window sill six stories off the ground a few days before. The older man with the nice hair stammered his response to her. "Not really a dinner party, just a little get together with my new friend Paul here. I didn't want to trouble you and I know you have your meeting tonight, don't you?"

Sheryl pointed at the stairs behind her as Paul had just pointed at the kitchen. "Not anymore. I just called Nancy and told her I would not be able to make it to the meeting."

Oliver walked to the corner of the room where a bottle of sherry sat on a small table. Four glasses were turned upside down, much like the small desk in his office. He began fixing himself a drink. "Oh I see." He poured a small amount into the glass and threw his head back like he was taking a pill. "How was your day?" It was only after having the drink that he walked over to her and kissed her on the cheek. Sheryl turned her face further away from him giving confirmation to Paul's earlier thought that she was repelled by her husband.

Oliver played off the rejection by addressing Paul. "Paul, have you and my wife been properly introduced?"

Sheryl interrupted. "Oh we've been getting to know each other quite well in fact. Isn't that right, Paul?" She walked to him and put her hand on his shoulder and left it there. Paul was very uncomfortable.

"Yes, ma'am."

Sheryl turned back to Oliver. "So, Oliver, this is the disturbed young man you saved from jumping to his death last week?" The respect she had shown Paul when he first arrived seemed to be fading. She was talking to him like he was in fact not their kind of person. He was a janitor after all.

Oliver was sipping his second drink and swallowed

quickly to answer her. "That's right." He turned his attention to Paul. "Do you want a drink?"

Paul held up his hand to indicate that he did not.

"Oh, that's right. You don't drink. I don't understand that. Do you understand how a person could go through life without drinking, Sheryl?"

Paul felt inferior again like a child talking to a patronizing adult. The feeling he had before, while alone, was now escalating. Oliver acted as though there was a right answer in life and anyone not like him was missing that answer by a wide margin.

Sheryl did not want to leave the topic that most interested her. "I was curious dear, how did you know he was out there, on the ledge? Was he screaming?"

Oliver walked back to the table in the corner. He shrugged and answered her with a matter of fact quality making the question seem silly. "No, I saw him through my window and went out to help him."

Paul looked at Sheryl knowing that she had heard two different accounts of what happened. He waited for her to point out the contradiction. Instead Sheryl smiled. "Interesting. My husband, the hero."

Oliver shrugged but without humility. "I don't know about that." He wanted to hear it again. His wife obliged.

"Oh no. You risked your life to save his. That is a hero. That's the definition of it, plain and simple."

Oliver shrugged again and looked down at the glass in front of him. Paul wondered if it was the sign of guilt. "I guess so. Who can argue with Webster? Say, honey, aren't you going to miss your meeting, saving the whales or whatever it is? What if an important issue comes to a vote? As President you should be there."

Sheryl would not miss this interaction for anything. "I can miss one week. Is anyone else expected tonight at this get together?"

Oliver shrugged again and stuck out his bottom lip as if at a loss for who else may be coming. "Uh, no, not that I can think of. Just going to be me and Paul here. Boring time. I don't know why you would be interested in that." He looked at Paul with pleading eyes. Paul was still mad about the hero talk so he did not oblige Oliver's silent plea to agree with him.

"And Holly. Don't forget Holly is coming."

Oliver put his finger in the air as if the answer had just occurred to him. "Oh yes, a friend of Paul's. Holly? Was that it?"

At that moment the doorbell rang. Oliver set his drink down quickly. "That may be her now. You two stay here. I'll show her in."

Oliver walked down the hardwood hallway wanting to run. He imagined opening the door and getting in his car and fleeing. That thought had occurred to him more and more lately. He looked behind him, back down the hallway to see if anyone was following him. He saw Paul in the doorway of the living room like a kid wanting to come downstairs to see what Santa had brought to him. Oliver hated the situation he found himself in.

Oliver opened the door to Holly. Wearing a tight red dress with a low cut her large breasts were on full display, the top of her nipples just barely covered. Oliver could not help but look down at her body and Holly was pleased at the intended reaction. This Paul guy, he could rot and die for all she cared but Oliver, it was her lover that she wanted back. He had been slipping away from her. She did not understand the dynamics of this dinner invite. She knew Paul was getting what he wanted and she knew Oliver well enough to know that he was receiving something in return. But she wanted something also and just as Oliver could wield his cunning and power and influence to get what he desired, she could do the same with her assets.

"Oh my God." Oliver covered his mouth and looked behind him grateful no one had followed him down the hallway. His libido had suffered in the previous days but something overcame him at that moment and he knew he would have taken her there if the circumstances had been different. Holly began to walk through the door, a confident woman but Oliver put his hands on her arm and stopped her.

"Listen, Holly, we have to talk before you go in there. My wife is," but he did not get a chance to explain the situation and command her to act accordingly. Sheryl's voice came from the hallway.

"Oliver, are you lost? Who was at the door?"

Holly looked at her lover through narrow eyes. Her

134

anger was obvious. "Is that your wife? What is she doing here?" The whisper was too loud. Oliver let go of her and said only, "You've got to calm down. I'll explain later."

"But you said that it would only be the two of us." Holly wanted an explanation for this turn of events but did not get it.

The third person, whom she had just forgotten, rose from his seat on the sofa as Holly walked into the living room. Paul had been up and down from the couch continuously, the nervous energy pulsating through his body prevented him from staying in one place and relaxing. Now the energy came to a crescendo. This was the moment Paul had rehearsed in his mind, and being honest, had rehearsed in his apartment many times over the weekend. He had decided he would rise from his seat and walk to her but the question had been would he hug her or merely, in this infancy of their relationship, shake her hand. He walked to her and misjudged the two steps in front of him to go from the carpet of the living room to the height of the hardwood. His toe caught the first step and he tripped and had to catch himself by putting his hands on the floor at Holly's feet. All of the rehearsing had been for naught. He recovered and bounced up the two stairs to stand next to the love of his life. He ran his hand across his forehead as if pushing hair out of his eyes but with his short hair the effort was unnecessary.

"Hello Holly, I'm so glad you could make it." Already he was going off script from what he had decided to say. He resisted the temptation to glance at her cleavage and showed her respect by only looking her in the eye. The hug or hand shake dilemma was still between them. He decided on the hug while she stuck out her hand effectively punching him in the stomach. Not hard but enough to be uncomfortable. He stepped back and shook her hand while Oliver could only roll his eyes from his spot next to the table with the alcohol.

Oliver stepped in. "So, Holly was it? You remember Paul. He was the fellow I met at work the other day and he was telling me about you."

Holly still did not know what was going on and did not like the insinuation that she was a stranger to this man she had been sleeping with for six months. Holly had been apprehensive about meeting the crazy person for dinner and had only agreed to do so knowing that Oliver would be there and provide comfort and support to her. Now it was as though she was on an island alone in an unknown sea and wanted nothing more than to jump in the ocean and try to swim back to the main land. She felt tricked and hurt and could only hope time would pass quickly.

"Yes, I remember Paul. How are you feeling today?"

Paul resented the notion that he had been sick and still fought with the desire to set everything straight and tell the truth about his and the mayor's encounter on the ledge. After all, he and Holly were in the same room and it was now his chance to prove his worth. He no longer needed Oliver's help. But out of respect for his host he decided he would let this first question about his mental health slide as long as it was the only one. "I am much better. Thank you."

The doorbell rang and Sheryl gave a suspicious look to Oliver. "And what surprise is that Oliver? Are you expecting someone else? A pimp perhaps?" She did not take her eyes from Holly's red dress and exposed cleavage but said it so that only Oliver could hear. He ignored the comment.

"If you'll excuse me that must be Rebecca who is here to prepare the meal."

Oliver left the room while Paul and the two women could only look at each other. Paul noted Sheryl's look of disgust at the over exposed Holly. He tried his best to make conversation.

"So Holly, isn't this house great?"

Holly did not break her concentration from Sheryl. "Yes, it is. How long have you and the mayor lived here?"

Sheryl needed a drink and walked to the table in the corner. "Sixteen years I suppose. I remember very clearly having to move this furniture into the living room and carrying the countless boxes of things to put on the shelves. It was quite a chore and being pregnant at the time made it no easier."

That was an obvious jab at her defenseless husband whose voice could be heard in the hallway.

"Well, it is a lovely home your husband has provided you." Holly jabbed back as Oliver and an older lady walked into the room. Paul noticed Oliver's arm on

137

the woman's back and how he appeared more comfortable with her than his wife. The lady carried grocery bags in each arm and Paul noted that Oliver's hands were free. He laughed to himself in light of what Sheryl had just said.

"Everyone, this is Rebecca. She is a few minutes late but that is okay. She'll be preparing our meal for us tonight."

It was obvious the woman would not have much to do in the way of cooking as the scent of a fast food restaurant filled the room as she walked through. "Right this way Rebecca. I'll show you where to put everything."

"Thank you, Mr. Gartrell." The elderly woman struggled with the bags as she walked to the kitchen. One arm load of bags hit the door frame as she walked through it. Paul considered going to help but knew that it was not his place as Oliver was the man of the house.

"Oh Rebecca," Sheryl called out to her and she turned again in the doorway and banged the other bags into the wall. "Could you fix another place at the table tonight? I have decided to join our guests this evening."

"Okay, Sheryl." Paul made note that Oliver was 'Mr. Gartrell' to the woman but his wife was 'Sheryl'. He decided this was not because of a level of friendship between them but more than likely a dislike the two women had for each other and a show of disrespect more than anything else.

Paul turned his attention back to Holly, this time unable to help himself, glancing down at her impressive chest. "So Holly, how long have you lived at Oak Ridge apartments?" Paul knew the answer to his question. He remembered the first time he had seen her eight months before in March when she moved in but he was scrambling to have something to say.

"About a year, I guess." Holly was wrong but Paul did not correct her knowing that would seem odd. "I may go help the Mayor in the kitchen. If you'll excuse me." Holly made her exit from the room. Sheryl stood in the corner still sipping her drink.

As Holly walked into the kitchen she saw Oliver at the sink wiping his face with a paper towel. He looked a little pitiful, with beads of sweat on the back of his neck and his shirt coming untucked. She did not show him sympathy though, staying firm in her anger and feelings of being tricked. She walked to him and whispered, "Oliver, what is going on? You told me that woman would not be here."

Oliver turned the tap on so their voices could not be heard. "I can't talk about it now. She cancelled her meeting when she found out we were doing this. The guy got here thirty minutes ago or something. She was supposed to be out of the house before anyone arrived. Please, please behave okay. I don't know you and you don't know me, okay?"

Rebecca interrupted. "Mr. Gartrell, are you going to eat at the dining room table?"

Oliver showed a kindness to Rebecca greater than

what he showed to anyone else in his life. She served him without needing anything in return and that set her apart from everyone else. "Yes, thank you Rebecca. Perfect timing."

Sheryl entered the kitchen and saw her husband and Holly at the kitchen sink. Paul followed her and thought nothing of it but Sheryl's suspicion heightened seeing her husband's reaction. Oliver snapped to attention upon seeing his wife and walked to the refrigerator as if unaware of anyone else in the room. "Okay, everyone, Rebecca is preparing everything. Let's go to the dining room and be seated." The misery Oliver was facing he decided may exceed the misery he would have to feel in a few days if he did lose the election. He had done many things in his life to get his way or have the pleasure of seeing an enemy lose but this dinner, whether it took thirty minutes or an hour, anything longer than that was out of the question he told himself, was the most grueling thing he could endure.

The four people in the kitchen lined up single file to walk through the door to the dining room. Oliver took his customary place at the far end of the table and Sheryl sat opposite him with six chairs in between. Holly walked to the far side of the table and sat in the chair on Oliver's left. Sheryl made note of that as well while Paul sat in the middle chair on the opposite side of Holly to not leave Sheryl isolated at the far end.

Paul placed the napkin that was at his place setting in his lap as the other three at the table had done. He was not classy. He was not sophisticated. He knew all he could do in these situations was mimic those around him so he watched each, paying special attention to Oliver. Paul would do what Oliver did.

"So Holly, what hospital do you work for?" Paul sipped his water after asking the question. His throat was already dry.

Holly seemed puzzled and looked at Oliver and then back to Paul. "Um, hospital?" She shook her head. "I don't work for a hospital."

Paul felt the now familiar sensation of his face growing hot. First question and already he appeared foolish. He thought he had known as much as there was to know about his neighbor from studying her over the previous eight months. "Oh, I thought you were a nurse. Sometimes I see you leave your apartment at night and you have on a nurse's hat, one of those old timey ones, and an overcoat. I assumed you were a nurse working third shift."

Holly shook her head and looked down at her empty plate. "Oh no, I'm not a nurse."

Sheryl took special note of the conversation and an interest in Holly. Her eyes narrowed studying Holly as she had Paul when he arrived. "If you're not a nurse, what do you do?"

Holly looked at Oliver. Her eyes sought guidance and help. He did not oblige immediately. "Oh, well, I'm a,"

Oliver realized he was needed. "You're a waitress, aren't you? Isn't that what you told me, Paul?"

141

Paul was feeling confused. "No, I don't think I would have told you that. I thought Holly was a nurse."

Oliver nodded. "Oh okay, I thought you told me she was a waitress. I just talk to so many people every day. It's hard to keep up."

Sheryl threw in her comment with a snide tone in her voice. "I'm sure it is."

Rebecca walked from the kitchen to the dining room carrying a big platter of fried chicken and a bowl of mashed potatoes. She set the food down into the middle of the table. She had been told specifically by Oliver to not leave the food in the bucket it came in. As everyone else focused their attention on the food in front of them Sheryl went back to the question. "So what do you do, Holly?"

Holly glanced quickly at Oliver and then to Sheryl. "He's right. I'm a waitress."

Sheryl raised her eyebrows. "Wow, lucky guess, honey. A waitress in a nurse's hat. Who would have thought it?"

Each of them reached to the middle of the table and took a piece of chicken. The atmosphere was more like that of a picnic than a formal dinner, the paper plates and the stack of paper napkins Rebecca had dropped into the center of the table created the informal ambience.

Paul wanted someone else to ask a question as he wished to be conservative with his topics of conversation but no one else was saying anything. "It was nice of you to come see me on Thursday, Holly, when I was out on the ledge."

Sheryl jumped on that also and asked the same question for the third time to a third person. "Yes, that was nice of you. And tell me again Holly, how did you know he was on the ledge?"

Holly was chewing but swallowed quickly. Paul thought it was cute that she seemed ill at ease. "Who? Paul? Oh, uh, a girl I work with at night also works in the cafeteria there at City Hall. She called me."

Sheryl pressed. "So she's a waitress too?"

Holly wanted to be left alone. "No, she's a, uh yes, she's also a waitress. I thought you meant in the cafeteria."

Sheryl had a piece of chicken on her plate that was forgotten. She placed her elbows on the table and put her palms together over her plate. For a second Paul thought she was going to give a blessing. She had no intention of eating and the fact fried chicken was her only option was not the sole reason. "Interesting."

Oliver shifted in his seat and looked at the large clock hanging on the wall next to the china cabinet. "So Paul, how long have you worked in City Hall?"

Paul did not want to talk about his job. "A year and a half, I guess."

Sheryl still had her hands clasped in front of her. She looked at Paul. "Do you plan on being there in January?"

An odd question that Paul was not sure he

143

understood. He shrugged. "Uh, yeah, I guess so."

Sheryl looked back at her husband on the other end of the table. "Oh, then Oliver, he'll be there after you leave."

Oliver laughed uncomfortably, the coldness of his wife becoming apparent to the two visitors in the house. "Sheryl, dear, I have been there four years now and I plan to be around for quite a few more."

Holly had just met her lover's wife and already hated her. Her thoughts had not gone deep enough to realize that a kind, loving wife would not have boded well for her and her long term plans with Oliver. She felt the need to help her boyfriend. "Now that you saved Paul's life I'm sure you have nothing to worry about. He was going to kill himself and you saved him. You're a hero."

The word 'hero' caused Paul to interject. His voice was a little louder than he intended it to be. "I don't know if I was actually going to kill myself." He emphasized the word 'kill' to call into question his true motive.

Sheryl continued to manipulate. "Oh? You were going to bounce?"

Paul could feel his face get hot yet again with all eyes on him. He hated to blush and had the urge to flee when he could feel his face redden. "Problems can build up and make you, you know, just," he mumbled wanting the subject to change.

"Go out on a ledge and kill yourself, right?" Sheryl had turned to a nemesis. "Paul, you know that is not

144

normal behavior. Of course I did see in the paper that story about your horrible, horrible life and it is no wonder you're crazy. They don't let you use anything dangerous at work, do they? No chemicals or sharp objects. I would expect a janitor would normally have to do that kind of thing."

Paul's hands were now on both sides of his plate, his fists clinched. "I'm a maintenance man. And the truth is, the real truth,"

Oliver could see what was going on. He could see his guest was about to crack. He wanted the dinner to end without any truths being exposed. He stood up quickly, "Would anyone like a drink?" He picked up the bottle of wine from the table and pulled the cork out.

Paul was not to be distracted. He had enough of the charade. "The truth is you know how newspapers have to make everything seem so much worse than they are. Actually, my childhood was a very good one and I have lived a great life. My father was a great man and I plan to one day be a great father." He looked at Holly when he said it but she quickly broke the eye contact and looked down at her plate.

Oliver had remained standing. His tone of voice was now convivial as if he had just entered the room. He was determined to change the course of the conversation and began by pouring himself a glass of wine. "Tuesday night at the Weatherton Inn is my victory party. I want both of you to be there. It's going to be a huge party, music, food, balloons, the whole deal. You're not going to want to miss it."

Sheryl had leaned back in her seat, satisfied with the torment she had inflicted on Paul. Now she turned her attention back to Oliver.

"Are you going to be in the big banquet room?"

Oliver was visibly annoyed by the question. "Uh, no, unfortunately I was not able to book the big banquet room but there is a smaller one, Banquet Room Number Two, down the hall. That's where the party will be. A much more intimate atmosphere." He put the cork firmly back into the bottle. "Cozy."

Holly resisted the urge of standing up and walking to Sheryl's place at the table to slap her. Instead she remained focused on Oliver. "I'll be there, Mr. Mayor. I know you're going to win."

Sheryl now shifted her focus again. Enjoying the aggravation she had caused Paul and Oliver, she did not want Holly to be left out. "Holly, are you into politicians the same way my husband is into waitresses?"

That question drew the sharpest protest from Oliver. "Not now, honey."

Holly did not hide. "No, I just keep up with it a little."

Sheryl leaned forward again and put her hands on the table. "Good for you. It's nice to see our young people take such an interest in our leaders." She turned her attention to Oliver and then to Paul, addressing all three of them. "Perhaps you've heard of Melanie Myers who is running for mayor. She is going to crack down on drugs when she's elected. And not a minute too soon if you ask me. The last few years this city has just gone to pot, don't you think? Maybe you've seen her billboards."

Paul and Holly finally shared a bond as they both realized how much this man and woman at the table whose house they were in, absolutely despised each other. Holly felt more hatred for Sheryl. Paul, for the first time, felt a slight touch of sympathy for Oliver.

Oliver slammed his hand on the table. "Of course they've seen the billboards. Everybody has seen her billboards. They're everywhere you look. I want to know how she can afford all of the advertising she's doing. It doesn't make sense."

Sheryl nodded. "She certainly is not relying on campaign buttons that look like an eighth grader's attempt to be elected for student council. That's for sure. I know she collected a lot of money the day she spoke at the Garden Club. She's sharp. And to rid the city of drugs, that's something we need."

Oliver forgot where he was and who he was with. He could just as well have been standing behind a podium addressing a room of civic minded citizens at their weekly meeting and was being challenged by a rogue, discordant opponent in the group. "Now hold on a second. The drug problem in this city is about the last thing we need to be fixing. What we need are more businesses, more jobs, better salaries. That's what I'm for. Paul, wouldn't you like to see a new hotel come to this city? Wouldn't that be nice? Or a few more restaurants?"

Sheryl remained seated and calm, adding kindling to the fire as it began to blaze. "Hmmm, more restaurants and hotels in the same town? That would certainly make life more convenient for you, Oliver. With more restaurants that means more waitresses." She looked at Holly directly to make her point. "You'd be in heaven, wouldn't you? You could stay at the hotel right here in town. Of course the irony is if you're not reelected you'll have all that time on your hands to go visit your friend in Atlanta whenever you want."

Oliver grew more stern. "Sheryl, I don't think this is appropriate dinner conversation."

Holly though was already drawn in. "What kind of friend?"

Sheryl took Holly's question and demanded Oliver answer it with her expression. "Oliver, what is that supporter's name again in Atlanta that you've been going to see? Natalie? Was that it?"

Oliver's jaw locked into place and he spoke through clinched teeth. "Sheryl, let's change the topic, please."

Holly looked at Oliver and back to Sheryl and then back to Oliver. "Who is Natalie?"

Oliver thought he could end the conversation by changing it. "How do you like your job, Paul? Is it fulfilling?"

Holly was angry and could not suppress the emotions beginning to boil inside of her. "Oliver, Mr. Mayor, who is this Natalie person? I want to know who Natalie is?"

Oliver looked down at the table and ran his fingers through his hair. In a calm, even tone Sheryl answered the question. "Natalie is my husband's girlfriend. Is that a fair description, dear? At least she's one of his girlfriends."

Holly's mouth was open. Paul could see the moisture collecting in her eyes. The light from the chandelier illuminated the blue. "Is that true? Oliver? Is it?"

Sheryl put her hand to her mouth in mock concern. "Oh, I'm sorry, honey. I had no idea you were in the club also. Oh, I bet you thought you were the club. A club of one. How awkward." She reached out and picked up the glass in front of her and sipped it. "Paul, how is the chicken?"

Paul did not look at Sheryl but instead pointed a finger at both Oliver and Holly. "So you two know each other?"

Oliver tried to calm the fire beginning to ignite in Paul's chair to his left and with a soothing voice said to him, "We're just friends. That's all." Trying to calm that fire threw gasoline on the match burning to his right.

Holly screamed, "Just friends? How many friends do you have Ollie, huh?"

Sheryl was still calm. Her monotone voice was oxygen for the fires burning in front of her. "Yes, Ollie, how many friends do you have?"

Oliver looked only at Sheryl. "Oh, don't pretend like

you're all innocent. That van has been in our driveway every day for the last week. I know all about your little fling with the good looking man who comes by the house in the morning."

Sheryl laughed. "Oh Henry. Henry Wilder. Yes, he's good. He's real good."

Oliver sat back down in his chair and raised his hands towards her with his palms up. "So you admit it then? You've had some man coming to the house during the day while I'm at work?"

Sheryl nodded. Still a monotone voice. "Yes, yes that's true. Every word of it."

Oliver slammed both of his palms on the table making the pieces of chicken in the middle jump. "Ha, so you do admit it. You're as guilty as I am then. Sure I've had my flings, a few girls on the side but what about you?"

Holly was crying now and wiping her eyes with the paper napkin that had been in her lap. "A few?" She pushed her plate away as if the chicken was about to attack her.

Sheryl shrugged. "That was business."

Paul had not taken his eyes off of Holly and was still trying to comprehend what he had heard moments before. He spoke to Oliver though no one was listening to him. "I knew something didn't seem right about our deal. You being able to arrange all of this in just a matter of hours. I shouldn't have believed you."

Oliver stayed transfixed on his wife at the other end of the table and ignored the two people beside him.

"Business? What do you mean business?"

Sheryl laughed again. "If you think I'm confessing to you that I'm a prostitute working from home, I am not. Henry Wilder is a private investigator I hired. Barbara Joiner down the street recommended him. That's who she got before her divorce and that's why she got the house, the cars, the summer home in Savannah. It was an excellent investment."

Oliver threw his hands up in the air. "Oh, so that's it. You don't trust me!"

Paul could not believe the statement and realized in that moment Oliver was not as intelligent as he wanted people to believe. Oliver's emotions overpowered his logic. He was cracking before Paul's eyes.

Sheryl said, "According to Henry I shouldn't trust you. What do you think, Holly? Should I trust him?"

Holly shook her head. She was looking down at her plate. Pressure was building up inside of her. Her breasts in the low cut dress began to move up and down as she took deep breaths.

Paul had the instinct to cover his face not knowing what was about to happen. Holly stood up and looked at Oliver. Her hands were shaking. She grabbed the mashed potatoes from her plate and flung the handful at Oliver. The potatoes covered the front of his suit and his face. She reached for the bowl in the middle of the table and grabbed another, larger handful and flung those at him too. Oliver remained motionless the entire time.

Holly screamed. "I can't believe you did this to me, Oliver. Stop coming to my apartment. Stop calling me. Stop giving me flowers, stop, stop, stop."

In actuality Oliver had done none of those things in the past month. He could have objected but did not and chose to remain silent. Holly left the room, her high heels clanking as she walked down the hardwood hallway. The three remaining at the table could hear the door open with a jerk and Paul and Oliver flinched slightly as the door slammed against the frame. Sheryl tossed her napkin on the table in front of her.

"You know, I may be needed at my meeting tonight after all. I would like to say this has been an enjoyable experience but that would be a lie and Oliver that is one thing I have not done to you."

As Sheryl stood up to leave Paul called out his confession feeling it could not be the worst thing that came from the dinner. "I'm not crazy. I was just out on the ledge taking a break. That's where I always go. To hide from my boss."

Sheryl ignored Paul's explanation and continued looking at Oliver. "I may have not been the most supportive wife, I guess we all could have done better but I have always been up front and honest with you." She stood with her finger tips touching the table.

Oliver wiped potatoes from his eyes. "I don't deny that. When you thought I was stupid, you told me I was. When I failed at anything I could always count on you to point it out to me over and over again. Your honesty has always been so appreciated."

Paul could tell Sheryl was a little caught off guard by the response. It was such a rapid return and Paul assumed it was something Oliver had rehearsed saying to her many times before. For a brief moment and for the only time that night, Sheryl was left speechless. Paul saw her lip tremble, but only slightly. Her silence lasted only for a second as she, for possibly the first time, considered that she was somehow at fault for the demise of their marriage. "You're welcome. Now if you'll excuse me. When I return I expect the house to be free of all trash. Oliver, that includes you. Paul, it was lovely meeting you. Next time you find yourself on a ledge I hope you take your hero here with you. Good night." She turned and walked through the door leading to the kitchen.

Paul called out after her. "I was just out there on a break. I always go out there. Honest."

Oliver snapped his fingers toward the table to shake the mashed potatoes from them that he had just removed from his shirt. He looked up at the ceiling and shook his head. "Unbelievable."

Paul did nothing but stare at the man for a minute. He hated having been tricked but in light of what had just happened, actually watching a man's marriage crumble in front of him, he felt sympathy for Oliver. Paul was not the type to take joy in another person's agony even if that person had wronged him. To call it karma was not in Paul's magnanimous nature. Perhaps that explained why Paul lived where he did and why Oliver was looking up at his twelve foot ceilings with

153

the massive chandelier hanging from it. Oliver took joy in seeing others lose when they wronged him. Now it was Oliver who had suffered.

Paul wanted to excuse himself but not as abruptly as the two women had. "So you and Holly, huh? Is she your girlfriend?"

Oliver wiped his face. He still had potatoes on his ear but Paul did not point it out to him. "It's complicated. Maybe you should go check on her, make sure she's okay, huh?"

Oliver was inviting Paul to leave and the prospect of talking to Holly regardless of who she was with or had affections for did not matter. Paul thought of her dress, her cleavage and combined with her sadness was compelled to leave. "You're right. Have a good night, Oliver. And thank you for dinner."

Paul placed his napkin on the table in front of him. He left the dining room and made the long walk down the hardwood hallway to the front door.

14

As Paul stepped from the front door to the porch of the Gartrell's mansion he noticed how the outdoor lighting illuminated the yard much like a football field. The woods in the distance, past the realm of the lighted house, seemed ominous and threatening. The chandelier he had noticed on the way in was now shining like something from a movie. Bugs flew in front of Paul's face but the November night was pleasant with a slight breeze blowing. His car sat alone in front of the house so he assumed Holly had gotten in her car and left the premises just as quickly as she had left the dining room.

As he walked to his car he heard a noise echoing off the tall pine trees. The worrisome sound of loud thuds hitting metal was coming from the direction of the garage. Not wanting to return home so early with only his thoughts of what had transpired on what he had anticipated to be the best night of his life, Paul made the decision to investigate. He walked across the front of the house toward the garage. He became more curious when he approached the corner of the house and could see the trunk of Oliver's Mercedes open.

Paul recognized the car from work. He had seen the expensive, silver, two seater in the space designated for The Mayor many days and always dreamed of owning a car like that. It was odd to Paul to now be seeing it out of the context of the City Hall parking spaces but instead in its natural environment, where the car was parked every night.

Paul remained behind the short hedge that separated the driveway from the front yard. Trimmed perfectly, the bushes looked more like a low wall of concrete than shrubs. From that vantage point all he could see was the back end of the car. He jumped when he heard the next loud crash now only a few feet away from him. He walked cautiously out onto the driveway and into the illumination of the floodlight. Next to Oliver's Mercedes was Holly's convertible. Her car was an older model sports car that Paul made note of every time he drove into or out of the parking lot of his apartment complex.

The first time he had ever seen Holly was in that car, with the top down and music playing loud enough for other people in the apartment complex to complain. Perhaps he would have complained too but he never did because the woman driving the car was beautiful. He was well aware of the fact beautiful people were granted a reprieve of certain rules and perhaps beautiful people purposefully pushed the limitations of the rules as an appraisal of their beauty. But he did not care. Holly liking him, or at least Holly not hating him as she did the other tenants in the apartment complex who complained, was more important to Paul than getting a good night slumber without the interruption of loud music from outside his apartment window.

Now to see two cars that he had always made note of side by side outside the mayor's house was surreal to him in some ways and also symbolic he decided of their relationship.

He looked around for the source of the noise he had heard a second before. Holly had been crouched down in front of Oliver's car. She was shaking her hand with a painful look on her face. He walked towards her to find out what had happened as she had still not seen him standing there.

Just before calling her name he stopped himself and took a step back. Paul saw the golf club rise over Holly's head and come crashing down on the hood of Oliver's car. Again, Holly dropped the club and shook her hands from the pain it caused in her fingers. But not to be deterred she picked the club up from the asphalt and raised it again. She brought it down with all of the strength in her arms and made another dent in the hood. The pain felt in her hands was not enough to stop her from exorcising the pain of her emotions.

Paul stepped closer to her in between swings. He could not imagine the monetary damage she had already done to the car but he was not going to stop her from continuing. He stood motionless once he saw Holly turn her head slightly acknowledging his presence. He remained calm as she remained angry and in a monotone voice only offered some advice. "You've got a wood. I would have gone with an iron."

Holly stopped in mid swing and was distracted by him talking to her. "What?" She threw the word at

157

him not wanting to be interrupted by this stranger.

"An iron. One of the metal ones. That one you've got there is for distance. But if you want to do some real damage the irons would be your best bet." He looked into the trunk of Oliver's car and saw the golf bag halfway hanging out. "And you have to get your body into it. Not just your arms. All of your body. Your legs, your back. You can do better than that I'm sure of it."

Holly pushed hair out of her face and tucked it behind her ear. The violence she had inflicted upon Oliver's car had left her out of breath and her shoulders would rise as she inhaled deeply. Paul tried to keep his eyes from drifting to her cleavage but he could not help himself. Holly dropped the club and brought both hands to her face, cupping them at her eyebrows and looking at the damaged car. "What am I doing? This whole night, this, this whole thing," she pointed at the house, "it's all so messed up."

"So the night did not go the way you had anticipated?" Paul said it sarcastically emphasizing the word 'not'. "Then that gives us something in common. I did not know what to expect but ending the night with you beating up the Mayor's car with the wrong golf club was not what I would have guessed either."

Holly leaned against the car and ran her hands through her hair. "I can't believe he did this to me. I thought we were something special. Damn, that sounds so stupid now. Special. I was just one his bimbo's. His toys." Her voice cracked with emotion and Paul waited for the tears.

"You're not a bimbo, Holly."

"Oh, how do you know? You don't know me. We live in the same apartment complex but that's it."

"Well, you are a nurse." The attempt to make her laugh was lost.

Holly threw her hands in the air and said loudly, "I'm not a nurse."

Paul nodded, pretending to remember, "Oh that's right. You just dress up like one."

"That's right. It's my character when I.....￼" She did not want to say the word but not out of shame. Her hesitation was a test to see if Paul had figured it out yet.

"Stripper. Okay, yeah, I got that now." They stood in silence on the driveway. Holly was still breathing heavy from her workout with the golf club. Paul did not want her to leave so he thought of something to say. "Look at this house. It's huge. And the car. I mean, come on, right? Did you know your boyfriend was loaded?"

Holly pushed herself off of the car and looked at him with her head turned sideways. Paul thought of his cat Daisy. "Is that what turns you on? Seeing other people's stuff? Drooling over what they have and wishing it was yours?" She was angry. Paul understood why but was hurt she was taking it out on him. She had been betrayed and needed to hurt someone else to feel better. "Thinking that because somebody drives some expensive car that they're better than other people?   That they're allowed to use people however they want to and throw them away when they're done?"   She turned and fell back against the car. The golf club was on the ground at her feet.

Paul's immediate answer to her question would have been, "Yes, yes, and yes." But he could tell by the way she asked it, the tone in her voice that this was not what she wanted to hear.   Instead Paul got defensive. "Hey, you're the one sleeping with the guy. I just came to his house for dinner."

Holly snorted in derision. "Not anymore. Not after tonight. Not after finding out I'm nothing more to him than that."

Paul pointed at the hood of the Mercedes and saw it from the other side. "Not after he sees what you did to his car." He was trying to make her laugh, at least smile. That was how Paul operated around anyone but especially the pretty girls who were down on themselves. It had never paid off in any way besides being the pretty girl's friend but it was how he was. If he did not invest he did not have anything to lose.

Holly looked down at the pavement between her feet. "Why can't I have a simple life? What is so wrong with me?"

Paul decided to be blunt as he was no longer trying to impress the woman standing in front of him as he had been an hour before. He was still hurt from the series of events that had led him there and tricked him into agreeing with Oliver's plan. He had not taken the time to consider that Holly, as far as his feelings were

160

concerned, was completely innocent of any malice toward him. But still he answered her question sharply.

"The simple life is hard to come by when you're dating the mayor of our city. The mayor of our city who is married," to make her laugh, "and lives in his humongous house. Did you see that fountain when you drove up? I could swim in the thing."

Holly half way laughed at his animated reference to the house. "I can't believe he did this to me. I just can't believe it. I'm such an idiot."

"I doubt the other nurses think so." Holly looked at him with a disgusted look on her face and realized he was again just trying to make her laugh and she smiled slightly. "So you're a stripper. That clarifies a lot by the way. I would see you leave the apartment in your nurse's outfit but I would always think those high heels would have to hurt after taking care of patients all night."

Holly inhaled deeply. She leaned over and picked up the golf club and looked at the scarred head. In the floodlight's glow it was obvious the club was badly bent. "I'm so tired of being used. I'm sick of it. Sick of it." In one last violent outburst Holly raised the club over her head again and brought it down quickly into the passenger side window of the car. The shattered glass fell onto the pavement and the car alarm began blaring.

Speaking loudly over the car alarm Paul offered encouragement. "Now THAT was a good swing. See, you got your body into it like you're supposed to. Did you feel the difference?"

Holly shook her head at him and smiled. "You're one strange guy, Paul. You know that. It's cold out here and I've got to get to a work engagement. I'm supposed to jump out of some guy's cake in thirty minutes. I'll never make it." She walked around the Mercedes to her car and opened the door.

Paul said one last thing to her before she disappeared into her old convertible. "Hey Holly," she stopped and looked at him, "be careful in those heels okay?"

Holly smiled and closed the door. Paul watched her back down the driveway. She did not worry about running over any landscaping. A few azaleas took the brunt of her exit from the situation at excessive speed. The back of her car narrowly missed the golden brick mailbox. The headlights spun out onto the neighborhood street and disappeared. Paul held up one hand, "Night Holly." With his fingers over his ears to protect him from the penetrating alarm he walked to his car. As dogs barked and a neighbor screamed an obscenity to Oliver Gartrell from somewhere across the street, Paul had nothing else to do but escape what he thought three hours before was to be a wonderful night.

Monday, November 6

15

As usual Lane was late to work. She turned the knob of the office door with the frosted glass and was puzzled that it was still locked. She had never in her four months of working in the mayor's office found herself in this position. Always either the mayor or Ms. Connors had unlocked the door before she arrived.

She rummaged through her bag. She had been given a key the first day of work but knew she would never have an occasion to need it. Kneeling in the hallway and putting a brush and her wallet and car keys on the floor next to her she finally found the single, lonely key beside the forgotten receipts and crumbs that had found their way to the bottom of her bag. She put the key in the door and was relieved when she was able to turn the knob. She imagined how impressed Oliver would be when he walked in to find her already at her desk with her computer on and working. She, of course, would not really be working, she had seen a dress over the weekend that she was determined to find online and order. But she felt that Oliver should be impressed with her punctuality if not her work ethic.

As she walked to her desk she shivered slightly. The office was not cold but being there before anyone else, and everything turned off--the lights, the computer, the copy machine, the coffee maker, with only her energy in the room-- gave her an eerie feeling. She had just made it to her desk when the phone rang. She almost did not answer it still feeling like it was early in the morning but the clock above her desk said 8:15 so she felt obligated to pick it up though she knew she would have to take a message. Never had she answered an incoming call that was not for Oliver.

"Yes, okay, okay, I will tell him." She was careful to not tell the man from the newspaper that her boss had not yet arrived to work and she felt she should be rewarded for that in some way. That was proof, she felt, that she was in fact an ideal employee.

She wrote the message on the notepad carefully, 'Guy from newspaper will be here in thirty minutes', and left the note on the corner of her desk so she would be certain to give it to Oliver when he walked in. In the meantime though she saw no reason to not go online and begin her search for that dress.

After several minutes she decided to walk down the hall and use the restroom before her day began. She saw the note on the corner of her desk and thought it best to put it in Oliver's chair so he would see it when he arrived in the event that she had not yet returned when he got there. That was a distinct possibility as Lane was always seeing someone in the hallway to talk to and she would have the obligatory, 'How was your weekend?' question to ask and answer.

She felt uneasy doing it but she opened the door to Oliver's office slowly. She would go in the office quickly so if Oliver were to walk in on her while she was there he would not think she was snooping around for anything. He had seemed more paranoid lately than usual. She could imagine him accusing her of spying on him or being in his office at the direction of some person running against him for mayor, like that Melanie what's her name.

She opened his office door and saw the desk chair. She made a quick dash for it as the light from the common area shined into his office.

"Hey hey hey, what the hell?" The voice made her scream. There on the couch covered by his jacket was Oliver. He rose and wiped his eyes. Getting her wits about her and taking a few deep breaths Lane was able to talk.

"Mr. Mayor, oh I'm so sorry. I didn't know you were in here. The door was locked when I came in and I thought I was by myself and I'm so sorry that I came in here and woke you up."

Lane took note of the dark circles under her boss's eyes, his disheveled hair, his skin seemed pale and ghostlike. He looked like death. She imagined the circumstances that had made him sleep in his office. No hypothetical situation came to mind that involved good news. She thought for a minute he was going to tell her he was dying. "Are you okay, Oliver? Did you sleep here?"

Oliver held his hand to his face to block the light from the other room. Despite the circumstances he still played his part well. "You know politics. Sometimes you gotta spend the night to change the world."

Lane felt bad about waking him up and she was still taken aback by his pitiful appearance. She decided to act humbled by his work and giving him a compliment would not be a bad thing. "You are so dedicated." She stood staring at him. The hair, the clothes, the bags under his eyes, even his smell, was unlike anything she had experienced in the mayor's presence. She was lost in her thoughts as she looked at him.

"Uh, Lane, did you need something?"

She remembered the note she held in her hand. "Oh yes, yes, this note. I took a message when I got here. The guy called and said he would be here in thirty minutes."

"The guy?" Oliver was still half asleep. Lane noticed the white splotches of something on his shirt.

"He said it like you would know what he was talking about."

Oliver was still squinting. "How could he say it like I knew what he was talking about if I wasn't talking to him?" His conversations with Lane were always exhausting but on this morning he had no patience for it.

Lane thought hard and snapped her fingers. "Interview. Newspaper. He said he would be here for the interview in thirty minutes." She was proud of herself for remembering that piece of information.

"Oh no, oh no," Oliver rubbed his face harder this time and stood up. "What is today?"

"It's Monday morning."

Oliver started looking around him as if a cat was biting his heels. "I've gotta get cleaned up. When did he say he would be here?"

Lane held her shoulders back, happy she was being so much help. "In thirty minutes."

Oliver stopped and looked at her like she was stupid. "And how long ago did he call?"

Lane looked through Oliver's office door at the big clock on the wall near her desk. "About," she did the math in her head, "25 minutes ago."

Oliver glared at her and she explained, "I didn't know you were here. I thought you were out there somewhere doing mayor stuff."

Oliver ran to his desk. "Unbelievable." He was looking at papers on his desk. He was trying to collect his thoughts. He heard a slight tap on his office door. "Hello, Mr. Mayor? I'm Jack Reed, from the paper."

In the doorway was a man in blue jeans and a white button up shirt holding a legal pad. Oliver laughed nervously, "Oh yes, yes, come on in. Come in. Have a seat."

Jack stopped about ten feet in front of the desk. "Do you feel okay?" He was not concerned for the mayor's health but for his own, not wanting to catch anything going around. An early flu season had ravaged the newspaper's offices.

Desperately wanting to help her boss make the best impression possible after feeling like she had wronged him in some way, Lane stepped in to answer the question as a third party witness for the journalist.

"He's fine. He slept here last night. Right there on that couch there. I just woke him up. He is so dedicated."

Oliver interrupted. "Thank you, Lane. That will be enough for now." Lane made her exit from the office and closed the door behind her.

Jack approached the desk and sat down in the chair, placing the legal pad on the desk in front of him. "So you slept here?"

Oliver tapped his desk. "Yes, yes, just trying to, you know, work on some things. City never sleeps and all that. Dealing with a kind of, um, a sort of emergency."

Jack looked suspicious. "You were expecting me, right?"

"Oh yes, yes, absolutely but you know what, something has come up this morning and if there is any way, any way whatsoever to postpone our interview I would be very much obliged. Would that be okay?" At that moment, though not intentional but helping to earn his reprieve, Oliver coughed into the elbow of his shirt.

Jack stood up, unsure of himself and what he was being asked but taking two steps away from the mayor. "Oh, of course, okay, sure. I guess I'll see you downstairs at the debate then. Will you be addressing the Albert King matter?"

"Yes, the debate I will see you then." Then it registered with Oliver what he had just heard the reporter say and the room spun just slightly around him. "Wait! The what matter?"

Jack looked at him now the way Oliver had looked at

Lane a few minutes before. Like he was stupid. "The Albert King issue. He made some very interesting comments in the paper this morning and I wanted your reaction to that."

Oliver smiled but realized at that moment how much he had to go to the bathroom. "Oh yes, Mr. King. That's right. Well, sure. I plan to comment on what he said. I'll see you downstairs in just a little bit. I have to go right now though, I'm sorry again for cancelling on you."

Jack clarified. "Postponing."

Oliver gave a labored laughed. "Yes, postponing." He walked Jack to the door and closed it behind him. As soon as the door was closed and Oliver was sure no silhouette could be seen through the frosted glass he turned to Lane. "Hold all of my calls for the rest of the day. And for God's sake, get me a newspaper and have it on my desk when I get back. I'll be right back."

Oliver opened the door and ran into the hallway toward the bathroom wishing again he had made City Hall add a bathroom to his office during his first term.

Minutes later, Oliver walked back down the hallway to his office with everything ahead of him running through his mind. He had become adept at visualizing things the way he wanted to see them happen, telling himself he was unstoppable and believing that to be true but he realized in this current predicament his positive self-talk would be put to the test on its greatest level. He had the debate. He had an interview to do. He had to make his last push for the election the next day but at that exact moment he had to figure out the best way to remove dried mashed potatoes from his hair. On his way back to the office he heard a voice behind him that he knew he had no time to entertain but it was persistent.

"Oliver, Oliver." Paul was trotting behind him in the hallway. He had taken the night before to think about the events of the previous days. The ledge kept coming back to Paul and the mere thought that while he was out there to hide from his boss, Oliver was out there for another purpose. It was his final realization that Oliver was not to be hated but pitied.

"Oliver, hold on a second, I wanted to talk to you about last night."

Oliver did not break his stride and continued looking straight ahead. Paul trotted down the hallway to catch up to him. "Sorry kid, no refunds. I know it was a bust but believe me, you got the better end of the deal even if you did hate it. You don't happen to have a newspaper, do you?"

Oliver's shortness towards him was something Paul had not anticipated. Paul had foolishly expected an apology from the mayor for using him as a pawn in his game. Oliver though had no intention of apologizing or for that matter even recognizing how any other person had been wronged.

"You didn't tell me she was your girlfriend. You lied about that."

Oliver stopped walking and Paul looked at him waiting for the apology to come. "Hey, hey, buddy, not so loud. There are people listening to everything we say and last night is one topic I don't want to overhear being discussed in the men's room. I've got enough trouble today as it is."

Oliver smiled wide to a couple that passed him in the hallway. "How are you two today on this fine morning? Remember to vote. Tomorrow morning is election day." After the couple passed Oliver redirected his attention to Paul and put his hand on his shoulder and his mouth near Paul's ear. "As far as I'm concerned last night never happened."

Paul did not like that statement and refused to accept it. The pity he had felt for Oliver began to fade and the anger returned. "What do you mean last night never happened? Look you got your picture in the paper and I've got strangers looking at me like I'm nuts. No, I don't like the way this has turned out at all."

"Oh really? Really?" Oliver's voice echoed in the hallway before he looked around and gathered himself. "It's all gone perfectly for me. Just like I planned it. Hey, you got your date with Holly. That was your side of the deal. What do I have? I've got a broken car window. You wouldn't know anything about that would you?"

Paul did not realize he was being accused of anything and his smile in remembering the circumstances of the previous night told Oliver as much. "Yeah, Holly did that. She's a lot stronger than a person would imagine. Of course you probably already knew that."

"Yeah, sure, listen I've got to run. I'm late for," he paused not sure where he needed to be or what he should be doing, "I'm just late."

He took two steps but was stopped by Paul with one more question. "I wanted to come and see how you were and find out what happened. Did you and your wife make up?"

Oliver clenched his fists but knew that punching the person would be seen by someone turning the corner in the hallway at that exact instant. "Yeah, we made up. We talked all night long and then she forgave me and we made wild, passionate love in front of the fireplace. It just so happens when I got up this morning I put on a suit just like the one I had on last night and at breakfast, what do you know, I spilled mashed potatoes on my tie again."

Paul looked at him with a confused expression. "You eat mashed potatoes for breakfast?"

"No!" Oliver screamed. Again the echo. A man walking into the restroom looked in his direction. His anger was getting the better of him and he realized it. He smiled again to a lady walking down the hallway before leaning in to Paul's ear to whisper. "We did not make up. She kicked me out and I slept in my office."

Paul felt sympathy for the discombobulated man before him. "That's horrible. Let me know if I can do anything, okay."

Oliver turned his back and walked away from Paul. "You'll be the first person I call. Trust me. Everything has been working out great since I met you. You must be my good luck charm."

Paul smiled and called out after the mayor. "Thank you."

Oliver shook his head. "Unbelievable," he muttered through gritted teeth as he continued down the hallway.

16

Oliver went back to his office. He was not surprised to see Lane's empty seat but he was relieved as well. He had the entire office to himself. He had to take time to think, to prepare, to clean up. He had to take time to assess and assuage the predicament in which he found himself.

"Come on, Oliver. Come on. You're a calm, cool, collected individual that can do this. You can handle any problem that may arise." He repeated the words to himself under his breath as he had done since he was in college. Those were the words he lived by and he believed those words had helped transform him from the shy, awkward eighteen year old he was when he arrived in college to the confident leader he was when he graduated.

Oliver walked to the mirror that hung over his couch. He had retrieved the brush and breath mints from the top desk drawer. As he sucked on two mints in his mouth he brushed his hair. "Come on Oliver. Come on." He was his own coach and this was minutes before kickoff of the big game. Satisfied with his hair he began working on the mashed potatoes on his shirt and tie. He remembered his good fortune and walked back quickly to his desk and opened the bottom drawer. Only two things were in it, a bottle of aftershave and a new, crisp red tie that had never been worn. He could not remember the occasion that had brought that tie to his desk drawer but he was glad to have it. Quickly he pulled off the stained tie from around his neck and put the new one on. He flashed his smile at the mirror and clapped his hands. He shouted, "Come on, Oliver." He was ready. He walked to his door and saw Lane there.

"Is everything alright, Mr. Mayor?"

Oliver was smiling. "Better than alright. I'm going to be fine. I'll be out for a little while at this debate. Take messages if anyone calls." He walked to the door with the frosted glass and banged his hands together again. "Come on," he shouted again. The noise and shout startled Lane. He pulled the door open and charged out into the hallway. A man transformed.

A short walk down the stairs and Oliver was standing outside the large meeting room on the second floor. The doors were closed. He put his hand on the door knob and took another deep breath. "I am a calm, cool, collected individual who can handle anything that may arise." He opened the door and stood with his shoulders squared to the people in chairs waiting for him. Melanie Myers was on a small stage at the far end of the room with a podium in front of her. She was in midsentence when everyone else in the room turned to see Oliver standing in the doorway.

"Good morning everyone." Oliver held up a hand to the audience and began making his way to the empty podium on Melanie Myer's left. Her statement had been cut off by everyone's withdrawn attention. She had to pull them back to her.

"Well, if it is not our distinguished mayor. Look everyone, he was able to take time out of his busy day after all to come and be with us. Let's give him a hand for his effort, shall we?"

Some in the room did not note the sarcasm in her voice and clapped once or twice before realizing it was not a group effort and they put their hands back in their lap.

Melanie Myers was a stout woman with stubby fingers. She was no taller than Oliver's chest and seemed dwarfed by the podium standing there in a red blazer. She looked like a child on Easter Sunday, Oliver thought to himself. She wore a ring on each finger which Oliver found to be annoying for some reason but it was her heavily dyed, jet black hair on which he focused his attention. To gain confidence in these situations Oliver would imagine his opposition in a vulnerable or embarrassing situation. As he walked to the podium and saw her lightly tapping one hand against the other in a sarcastic manner he imagined the heat in the room being turned up and the pressure she was under causing her to sweat. He could envision the lines of black dye that would stream down her face. He smiled at the thought.

He could not believe this was the woman challenging him for mayor. She was an insipid human in his eyes and he could not understand how she had garnered such support from the people in Weatherton.

Oliver responded to her deprecating quip. "Yes, Ms.

Myers, I've had a little bit more on my agenda this morning than you have. I'm sure you had no trouble checking 'pedicure and manicure' off of your 'to-do list' today." He was still looking at her hands and the gaudy rings.

Myers was quick with her comeback. "Yes, and it would appear you have not yet had the chance to mark off 'shower' from yours."

There was a small splattering of laughter in the room but Oliver ignored it.

Oliver was at the podium now and tapped the microphone in front of him though it was a bit silly in the small room. "I'm a busy man, running the city."

Under her breath but to her microphone Myers responded with, "Running it into the ground."

Judge Steve Powers sat before them at a folding table. He stepped into the bickering. "Okay, okay, let's get this started shall we?" He looked at his watch and Oliver understood that Steve was no more interested in being there than he was.

"Sure Steve, uh your Honor. Let's do that." Oliver had used his first name on purpose to make the connection with the distinguished man who would be serving as the moderator of the debate. His sole intention was to intimidate Ms. Myers as she surely had never spoken to Judge Powers before in her life.

Judge Powers addressed Oliver. "Mr. Mayor, would you like to open with any remarks."

Oliver could not keep his hands away from his hair. It was not vanity as the people in the room likely

178

assumed but it was instead the overwhelming feeling that he still had mashed potatoes stuck to him. "No Steve, I don't have any opening remarks." He looked at Melanie Myers' smug expression and decided to not be that short. "Except to say I have served this city well during my first term and I plan to serve it just as well in my second."

Judge Powers nodded and again stole a look at his watch. "Okay. Mrs. Myers, do you have any opening remarks?"

Melanie nodded. "In fact I do." She reached to the pocket of her blazer and pulled from it a piece of paper and began unfolding it on the podium in front of her. The microphone magnified the crackling sound of the paper moving. "As a young girl,"

Oliver did not mean to say it loud enough to be heard but he only said aloud what Judge Powers was thinking, "Are you kidding me?"

Melanie shot a glare at Oliver. "Excuse me, Mr. Mayor. I believe I was speaking." She turned her attention back to the paper. "As a young girl I had visions of what this city would one day become. I had a vision that all of the citizens in this city would enjoy the same levels of security and freedom and,"

Oliver was clutching the side of his podium. He interrupted. "Steve, can we get on with this?"

Melanie was outraged. "Your Honor, I intend to be given the same level of respect and opportunity to speak as Mayor Gartrell is given."

Oliver shrugged. "In that case I'll shut up." Judge

Powers got the joke and laughed but the sarcasm was lost on Melanie Myers who only looked at him still fuming. "Thank you."

Judge Powers wanted things to move along quickly as well. "Ms. Myers you will certainly be afforded that right but we have scheduled this short debate really as only a last minute chance for you to answer one or two questions and frankly so Mr. Parker over there will have something to put in his newspaper tomorrow morning."

Melanie seemed about to cry. "Your honor, if you don't mind me saying so, it certainly appears that you do not want to be here today any more than Mr. Gartrell."

Judge Powers smiled. "You are a perceptive lady. But unfortunately you don't get points for keen observation. Now, where were we? Who had the first question?"

Oliver could only look at the ceiling when the woman in the back of the room stood up. "Yes, I have a question." Ann Strickland rose from her seat. "I'll go first, your Honor. My question is for Mr. Gartrell. Is it true that the city's finance department has been asking you repeatedly over the last several weeks to explain several questionable and unusual expenditures coming from the Mayor's office?"

Oliver used the tone of voice he had refined during his time in politics when being put on the spot in front of a group of onlookers. "Now Ann, you know the answer to that. My door is always open to you or anyone else who has any question for me at all. That is my policy and always has been."

Ms. Strickland did not have the opportunity to ask anything else as Mr. Reed jumped in. "Mr. Gartrell, please explain to us your relationship with Albert King. Is it true you have been working with Mr. King behind the scenes to move forward on the River Mill site despite the zoning limitations?"

Oliver leaned into his microphone. "What was that name again?"

"Albert King."

Oliver stood back up. "Oh yes, Mr. King. I do know Mr. King. Known him since I was a child. He was a friend of my father but as far as the River Mill project, that's a dead issue. Our board of commissioners voted against it and you know as much as I do, when that happens, that's the end of it."

Jack Reed did not concede the floor back to Ms. Strickland. "Mr. King was picked up for questioning last night by the Weatherton police department on an unrelated matter and he had some interesting things to say that I would like your comments on. When he spoke to an investigator he demanded that he speak to you. Apparently you were not at your home last night at approximately 1:30 in the morning."

Oliver began shaking his head and looked only at Judge Powers as if he was the only other person in the room. "Steve, I am a very busy man with a lot on my agenda today and, well, it seems this is shaping up to be more of a witch hunt than a debate. So," Oliver dropped his hands on the podium, purposely making a loud thud resonate through the microphone, "if you will excuse me from the festivities. I will speak to all of you tomorrow night at my victory party. Everybody remember to vote tomorrow, for me, your incumbent or Ms. Myers over here. Thank you and have a good day."

Oliver had learned many years ago to size up a situation and determine early if there was any good that would come from it. If there was even an ounce of expectation for positive results he would stay in the middle of the fire and fight to prove himself. But in those situations when he deemed it a no win situation it was always better to make a quick exit and deal with the ramifications of running away than staying there and getting beat up. Not fully aware of what Albert King had said or not said and with Ann Strickland playing offense in front of a home crowd, Oliver felt he could only incriminate himself rather than attack Melanie Myers. He held his head high as he walked from the podium to the door. Melanie Myers was livid. "What? He can't just leave in the middle of a debate. That's absurd. The debate is not over."

Oliver turned to her and the rest of the group. "Well then, carry on without me."

He knew he was running away. He knew the press would be bad and he would be found guilty in the paper of any wrongdoing of which Ann Strickland or Jack Reed wanted to accuse him. But he could only hope, contradictory to what he had thought after being called a hero a few days before, that no one really reads the paper anymore.

Tuesday, November 7

17

Paul woke up Tuesday morning and went through his normal routine albeit half- heartedly. He got ready in the same way. He ate the same cereal. He said the same things to Daisy he had said to her every day in the four years since he had gotten her. Daisy was his only loyal companion he had decided and that likely was because she never went outside. If given a choice she surely would find some other home. Paul was in that mood. It was a languid state that he often found himself.

To Paul in his somewhat depressed mindset the day was a typical Tuesday with no difference between the Tuesday before or the Tuesday to come. It was no different than the Monday before or the same date on the calendar a year from that day. Monotonous and boring was his life. Any sense of control or power he had felt the week before, driving to the bank, driving to Oliver Gartrell's house, had disappeared as he focused on the feelings he had while driving away from those places. His was not a life that would involve winning or getting what he desired but rather a consolation prize with only, at best, a participation ribbon waiting for him at the end.

It was when he got to work that he realized this Tuesday was different for some people. For the important, influential people of Weatherton this was an important day. Every person Paul passed on the way into City Hall, with only a few exceptions, was wearing a pink t-shirt. He had not yet been able to read what one of the pink shirts said but he marveled at the sight of so many people wearing the same unusual color.

As usual his boss was waiting for him in the hallway. Before giving Fletcher the opportunity to address his tardiness, Paul asked a question.

"Hey Fletcher, what is with all of this pink around here?" Fletcher wiped his hands on a now blackened towel. He ignored the fact that his subordinate was ten minutes late to work.

Fletcher had a curious expression on his face. "It's that lady running for mayor. Looks like she's passed them out all over town this morning in some kind of last big push for the election today. Those sad little buttons your buddy has been passing out like candy to everybody around here won't hold a candle to this woman. I tell you what, this woman is good."

Paul watched more people pass. All of them were either wearing or holding the shirts. "So you think the Mayor is in trouble?"

Fletcher shook his head. "The guy doesn't have a prayer. And to think just four days ago everybody was talking about him saving your life. You could have just jumped and nobody would have cared. He was wasting his time if he was trying to look good to everybody."

Fletcher saw the hurt look on his employee's face

and hit Paul on the back. "Ah, I'm just messing with you." He let out a hearty laugh but he choked it back a second later when he saw Oliver walking down the hallway.

Oliver walked by with a serious look on his face, moving intently down the hallway with long strides. He acknowledged the maintenance men in the hallway but obviously had no intention of stopping to talk. "Gentleman."

Fletcher raised a hand to him for a full hearted high five but it went ignored. "Morning, Mr. Mayor."

Oliver did not break his stride but continued down the hallway. Again Paul felt like Fletcher's hand, slighted, as he had been a key part in the mayor's strategy to be reelected but was now being ignored by him.

Fletcher looked at Paul and leaned over to put his mouth next to his employee's ear though no one would have cared what he was saying anyway. "He doesn't have a prayer. Your buddy's about to get his butt kicked by a pair of high heels. You just watch."

18

Paul's day continued as it normally did. He checked off the things on his agenda. He put the date and time on the little piece of paper that hung on the back of each bathroom door in the building. He checked all of the trash cans, mopped up any spills. The pink t-shirts were a constant reminder to him of the previous days. People wore them throughout the day and he wondered what the tally was and how many votes had been cast

Paul found himself invested in the story but was now reduced to being only a bit player in the background. He waited to hear the news of who won the election just as everyone else waited. To say he wanted Oliver to win would not be entirely accurate as Melanie Myers had not wronged him in anyway as Oliver had but still Paul could not hope for the man's defeat. In spite of feeling like a pawn in Oliver's game, Paul knew Oliver was not a happy man as the episode on the ledge could attest. Paul had spent his life wanting more, hoping for more, but never actually doing anything to get it. And here was a man who had wanted more and had gotten more. Whether his opulence was earned through honest means or purloined was questionable and to Paul somewhat doubtful. But still Oliver was a man with feelings who had lost his wife, his house, and likely his job all within a matter of days. Paul could not help but feel some sympathy for the mayor.

After work Paul went home and changed his clothes, fed his cat, and watched a little television. But still he could not stop thinking about Oliver. Oliver had mentioned his victory party during dinner at his house. At 7:30 Paul decided to take Oliver up on the invitation extended to him Sunday night. Paul went back out to the hotel downtown.

Paul knew it was silly but he thought of Holly and wondered under what circumstances he may see her at Oliver's party. She had become something more than just his beautiful next door neighbor in the previous days. She was lonely. And sad. At the dinner party she had become a person to him. He knew he would likely never be with her in that way he had fantasized about but he felt he could possibly be her friend.

Paul walked down the carpeted hallway of the hotel after going through the automatic double doors from the parking lot. No one was at the desk so rather than wait he decided to wander. He would follow the people and listen for the voices. He turned and saw a group of three women, each in a pink t-shirt walking down the hallway. He knew these people were not going to Oliver's party but they would at least lead Paul in the right direction of Banquet Room Number One and Two.

The women stopped outside of closed double doors.

The doors were the color of the carpet and seemed to be an extension of the floor. One of the women leaned over and pulled the door knob and as the door opened Paul was met with the sound of music and laughter and chatter. He saw a quick glimpse of what appeared to be a room full of balloons and hundreds of people's backs and legs. It was a party indeed. A band was set up on the far end of the room. The electricity flowed into the hallway. And then just as quickly the door closed and the music and laughter and celebration was gone, replaced by a thumping that was now perceptible to Paul that he had not noticed before. He thought about going into that room. He could see who was there. Watching beautiful women who were drinking too much and being ignored by their significant others would be an interesting study of the human condition. But he had come to see Oliver and he knew the likelihood that Holly was anywhere in the room with the pink t-shirt clad women was unlikely.

Paul walked further down the hallway and found the door with the placard beside it designating it as Banquet Room Number Two. He stood back and put his hand on the door knob thinking of the music and party that he had witnessed a minute before. It was only 7:45. The election returns were probably not all in yet. He wanted to compare Oliver's party to Melanie Myers' to see which party had the most energy and a palpable excitement with an air of victory. He opened the door and was met only with the sound of a vacuum cleaner being used on the far side of the room. Tables were set up with chairs anchoring tied balloons reaching for the ceiling. The center piece of each table was a large flower arrangement. But other than the forgotten furniture and the hotel employee with the vacuum cleaner, the room was empty. Paul thought he must be mistaken. Perhaps there was a different Banquet Room Number Two. Or maybe he was in the wrong hotel altogether. Paul shrugged and turned to leave but turning to his left someone caught his eye. There he was. In the corner, at the smallest table in the room sat Oliver, alone, with a drink in front of him. Oliver was staring at the glass as he turned it with his thumb and forefinger.

Paul walked up to the table. He was not heard over the vacuum cleaner's low roar and not noticed by Oliver's blurred peripheral vision. It was not until he pulled out the chair across from the table that Oliver saw him and acknowledged his presence.

"Ah, it's Paul. My good luck charm." And then with a loud voice but devoid of emotion he addressed the empty room, "Everybody say hi to Paul."

It was obvious that he was more inebriated than Paul had ever seen him. His eyes seemed to droop toward his mouth.

"How are you, Mr. Mayor?"

Oliver leaned his head back with his mouth open and let out a loud laugh. "Ha! Mr. Mayor." Then he looked back to the glass and was back in his state of depression. "I'm not so good."

Paul noted the slurred speech. "I was just down the hallway and figured out what happened."

Oliver's eyebrows raised as if just hearing some interesting news. "Oh, how was that party? As lively as this one I guess. Did you happen to see my wife down there? If you do, tell her I won't be home tonight. No wait, she already knows that."

Oliver covered his face with both of his hands and Paul waited to see his shoulders shaking to indicate he was crying. Instead he pulled his hands away and looked at the wall on the far end of the room. Paul for a moment decided that Oliver had forgotten he was there.

Oliver did not take his eyes from the wall but began talking to himself as much as to Paul. "Do you know why I became mayor? Do you know how all of this started?"

Paul looked at the spot on the wall that seemed to be holding Oliver's attention. "No."

"For many years I sold insurance. That's how I got my start, how I made my living. And I was pretty good at it." He held up his hand, objecting to his own statement. "No, I was damn good at it. I would go into people's homes and I would talk. I would convince them that this is what they needed. If they didn't have insurance I made them feel stupid for their obvious oversight and then it was my job to make them feel smart for getting it, from me of course." Oliver took another sip of his drink. "I was good. Real good.

192

There was this other guy in the office, Rex. Rex Patterson. Oh boy, old Rex. We were the top two salesmen there for fifteen years or so. Not just in Weatherton, the whole southeast. Nobody could touch us. Nobody. And just like any two top dogs, we hated each other. Oh man, we had our little wars. Always trying to one up each other. If Rex drove to work on a Monday in a new car you better believe by the weekend I was in something new, not only nice but nicer than his. It had to be nicer than his. That's just the way we were. Everybody in the office hated us I'm sure but we didn't care. We were rolling, making more money than we knew what to do with. It was good. Maybe not healthy but good. One day we're sitting in the office. The city had kind of fallen on hard times, things were looking bleak for everybody. We knew things were going to get harder for us. So we're sitting there talking and somebody says something about the mayor and how horrible the guy was. And I said something like," Oliver sat up straight in his chair and spoke in a deep voice, "'Maybe I'll run for mayor.' I didn't really even mean it when I said it. But do you know what Rex did?"

Paul was leaning forward, engrossed in the drunk man's story. "No, what?"

Oliver sipped his drink again to let the anticipation build. "He laughed. He laughed at me. Not one of these, 'oh yeah right' kind of laughs. No. No it was a, 'You're out of your mind,' kind of laugh. Oh boy, that made me hot. I didn't say anything to anybody the rest of the day. I just sat in my office and let that laugh echo in my head. I went that afternoon and found out what I had to do to get in the race. The election was a year away but I started that day campaigning. And now after one term as mayor look at me. Look at this room. It doesn't look like the room I was in four years ago. That room was the place to be." He held his drink in the air and shouted, "The king has arrived!" Paul looked at the man pushing the vacuum cleaner as the man looked back across the room at them. He felt embarrassed for this man in front of him. "Do you know what I am, Paul? Do you?"

Paul always had an elevated sense of confidence around intoxicated people and his confidence and their inebriation were directly proportional. He did not fear the drunk man's judgment. Paul looked around the room and then back at the mayor to answer his question. "Uh, lonely?"

Oliver ignored Paul's answer. "Finished." Oliver looked around the room for affect and then poked his finger in the air in Paul's direction. "I'm finished. I needed to win this election, Paul. If someone had told me six months ago that I was going to lose I'd of said they were insane. And now, now, I'm not going to be the mayor anymore. My wife threw me out. My reputation, ha, what reputation? I got nothing. But you Paul. I've got you."

Oliver stood up and walked around the table to Paul and placed his hand on Paul's shoulder. "You're the only friend I've got left. Oh man," Oliver fell back into

194

the chair next to Paul. "I don't feel so hot." He put his hand on his chest and took some deep breaths.

Paul became concerned. "Does your chest hurt?" He saw Oliver nod without speaking. Excitedly Paul stood up and reached into his pocket to pull out a small bottle of pills. He handed the bottle to Oliver. "Take one of these. My doctor gave them to me. They help me out whenever I don't feel good. Sometimes I get kind of panicky and my chest starts to hurt but I just pop one of these pills and it fixes everything."

Oliver squinted at the bottle and held them out at arm's length from his face. "What is it?" He looked old doing it but Paul found some respect in the man's failing eyes.

Paul shook his head but was eager to help. "I don't know what they are but they work. Just put it in and swallow it. But don't bite it. My doctors says you have to swallow them whole. He says somehow it goes straight to your heart and the pain goes away and you become calm throughout your body."

As Paul spoke Oliver placed the pill in his mouth and bit down. Paul heard the crack between Oliver's teeth. Oliver looked at him with an exasperated expression much like he had on the ledge, in his office and at the dinner party. "This is a mint."

Paul was offended and took the bottle back from Oliver. He stood up and put the bottle in his pocket. "No, it's not. It's medicine."

Oliver's inebriation could not be suppressed. He never spared another's feelings but usually his criticism was given with tact and class. Now all he did was laugh. Hysterically. He covered his face with his hands but shook his head, unable to hide his delight in the situation. He leaned back in the chair and almost tumbled out of it. "Your doctor gave you candy." And suddenly it was as if his pain and public humiliation was gone and replaced by this other person's shortcomings. Barely able to talk he asked through gasps of breaths, "How much did he charge you for those?"

Paul was red faced and wanted to leave. "Did he, did he," Oliver could not get out the words and took a deep breath. He exhaled slowly and forced a serious expression on his face. "Did he write a prescription?"

Paul was angry now and spoke loudly. "They are medicine and they work." Oliver could see the anger in Paul's face and he feared his friend would leave him. Paul understood at that moment. Oliver had flaws, many, many flaws. But his most obvious one, the one that made him mean but also what likely made him successful was his inability to lose anything with grace. He had been alone in the room with no way to transfer his failure on to another person. But now, here was Paul, an unwilling volunteer. And Oliver could move his pain on to someone else. Paul would have to consider the fact that the medicine he carried around was perhaps nothing more than candy. But he knew for a fact that Oliver was poison.

"Okay, okay, I'm sorry. Maybe they just taste like mints." But still he laughed to himself, his shoulders moving up and down slightly. The maintenance man and the mayor sat in silence and listened to the vacuum cleaner. It turned off and Paul watched the man unplug it and begin wrapping the cord around the handle. Paul thought of his job and how much he hated it. He thought of his life and how much he hated that bigger picture. It was not lost on him that here before him, at the same table was the soon to be former mayor of the city whose life had fallen into shambles over the previous seventy two hours but yet he was still able to laugh heartily at another person's expense. But he could laugh nonetheless. Paul lacked that ability to be happy. His growing sadness moved him to ask Oliver a question.

"Have you heard from Holly?"

Oliver leaned back in his chair and crossed his hands over his stomach. He answered the real question Paul wanted to ask. "Oh Paul, Paul, Paul. No, if I had to bet I don't think she's gonna be here. I'm sorry there buddy. Look at us. I lost the election and you lost the girl. Just two losers sitting around in an empty room feeling sorry for ourselves."

The comment stung Paul. He maybe could not control who he was but he could determine where he was. He slapped his knees to tell Oliver he was leaving and stood up. He would refuse the poison on this particular night. It was his prerogative. "Oliver, I'm sorry you lost. I hope everything works out for you though. I'll see you at City Hall, huh?"

"Yes, I suppose you will. I'll need a janitor in a few

weeks to come help me clean out my office."

The word 'janitor' stung Paul again but he did not argue. He turned and walked toward the door.

Oliver called out after him. "Wait, Paul, don't go. Come on. I've got ten cases of ice cold beer back there. Stay for a while. I can't drink all of them by myself, you gotta help me out." Paul held up his hand to decline when the mayor remembered. "Oh wait, you don't drink. I just don't understand, Paul. I just don't get that."

As Oliver sat shaking his head his chin fell down to his shirt. Paul could have felt sorry for him if he was witnessing the suffering of a nicer person. But he knew he was not. "I'll see you tomorrow, Oliver. Have a good night."

Paul walked to the door he had come in through. As he walked out a man dressed in the hotel uniform walked in. "Mr. Gartrell, we're going to lock the doors to Banquet Room Two in ten minutes. You'll need to get your things together." The hotel manager spoke softly. Paul noticed the sympathy in the man's voice as if he was telling Oliver his dog was sick and there was nothing they could do. Paul turned and looked back at the man alone in the room. Oliver raised his drink to acknowledge what he had been told and said loudly, "Cheers."

Paul stepped into the hallway and walked toward the exit. He passed Banquet Room One as a man and woman fell through the door out into the hallway. The couple held each other up both too drunk to stand on two legs alone. The loud music and festive atmosphere once again spilled out into the hallway. Two women in pink shirts were stumbling down the hallway with beer bottles in their hand. One said to the other, "Mayor Myers puts on a good party." And the other agreed with a loud, "Hell yeah, she does."

Paul repeated the name 'Mayor Myers' to himself. He wondered when Oliver would say that for the first time.

Despite the happy people in the hotel lobby as he made his way to the parking lot, Paul could not help but feel very sad.

Wednesday, November 8

19

At work on Wednesday morning Paul stayed away from the sixth floor. He did not know if it was a fear that he would find himself consoling the ousted mayor again or if even more so, it was a fear that Oliver would have completely recovered from the night before and losing the election. Paul did not want to see Oliver in the pits of despair but he most definitely at that moment did not want to find him fully recovered from his loss and in high spirits.

Paul assumed that Oliver would not be there. It seemed any person after having lost an election would not be eager to come back in to work the next day and put on the fake smile and say over and over again, "That's okay. She'll do a fine job."

Paul felt that with the election over it was time to put the silly charade behind him. To him life was back to normal and the previous week may as well have never happened. Paul decided that morning on the way to City Hall he would work harder than he ever had. He would be focused on the tasks at hand, to checking off his 'to do' list with care and efficiency and he would make Fletcher proud. He could lose himself in his job though he knew that would be short lived.

Paul had pulled the bags of trash from the men's and women's room on the fourth floor and was carrying the bundles down the hallway toward the service elevator when he heard the familiar and dreaded voice call to him.

"Hey crazy. I see you made it to work this morning. Your lady friend must not be keeping you up very late at night, huh?"

Paul turned to see Sullivan walking toward him. He was holding only a towel that he wiped his hands on repeatedly to give the illusion of just having finished doing something. It was a trick he had no doubt learned from Fletcher.

"Leave me alone, alright. I've got work to do." Paul was in no mood to spar with Sullivan. To be reminded of the past week any more than what was already running through his mind in a continual loop was not a welcome chore.

Sullivan looked at his hands and paid careful attention in wiping his nails with the towel. "Just admit it, you made the whole thing up. There was no broad. That woman who came in here the other day doesn't know you exist. Just say that out loud to me and I'll leave you alone. Admit you lied."

Paul did not want to concede anything to his nemesis. "I did not lie. I did not make anything up. And why do you care anyway?"

Sullivan began laughing. "Yeah you did. You know you made it all up. Just the look on your face tells me so." Paul had always understood that there are people in life who have to win. Those people were easily identified on all of the playgrounds of his childhood through school, through college. Paul never found fault with the people in that group. The will to win was

202

an admirable quality to possess. But Paul had always identified another group that he loathed. The group consisted of those people who did not have to win but who found it very important to see other people lose. Oliver wanted to win and his competitiveness Paul could tolerate. Sullivan though was in the other group. Paul had run out of patience to entertain either but especially not Sullivan.

Paul put his hands out to his side. "Fine, if it will get you to leave me alone then I made the whole thing up."

With his hands in the air as if signaling a touchdown, Sullivan yelled, "Yeah you did. And do you know why you made it up? Cause you're a loser."

The comment did not make Paul mad. He was in a strange place of melancholy and tiredness and his insipid coworker would not get a rise from him on this day. He shrugged his shoulders and turned to continue his walk down the hallway with the bags of trash in hand. He did not have the desire nor energy to argue.

But then, in one of the greatest moments of Paul's life, it happened. It could not have been planned any better. Paul saw the expression on Sullivan's face change while he heard his name called from behind him.

"Paul, is that you?"

He turned around and there she was. In the hallway of the fourth floor of City Hall, Holly stood before Paul and had spoken his name. She was dressed far more conservatively on this day than at the dinner party a few nights before. She wore a buttoned up white shirt untucked that fell down below her waist. Her jeans fit perfectly. Her thick hair was not curled the way it had been at Oliver's house but was hanging straight to her shoulders. Her eyes though were the same.

"I've been looking for you. I was wondering if maybe you had time to go somewhere and talk. If you have time."

Paul was mesmerized by her beauty. He did not want to stop looking at her but knew it would be worth it to see once again the expression on Sullivan's face. "Hey Sullivan, could you take care of these for me?" He handed both bags of trash to Sullivan who took them without objection. "Thanks, buddy." He turned back to Holly. "Sure, I've got time. Do you want to go down to the cafeteria?" She nodded and followed him to the stairwell.

Paul walked behind Holly down the four flights of stairs. They were silent in the stairwell with only their footsteps echoing in the hollow chamber. Paul tried to think of something to say but not knowing the reason she had sought him out he decided to let her be the first to speak. The whole time he was unsure of himself and how to act. Questions were constant in his mind. Should he be in front? Should he be closest to the wall or let her walk next to the wall? How far ahead of her should he be to open doors for her? Holly still did not speak but said, 'Thank you,' as he let her pass through the door on the first floor before him.

He held the cafeteria door open for her and two more people walked in behind her.

They sat down across from each other at a table on the far end of the cafeteria next to a window looking out into the courtyard. It was an odd view for Paul as he normally would be on the other side of the window working in the courtyard while people watched him.

"So, have you been working on your golf swing anymore?"

It was his attempt to make her laugh but also to create common ground between them upon which they could build a conversation. Watching her beat up Oliver's car was an experience that he had shared with her that she had probably not repeated to anyone else. Paul chose to remind her of it, whether he was cognizant of it or not, because her response would allow him to gauge her current feelings for Oliver. He was prepared to match her disdain or sympathy for the man.

Holly looked away from him and he instantly regretted the comment. "No. Oh my gosh. I feel so bad about what I did."

The morning sun shone in through the windows of the courtyard. She truly was a beautiful woman. The symmetry of her face, the contrast of the blue eyes and blonde hair. But now that she was across from him he could see other features he had not noticed before. She had a mole just above her left eye. It did not distract from her beauty but Paul assumed that she did not like it. "Yeah, I guess we all do things that we're not proud of."

Holly saw this as a challenge. She squinted at him. "Now, I don't know you at all, but, I'm just being honest here, you don't strike me as the type of guy that would do something like that."

"Like what? Beat up a Mercedes with a golf club? No, I've never done that. But in a previous life I made a few wrong turns." Paul decided not to elaborate and would leave it at that.

"Oh, really? Are there some overdue library books in your past that you want to confess?" She decided to call him on what he said and the demeanor he was trying to convey.

"I've taken plenty of risks."

"Going out on a ledge to kill yourself doesn't really count as living on the edge."

Paul smiled but with a feeling of sadness. He looked into the courtyard and then back to Holly. "I was not out there to kill myself. I told you at the dinner party, I was taking a break. Relaxing. That's where I always go to hide from my boss."

Holly was looking at the door of the cafeteria, aware of every person who was coming in. "Yeah, you don't seem like a real risk taker. Oliver wasn't either when I first met him. He was innocent and sheltered."

It felt odd to Paul being compared to Oliver. Whether fact or not, it was something Holly needed to feel was true. "But you converted him."

Holly broke her fixation on the entrance. "I didn't

convert him. I helped him. I got him to loosen up. Put down his guard. Live."

Paul did not want to talk about Oliver but realized that was why Holly was there in the first place and he would oblige. "He seemed pretty loose last night."

Holly's attention was completely on Paul now and she leaned forward into the table. "You saw him last night? Where?"

"At the victory party. Banquet Room Number Two. And oh man, he was a mess. Sitting there at a table, all alone while somebody vacuumed in the corner. It was kind of sad really. Hey, where were you last night? You're sleeping with the guy and in his darkest hour he's only got me to talk to. I felt bad for him. Or at least as bad as I could under the circumstances."

"That's not really my thing. And besides, I didn't know who would be there. My first meeting with the Missis didn't go too well. You may remember." Holly looked out of the window into the courtyard. "That whole incident at his house the other night, it was…" She paused and touched the napkin holder on the table. "It's kind of sad. The way things change." She inhaled deeply and Paul thought she may cry. "The way they end."

Both of them looked down at the table and shared a moment of silence remembering what had happened. "He always comes by my apartment on Wednesday mornings, every week for the past five months or so and then this morning, he wasn't there. It's not really like I expected him to show up I guess, not after

Sunday night and all that but I don't know, I missed him. I need him to stop by my apartment and," she looked again at the table and then back to the door, "fix a few things."

Paul misunderstood. "I'm not a great handyman but I could come over and take a look at anything that's broken."

Holly made herself small in her seat, bringing her shoulders in front of her. She seemed embarrassed and Paul realized what he had misunderstood. "Oh."

Holly changed the subject. "I am worried about him. I came here and wandered around near his office thinking I may see him but he's nowhere. Just gone. I've called him. Texted him. No response. I just want to check on him."

The irony struck Paul. Holly acted towards Oliver as Paul acted towards her. He thought about how he walked slowly to his car each morning and the time he spent adjusting his blinds thinking maybe she would walk by. He felt an odd sense of satisfaction knowing she was guilty of the same behavior.

Paul tried to steer the conversation towards closure for Holly. "Maybe he's gone back home. She kicked him out, you know. But maybe after last night she's taken him back. She's there for him. Maybe."

Disgust came over Holly's face. Her dislike for Sheryl was obvious. "Oh, what does she care?"

"She is married to him."

Holly ran her hand through her hair and scratched her head and crossed her arms over her chest,

208

withdrawing from the comment. She was not trying to impress Paul. "I know it's stupid. But I miss him. It's been the best relationship I've had in a long time. Maybe ever."

Paul decided to be honest and judgmental if necessary. "Relationship? He'd write you poetry, you'd doodle his name on your notebook, call him every night, go to the prom, that kind of thing?"

Agitated, Holly looked back at the door. "It's complicated."

Paul leaned forward and put his elbows on the table. "Can I ask you something, Holly?" She said nothing but put her arms to her side, opening herself back up. "You could have anybody in this town. Anybody. Wealthy. Good looking. Maybe, I don't know, single even. Why him?"

Intrigued by the directness of the question Holly pushed herself up in her chair to put her elbows on the table. It was obvious she enjoyed talking about Oliver. "Why him, what?"

"You and him? What's there that made you, you know," he moved his hands struggling for the words, "make him your handyman? What's so great about Oliver?"

"I see where you're going with this. You mean, 'Why him?' and 'Why not you?' Is that what you're asking?"

Paul shrugged, embarrassed to have her contradict him and be right. "Oliver," Holly thought for a minute, "Oliver thought he deserved me. He thinks he deserves everything he has in life. That's what is different about him and most people. Most people go through life hoping that they'll get what they want. Wishing. But Oliver, it's like he demanded it. I found that very appealing."

Paul wanted to dig deeper into the line of questioning not to elicit her guilt but for his understanding. "There wasn't anything about him that made you question whether you should be with him?"

Holly looked again at Paul, accepting his challenge. "I knew he was married if that's what you're asking. Everybody knew he was married."

"But everybody didn't sleep with him. Just you, oh and that girl from Atlanta."

Holly did not like being accused of anything but she was there because of Oliver and welcomed the chance to talk about him regardless of the implications. "Falling for him was not what I planned. We had fun in the beginning. But I couldn't help it. He's never raised his voice to me, much less a hand or a belt or a broken beer bottle."

Paul stuck his bottom lip out and raised his eyebrows as if he was impressed by her comment. "Wow. Boyfriend of the year."

Holly raised her voice to defend herself and Oliver. "I've had plenty of abusive boyfriends in my life. For the first time in my life I thought I had found the other type of guy, the good guy. He was perfect."

"And married."

"Yes, and married. Why do you keep saying that? I

know he is married."

"And rich. That had to do something with it. If he was some clerk or office assistant or something you wouldn't have been interested. But the rich mayor of our city, living in his mansion, driving his hundred thousand dollar car. That was nice, right?"

Holly shook her head. "That's not important to me. I don't care about that stuff. I really don't. But you seem so hung up on it. Going on and on about his house the other night. I don't care about his wealth and money. I really don't."

"Everybody is hung up on it. Oliver is more obsessed with it than any person I've ever met but you don't notice it because he has everything he could want. At least for now."

Holly was getting more agitated. He had not meant to make her angry but she shifted in her seat as if challenged. "What about you? Who are you to judge? The guy who has to ask somebody else to help him get a date with his neighbor. Classy. Where are your guts?"

Paul was put on the defensive. "I just didn't think I had a chance any other way."

"And you were right." Holly snapped back at him. "You didn't have a chance. You know why? Cause you're a wimp. It wasn't Oliver's money that attracted me to him. It was his confidence. You never had a chance because you didn't think you did. Do you really think a girl wants to date a guy that doesn't think he can have her? Do you try to appeal to a girl's

211

charitable heart hoping she'll have mercy on you? Is that it? Because that's not the way it works. We save pity for three legged puppies and little old ladies. Not boyfriends. Girls don't want wimps."

Now Paul had to look away. He half smiled and looked out to the court yard. He had been punched in the face. This coming from the girl he had thought about every hour of each day for the last five months. She was a girl that he had given a voice to. He had formed her in a perfect way in his mind. She had a softness he assumed, a need to be treated tenderly and would treat people tenderly in return. Hers was a personality, a soul that he could fall in love with, he thought. But he was such a fool. He did not know her. She had never said those nice things to him that he imagined. What she said hurt him. It hurt him because what she said was true. Girls do not want wimps and girls apparently did not want him. He had to say something.

"You make a very good point." He wanted to leave her there. A pigeon in the courtyard walked to the window. Paul remembered what Oliver said to him on the ledge, about a fire in the belly and being like a pigeon. At that moment, Paul saw Oliver's wisdom. Paul had the answer to his question he had just asked Holly.

Holly was looking at the table in front of her and Paul realized she had a similar expression on her face that he must have had on his. Her voice softened. She spoke quietly, apologetically. "Listen, it's been a long, strange week, huh? I'm in a bad mood. I'm stressed out. Still thinking about my boyfriend having a girlfriend somewhere else."

Paul looked at her quickly and then back to the courtyard. She continued putting herself in the lower position that he currently occupied. "And I found out from his wife too. That's the real kick, huh?" The silence from Paul affected her more than she realized it would. She had been mean and she was sorry but it made her sad in light of what she had just been saying and what she had been going through. The tough guy had hurt her and she in turn had hurt the guy who liked her.

"Listen, Paul, you're not a bad guy. Hey, you're probably a great guy, I don't know. I don't really know what that even looks like to be honest. I thought I did but I realize sometimes that I have no clue. And you're not a bad looking guy but you have to understand people are not going to think any more highly of you than you think of yourself. That's just a fact. You have to understand that. Oliver thought he was a king and he expected to be treated like that, and for the most part he was. But that's wrong too."

Still Paul looked out to the courtyard. Her assessment of his looks was now added to the label of 'wimp'. He turned back to her but looked at the table between them. "I want to be your friend, Paul. I don't have many of those right now."

Paul appreciated her candor and apology for what she had said to him. She could have gotten up and left but she did not and he recognized the positive in that.

Paul noticed a woman behind Holly walking to her and acting strangely. She was on tip toes. She was a black woman about the same age as Holly and Paul. She had a bandana around her forehead to control the hair that exploded from her head. Her green eyes were mesmerizing to Paul and he looked at them while she approached. Wearing a very tight, white button up shirt that struggled to cover her breasts, Paul could see the gap between two buttons and her exposed bra. The woman put a finger to her mouth to tell Paul not to say anything to alert Holly of her oncoming attack. She stood beside the table and then in a loud voice to make Holly jump, said, "Girl, what are you doing here?"

Holly did jump, startled by the loud voice next to her. "Oh my God, you scared the hell out of me." Paul felt badly for not having warned Holly that was about to happen.

With Holly's reaction being her intention the girl tilted her head back and laughed loudly while clapping her hands in front of her. Again, Paul thought of Oliver and the mints. Then the woman beside Holly got serious. "What are you doing here? You're not in trouble, are you?" She pointed at Paul and spoke as if he was deaf. "Is this your court appointed?"

Holly smiled, embarrassed by her friend's loud demeanor. "No, this is Paul, my neighbor. This is Tammy."

Paul rose up slightly from his seat and shook her

hand. Tammy was impressed and tried to embarrass him. "Uh oh, look at the manners on this one. Is this the neighbor you were telling me about? How you doing, boy?"

Paul did not like being called boy but only smiled and nodded understanding that was her way of establishing herself as the dominant person at the table. It was a position that he conceded without care. Tammy looked back at Holly. "Is Nurse Holly on call tonight?"

Holly looked up at her, moving only her head to look back in an uncomfortable way without moving her body. Paul knew from Holly's body language she was silently telling Tammy to leave her alone. "Yeah, I go in at ten. What about you?"

Tammy was not worried at all by who may hear her talk. "Oh you know I'll be there. I've got to go to work. Just walk around, whisper in a few rich guy's ears, rub up against them." She looked toward the kitchen and said loudly, "I still make more money in an hour there than I do at this place in a whole day. You know what I mean?" Her lack of discretion made Paul ill at ease which intensified when she turned her attention back to him. "Hey, I've never seen you at the club. Why don't you ever come by and support your neighbor Holly in her career, huh? Save you from peeking through the apartment wall at her and seeing everything she's got."

With that comment, Holly shared Paul's discomfort of the unwelcomed presence and shifted her weight in her chair. A loud voice came from the kitchen area telling Tammy to go back to the counter. Tammy looked in the direction of the voice and swatted her hand as if being threatened by a bee. "Listen to him yelling at me to get back to work. We need big Max up in here to protect me. He'd snap somebody's neck if they yelled at me like that." She yelled back in the direction of the kitchen, "I'm working over here." Then she turned her attention back to Holly. "Hey, here, have some condiments." She reached into the small apron tied around her waist and pulled out two handfuls of honey mustard sauce and threw them on the table.

The voice came again commanding her to return to her place behind the counter. Tammy began walking away and Paul relaxed. Then Tammy remembered something and walked back to the table. "Hey Holly, I've been working on a new pole move that I'm gonna try tonight for the first time. I tell you what, if I can do it without landing on my head the fellas are going to love it. I'll need a money strap to carry all those bills around." She turned back toward the kitchen and yelled, "I'm coming." And then to Holly and Paul. "Here, have some more of these." She tossed more packets of honey mustard and ketchup on the table in front of them.

The loud voice came barreling from the kitchen again. Paul looked around at the other people in the cafeteria. There was a middle aged man, sitting alone, sipping coffee and holding a newspaper in front of him.

216

To the other side was a twenty something woman, zipping through messages on her phone but now each of them was looking at Paul's table. The paper and the phone ignored. The looks of consternation and annoyance were obvious. Tammy quickly left the table and did not look back at either one of them. Holly looked at Paul and felt the need to explain.

"That's a girl I work with."

Paul had an incredulous look on his face. "Oh really, I thought maybe you sang with her in the choir at church." He looked out of the window again wondering if he should ask the other question that had been on his mind and decided he had nothing to lose. "Holly, why do you do that?"

Holly acted confused. "Do what?"

Paul leaned into the table and whispered, "Strip."

"Oh strip? You want to know why I'm a stripper." She said it loud enough that the middle aged man and the twenty something woman looked up again from their paper and phone. Paul felt a slight embarrassment. "The 401k by itself makes it worth it but when I heard they had dental also, well that just sold me on it."

Knowing he was being answered with sarcasm to tell him it was none of his business, Paul played along. "Is there a large pension if you stay until you're sixty five?"

Holly had calmed down and seemed only slightly embarrassed being as loud as she was. She laughed at his question. "I won't be doing it that long. Tammy on the other hand, who knows. I think maybe one day I'll go back to school, be a teacher or something like that."

Paul remained focused on her and leaned into the table. He was paying close attention to her and listening. "I could see you doing that. I really could. And hey, you're already comfortable standing up in front of people so you have that going for you."

Holly laughed. She put her hands up on the table and seemed comfortable and at ease. "It's just kind of a pipe dream. I had a pretty rotten childhood. Parents who didn't care. I was on my own by fifteen. Some drugs and stuff. Bad boyfriends. Maybe I could save somebody else from going through all of that. I don't know." She waved her hand, dismissing what she was saying. "It's probably never going to happen."

Paul was excited she was opening up to him. She was beginning to trust him and he welcomed that. He had to be positive and encouraging. "You should go for that. You'd be good at it. Look at Oliver. That may be one reason you two were together. He's so," he searched for the word, "childlike. Immature. He doesn't really have any concept of how the world works. He just assumes he's always going to get his way."

Holly smiled and nodded her head slightly. "You may be on to something there." She laughed again. "That guy is such a mess." There was still a fondness in her eyes that Paul could sense. Holly looked around the room and saw a clock on the far wall. "It's ten thirty already? How long have we been sitting here?"

"I don't know but I'm going to get fired. But hey, would that be a bad thing? Probably not." Paul was happy sitting there with Holly. He was not hiding out on a ledge or in a closet or out in the courtyard. He was there in the open spaces, breaking the rules of his job, at risk of being reprimanded but he did not care.

Holly looked at the entrance one more time.

Paul felt the need to tell her what she did not want to hear. "I doubt he'll make it in today." Paul shrugged as he said it.

Holly smiled. "Probably not. Not after last night. Did you see the final count of the votes? Oh my gosh. It was brutal."

They both sat in silence for a minute. Holly placed her hands on the table to push herself up but stayed there a few seconds longer than needed and then dropped her hands back into her lap. "So that's it then. Here we are. A stripper and a janitor hitting rock bottom chasing the wrong people. Story of our lives probably, huh?"

Paul chose not to correct the title and let the janitor word slide. "That's true. But this has been nice sitting here. So much nicer than our romantic dinner at the mayor's mansion."

Holly smiled. "That still makes me laugh. The whole situation. Oliver asking me to come to his house for dinner, telling me about you and how I'd be doing him a favor and you're a great guy. It was so strange. I didn't know what he was talking about but he has that way of getting people to do what he wants them to."

"I've learned that lesson the hard way. Everybody looks at me like I'm some nut job and all I was doing was hiding out there on the ledge to get out of working. And then an hour later he's setting me up on a date with you and I'm the happiest guy in the world."

Holly leaned forward. "But you didn't even know me. You thought I was a nurse." She got serious and looked him in the eye to make an admission that Paul felt was sincere. "Listen, you can do better than wasting your time chasing the stripper who lives next door."

Paul looked at the door. "Who is wasting her time chasing the married mayor."

She looked at him in a curious way. Absorbing what he had said. "That's true. Very true." She seemed reluctant to do it but forced herself. She put her palms down on the table and pushed herself up out of her seat. "Oh hey, listen, I've got to go. I may go back upstairs one more time just to see if he's there."

Paul stood up. "See, he's just like a lost kid on a field trip." Holly smiled. "I'll tell him you're looking for him if I see him."

Holly turned to leave and stopped. She turned back to the table, her body square to him. She pushed a strand of hair behind her ear. "And listen, Paul, I'm sorry about what I said earlier, the wimp thing. Sweet is not so bad and you are that."

Paul appreciated the apology but was uncomfortable with it. He deflected. "Oh perfect. Just what a guy wants to hear. Sweet. You forgot funny. If

I had a dollar for every girl that's told me that over the years I'd have more one dollar bills in my underwear than Tammy. Now if you'll excuse me," he pointed to the table at the packets of condiments Tammy had left behind, "I'll go drown myself in a tub of honey mustard somewhere."

Holly smiled, happy to have found an amusing friend. "And hey, if you're lucky, Tammy may come out and give you mouth to mouth." Paul smiled, pleased that Holly was playing with him in that way. "I'll see you around, Paul. And thanks." She paused and squinted her eyes slightly. Paul assumed she had one more thing to say but then she turned and walked towards the door.

She was gone. Paul had no choice but to leave the cafeteria but knew it would be awkward to follow her. He walked to the door that exited to the courtyard and went outside.

With the exception of his hiding place on the sixth floor ledge, the courtyard was Paul's favorite place in City Hall. The courtyard was much bigger than it needed to be. One or two benches would have been sufficient as Paul had never seen more than two people sitting on them at a time but instead there were eight benches along the brick pathways that went from one side to the other. Paul preferred working in the raised flower beds and sweeping the stones over cleaning toilets and mopping linoleum.

When Paul stepped outside from the cafeteria he was aware that someone had come through the door behind him. He decided to make a quick exit to the other side but the person called out to him.

"Excuse me, young man. Excuse me." Paul turned without thinking, assuming someone needed help with directions. The attractive black woman in the business suit was standing in front of him. He did not know her name was Ann but knew that she was some distinguished person with the county. "Can I ask you a question?"

"Okay." Paul knew that a request for directions would not be it.

"How much did he pay you?"

Paul was confused and looked around the courtyard. He did not know if she was referring to Fletcher or if she had mistaken him for someone else.

"I'm sorry. Who paid me for what?"

Ann was confident and accusatory with slits for eyes. "He paid you, didn't he? Oliver Gartrell paid you to go out on that ledge and pretend like you were going to jump so he could save you."

Paul shook his head and noticed how hot the courtyard was despite it being November. "No, not exactly."

She was adamant in her inquisition. "I know that man did not see you outside his window and go out there to save you. Now tell me what happened."

Paul was tired of discussing any detail related to the election. "Why does it matter at this point? He lost. It's over, right?"

"I need to know. I just do."

Paul thought of the reporters in Oliver's office that day and everyone shouting out questions to him wanting to know the truth not for the sake of having the truth but for the sake of having the story. Paul became defensive of Oliver and vague to not be rude.

"We were both out on the ledge. I was on one side and he was on the other. I had never met him before that encounter so no, he did not pay me to go out there."

Ann tilted her head and put her hand on her hip, breaking her rigid posture. She was confused and did not like the feeling. "What was he doing out there? Was he going to jump?"

Paul took a step back from her fully aware of his long absence from doing anything work related that day. He knew Fletcher had to be looking for him. "I don't know what he was going to do. I really don't. I don't think he knew either. I was just out there taking a," he paused and redirected his excuse, "cleaning up."

Ann looked at the bed of dying marigolds to her left that Paul needed to dig up. "Hmmm, interesting."

Paul took her silence as a chance to leave. "You have a nice day." And with that he turned and walked quickly across the courtyard through the middle of the pigeons rather than around them, making them ruffle their feathers and quicken their step to move out of the way to avoid being stepped on. They squawked at him to show their displeasure.

20

Nights were never very different for Paul except for the rare occasion he found himself at the mayor's mansion for dinner. His typical night consisted of a little television, maybe flipping through magazines collected over the years and cereal. Cereal was a staple of Paul's diet. It did not matter if it was breakfast or eleven o'clock at night.

On this night he had just fixed the bowl of cereal and was prepared to sit down at the tiny table to eat it. Milk had splattered from the bowl to the counter around it. He would often let Daisy climb in his chair and lick up the milk that would otherwise be wiped up by him. The night had not been unusual up to that point. Paul's lonely existence was a constant. The phone rang.

Paul had always considered himself a good listener. He could hear not only the words spoken but the way they were spoken, the emotion behind them whether fear, anger, despondence. Hearing only the words, 'Is this Paul?' he knew this was a desperate person, alone and afraid. As the woman told him who she was it was obvious she was crying. Paul had difficulty making out all of the words she said. He understood 'Oliver' and 'ledge' and 'marriage' but with her heavy breathing, sobbing, and apparent drinking, those were the only pieces he had to put together. It was not until the words, 'Will you come over?' were spoken and he, being a person who could never bear to hear a woman cry, said he would that his plan for a normal night was to be abandoned. He turned from his drawer of silverware, where he stood holding the phone in one hand and a spoon in the other and looked at the bowl on the table. He hated to do it but he picked the bowl up, drained the milk into a smaller bowl for Daisy to enjoy and dumped the remaining wet clump of cereal into the trash.

Thirty minutes later his headlights illuminated the golden brick mailbox and he knew he had found his destination. After a few minutes in the car talking to himself he stood in the place he had been a few nights before and again knocked lightly on the door. He stood back and looked up at the high ceiling of the porch with the large chandelier hanging above him. The house was no less impressive on this night than it had been the time before but it seemed darker, almost haunted. It was not only the cold breeze on his neck that made him shiver slightly.

When the door opened he was immediately confused, scared, and impressed in equal measure. Standing before him was Sheryl Gartrell wearing only a negligee and holding a glass in her hand. She did not seem as upset as she had been on the phone. Her eyes were only slightly red. Her hair hung to her shoulders not brushed but not disheveled. Paul imagined the number of tissues she had been through and the number of trips she had made to the little liquor cabinet in the corner of her den over the previous thirty minutes.

"Oh good, you found the place. Please come in." She stepped back from the threshold and stood almost behind the door. As he stepped through she pushed the door closed behind him quickly to keep the cold air from coming in and to not be seen by anyone outside.

Paul began the conversation as he had the previous time he had been there. "This house is so impressive. It is like something from a movie." A stupid statement he knew. He was at a loss for what to say and fighting the temptation to look at her but knowing he should not.

"Please come in and have a seat." Paul followed her down the hardwood hallway. Now he could look at his own discretion. Paul assumed the woman was in her early fifties if Oliver had just turned fifty four but her body was toned and tan. She had a very impressive physique and was in as good of shape as any woman he would pass on the street regardless of age. Her legs were small but strong, her back broad and muscular. He thought of Oliver and how he was married to this woman and had Holly as a girlfriend. Paul could not help but shake his head and sigh under his breath, "Money". He recalled what Holly had said to him in the cafeteria. It was a statement he had forgotten while reflecting on their conversation. Oliver did not ask for things, he demanded them. His income was not the reason for what he had and who he was with but rather his confidence. The thought gave Paul a heavy heart while simultaneously it filled him with hope as he followed Sheryl to her living room.

Sheryl sat down on the couch and directed Paul to sit next to her. He did but propped his elbow up on the arm rest keeping a distance of two cushions between them. "I really do love this house." Tension.

"Oh my goodness. How rude of me." Sheryl sipped her drink one quick time before setting it down on the coffee table in front of them. "What would you like to drink?" She stood up and walked to the table with the liquor on it. Again he watched her. Her tan thighs being exposed with the negligee covering only what the smallest of bikinis would. Paul held his hands in front of him, "Oh, none for me. I don't drink."

Sheryl stood at the table holding a glass in one hand while dropping two ice cubes into it with tongs held in the other. "Oh that's nonsense. Everyone drinks." Her tone of voice turned stern and slightly annoyed. She uncorked a bottle and set the cork on the table and then poured it into the glass filling it up halfway. "You'll try this."

She walked back to the coffee table in front of him and picked her glass up. In the first instance of exposing her level of drunkenness to him, she handed him the glass she had been drinking from. She pulled it back quickly. "Silly me. This one is yours." She extended the glass to him and he had no choice but to take it. He was uneasy holding the glass and set it down on the end table when she turned her back to him. He told himself to ignore it until he was permitted to leave.

With her back to him, Sheryl sat down half landing on his thigh. She moved over so she was no longer sitting on him but pressing her body to his as much as she could. Drunk.

"I guess you're wondering why I asked you to come over."

The strap of her negligee fell from her shoulder as she asked the question. The strap remained across her upper arm ignored as she did not make any effort to push it up.

Paul was trapped between her body and the end of the couch. "The question had occurred to me." He was desperate to escape the tight position. He looked behind him toward the kitchen. "Is Oliver around?"

Sheryl leaned toward him and put the drink in her left hand further away from him. "No, and that's why I called you." She raised a finger and touched his temple and ran it backward to his ear. Paul felt a nice sensation. "I was curious to know if you had seen him."

Paul struggled to swallow the large amount of saliva collecting in his mouth. When he finally swallowed he knew she could hear it. His nervousness exposed. He normally would have hated that being so ill at ease was obvious but in this circumstance he felt he was not the one to blame and his discomfort was warranted. "I saw him Monday morning and he said he slept in his office."

She cut him off. "How did he look?"

Paul looked straight ahead but cut his eyes to her.

228

"Like he had slept in his office. And then I saw him last night at his victory party." Paul still did not know what else to call the event that only he had attended.

"Did he say anything about me?"

"He said you kicked him out. He was very depressed and down."

Sheryl took her hand away from his head and looked straight ahead. In an instant it seemed her intention changed. Paul was relieved and a little disappointed in a way he did not want to consider. "That's what I'm worried about. You and I are the only people who know he did not go out on that ledge to save you."

Finally, finally Paul was hearing the truth from another person. All that he had said the other night had been heard. He felt vindicated for the scam in which he had been involved. But he was curious what Sheryl meant.

"How do you know he did not come out to save me?"

"He would never have gone out there to save you. I can only think of one possible reason why Oliver Gartrell would go out on a six story ledge or any ledge for that matter. And," she did not finish her thought. She put her hand to her face and shook her head. Taking a breath she collected herself.

Sheryl leaned forward and set her glass down on the coffee table in front of her. As she did Paul stole another glance of her physique. He was reminded of a competitive swimmer, broad and strong but also, in a way, petite. He could see the definition of each muscle. He thought of Oliver's corpulence and noted the difference between husband and wife.

Sheryl leaned back to look Paul in the eye. "I can't help but wonder if," she shook her head again, "I can't even say it." She looked at Paul, her eyes pleading with him to tell her something different than what she assumed. "Was he out there to, you know?"

Paul moved his hand in the arc motion to signify a person jumping and Sheryl nodded. Paul answered her. "I think the thought had maybe crossed his mind. He was very distraught. He talked about the election and people asking questions and you and the car outside of your house."

Sheryl rose from her seat and picked up her glass. She walked back to the assortment of liquor bottles on the table and Paul thought she maybe was going to pour out the alcohol that remained in her glass. She did, but not into the sink. She tilted her head back and swallowed in one gulp much like Paul had seen her husband do on occasion. She pulled the cork from the bottle again and poured herself some more and sipped it.

"You know this is the longest we've been apart. I called his secretary and Lane hasn't seen him. He told her he had to go somewhere and when she asked, 'What should I tell people who are looking for you?' he said," Sheryl paused again to collect herself and take another sip from her glass, "he said, 'Tell them I'm dead.'" She cried out at that moment and put her drink back on the table.

Her speech was decidedly more mumbled than it had been just minutes before. Paul was not positive he had understood what she said and tried to steer the conversation toward a favorable outcome. "So you miss him? You wish you had him back?"

Sheryl stood upright again and walked back to the couch with her drink in her hand. Again she fell into the couch right next to him landing on his jacket so that now he was essentially pinned to that spot. A splash of her drink landed on his trousers.

"You know what my problem is, Paul?" Her eyes were half closed. Paul did not know if she was waiting for an answer so he remained silent. "My problem is I never get my wish. I never, never, never get my wish." With her slurred speech and rolling eyes she leaned toward the coffee table and Paul held out an arm to catch her from falling off of the couch. She regained her balance and Paul felt obligated to seek clarification.

"What is your wish?"

She held out a finger to him and shook it but her eyelids closed in a very long blink. "I wish I liked him but I don't. I don't like him at all. But if I don't like him then I wish I didn't love him but I do. I can't help it. I love him. I always will. See the kind of bind that puts me in?" She leaned into him as she said it. Paul felt her breasts on his arm. With no choice he moved his arm over her head and rested it on the cushion behind her. That opened him up and she fell into his chest.

Paul looked at the ceiling but felt the cool, smooth silk of her negligee with the tips of his fingers. "Okay, yeah, I understand what you're saying. I get that."

She continued with her head on Paul's shoulder. "He's just a heartless, unloving man that I wish I could forget. But now it's been three days since I've seen him and I can't think about anything else. The man that I love."

"And hate." Paul added.

She sat up straight again and looked at Paul. The tips of their noses were almost touching. He thought for a second she was going to kiss him. Instead she spoke. "And hate." She put her head back on his chest and her hand on his stomach. "And now I don't know if he's alive or dead. He's out there somewhere but whether he's eating or being eaten I don't know. Part of me wishes he'd walk through that door but another part of me, oh this is horrible to say, another part of me is waiting for a policeman to walk through that door to tell me he has done the unthinkable, he has followed through with what he contemplated the day you met him. I imagine being asked to come downtown to identify the body." Her speech faded away as she spoke.

Paul made the arc motion with his finger again and she nodded.

"That would be horrible, I know." Sheryl said it as if answering an unspoken question. "Then we could all just," Paul waited ten seconds for her to finish her sentence, "move on. The election was all he cared about. I knew he didn't have a prayer of beating Melanie Myers but he just knew somehow it was going to work out for him the way things always do."

Paul was eager to change the subject from Oliver ending his life so he jumped on that line of thought. "She did have a lot of supporters. You sure seemed to like her."

Sheryl put her hand on Paul's chest and pushed herself up to a sitting position. She waved her hand at him and again almost fell off of the couch. "Oh I was just talking. Trying to rattle his cage, you know. I have to drive him crazy to keep my sanity."

Sheryl leaned back into him and placed her head on Paul's shoulder to steady herself. Her voice shifted to a softer, more intimate tone. "You know I've thought about divorcing him. I'd get half of his stuff. It would serve him right. Don't you think?"

Paul wished he had stood up when he had the chance. "Sure. Jackpot, huh?"

"Yeah, jackpot. And then maybe I'd move on. Start living and doing the things I've been missing all of these years."

In an instant her intention changed back to being focused on Paul. She was crazy he decided and a perfect match for her husband. She placed her hand on Paul's inner thigh and put her mouth to his ear and began blowing. The smell of bourbon invaded Paul's nose. She extended her tongue slowly and licked his ear lobe. Paul swallowed hard again but decided at this point he would not be judged for it as she was too drunk to notice. "Maybe you could take up a new hobby."

Sheryl brought her exploring tongue back into her mouth to speak. She whispered, "Or maybe pick up an old one. Paul, do you ever get lonely?"

"Sure I do. Everybody does." Paul sat up now and tried to free his jacket from underneath her.

She kept her mouth just an inch from his ear. "And what do you do about it? When you get lonely? Do you have someone to be close to?" She whispered the last two words and her hand moved up his leg. Paul shifted his weight on the couch to be more comfortable.

"No, not at the moment I don't." Her hand moved to its mark and Paul had to stand up for his own sake. "I think I'll get a refill." He reached to the end table and picked up his glass. He held it up and shook it knowing it would not matter that it was full. He walked to the small table and pulled the cork out of the bottle and added only another drop to his glass. "I'm sure there are some positive things in your marriage."

She leaned back on the couch and her arm fell limp on the seat next to her where Paul had been sitting. Her head tilted back in a weird angle. "Ha, I'm only married on paper. I'm a widow, or may as well be. I've been a widow for years. My husband is not dead, not that I know of, but our marriage, the life we had, it died a long time ago." She stood up. Even as drunk as she was Paul noticed her excellent posture. Her head was held high and her shoulders pushed back. The neckline of her negligee had fallen and her breasts were nearly exposed.

She took a step and reached out to touch his collar. Before she could move any closer Paul held up his hands. "Could I use your bathroom?" Sheryl reluctantly backed away from him, her intoxication and loss of balance making it difficult. She turned her back to him and picked her glass up from the table and sipped again. She pointed toward the front door and Paul assumed he was being given directions.

Paul walked down the hardwood hallway to the bathroom and closed the door behind him, thankful to be alone. He placed his hands on both sides of the sink and looked into the mirror. He remembered what was in his pocket. He took out the small bottle of pills and looked at them. In the past, a situation like this would have warranted a dosage of what he had believed to be medicine. But now he could hear Oliver's laughter. He put the bottle back in his jacket pocket and instead splashed cold water on his face and took deep breaths. He spoke to his reflection, "Go out there and tell her to have a good night and that if I see Oliver I will tell him you are worried about him and to call you. Don't let her touch you or talk to you. And for God's sake, Paul, don't let her lick you. Just get out. Leave." His expression was stern as if admonishing a child so his reflection looked back with what seemed to be a stubborn rebellion.

He stood up straight and pulled his jacket down

235

tight. He was intent on his mission. He exited the bathroom and walked back down the hallway ready to make his stand and then retreat. Sheryl was there on the couch, with one leg on the floor and the other stretched out in front of her. Her head was tilted back, her mouth open, and her eyes closed. The loud snore told Paul that she was okay so he quietly walked back down the hallway. Halfway he stopped and went back to the couch to look at her one more time. She was a beautiful woman. He looked around the room and saw a small blanket on the back of the recliner next to the fireplace. He picked it up and unfolded it. Gently he laid it down on top of her and quietly walked back to the front door. He opened the door softly and closed it behind him. He was thankful to be free. The crickets in the dark seemed to be screaming at him and a cool breeze blew as he pulled his jacket tight around him.

He walked to his car and looked back at the large front door shining in the chandelier's light. To a passerby his beat up, old car looked so out of place on the pea gravel driveway outside of the immaculate mansion. The oddity of life that had been unveiled by the strange night behind him made Paul laugh to himself. The irony was not lost on him. Those things that seem so perfect, those things coveted by others, whether a house, a car, a marriage, though appearing impeccable and impenetrable from the outside can be just as beat up and broken down as his old car.

He got in his car and turned the key. In a second he was driving away from the mayor's house. He was relieved and happy to be on the way home.

Thursday, November 9

21

Paul awoke on Thursday morning in a good mood. He did not try to explain to Daisy his high spirits but quite possibly he thought it was from his two encounters the day before with beautiful women. Seeing Sheryl in her low state the night before and talking to Holly in the cafeteria had made it one of the most unusual days of his life. It was not so much the opportunity to talk to them that had elevated his spirits but the new knowledge gained in knowing that everyone has pain. Everyone doubts themselves. Everyone wonders if they are loved. He had always felt alone in his life with those questions that plagued him. But now he realized those questions were common and not reserved for only him and people of similar means and circumstances but were also considered by the beautiful and the rich.

To be standing in the living room of a mansion with the wealthy, beautiful wife of the city's mayor who needed consoling was not an experience many people got to have. Or at least not people like him. People like him would only overhear tales of such things whispered in elevators or from tables in close proximity to his at restaurants. He was not a successful business owner or lawyer or judge but only a maintenance man who cleaned up behind those people. His life was not one prone to such excitement. He knew the alcohol had a lot to do with it but that fact was offset in his mind by the fact he had not acted on what he could have done. Sheryl's inebriated state and his clear conscious was a wash he decided. His own discernment was a source of pride. Still though a woman of her beauty practically sat in his lap, licked his ear, tried to seduce him. His high spirits could be explained with one word whether he realized it or not. Hope.

As he had in the previous days, he spent more time getting ready that morning than he was accustomed to do. He took longer to brush his hair. He took longer brushing his teeth. Shaving was a more tedious affair. He paid closer attention to the details of his appearance than he ever had before.

He knew the chance to talk to Holly sometime during that day was not just a wish but a likelihood. Holly had told him he was attractive. Maybe that was true. Sheryl had whispered in his ear. Maybe not because of the alcohol but because of him. He smiled at himself in the mirror and said aloud, "No, definitely the alcohol."

He bid Daisy goodbye. The air was cool and crisp as he walked to his car. He saw Holly's car pull into a parking space across the lot. Her car coughed one last time as she turned off the motor and the last bit of exhaust escaped and rose into the cold air. He felt his newfound confidence and their conversation in the cafeteria the day before had given him allowance to wait there in the parking lot and talk to her.

He walked to the back corner of the car and waited for Holly to open her car door and spoke. "Late night at work huh? Is that place open twenty four hours a day?"

Holly spoke to him without questioning why he was standing there. "No, the club is not open twenty four hours a day. But the hospital is." With that she swung her foot out of the car exposing a thick, black cast on her leg. The cast stretched from her knee past her ankle and left only her toes exposed. The crutches came out of the car next.

Paul walked quickly to assist her. "Oh my gosh. What happened?"

Holly placed the ends of both crutches on the ground and Paul noticed her tongue come out of her mouth, tilted up toward her nose. Though the look was not appealing he thought it cute that she did that to concentrate. "You know Tammy's new trick? The one she told us about? It involved shaving cream and peanut butter. I went on stage right after her and slid off the stage right onto some fat guy's lap."

"Lucky fat guy." Paul was unsure whether to touch her to help as she got out of her car and on to her feet. "Is it broken?"

Holly grimaced and nodded. "Two places. I've got to stay off of it for four weeks." With her apparent pain Paul did not hesitate but reached out to her and held her elbow so she could stand. It was the first time he had touched her besides the awkward handshake at the mayor's house.

Paul dropped his hands back to his side after she was stable on the crutches. He could at least carry her things. He was never forward enough to touch people assuming they did not want him to. He never wanted to put anyone else in an awkward position and as a result he lived in one every second of every day. "That's too bad."

Holly took exception to the careless phrase that Paul muttered while trying to help her, listen to her, and also look at her. "Too bad? Too bad? No, it's not too bad. It's horrible." Emotion began to come. "How am I going to pay my rent? How am I going to eat? What am I going to do?" She unleashed the pent up distress she had been feeling. She broke down in the parking lot of the Oak Ridge Apartments and Paul was there to catch her. The question Paul asked himself about touching her was answered. She fell into him and put her head on his shoulder. Paul could tell she was crying and that tears and snot would likely be on his shirt when she stood up but he did not care.

"I'm sorry." Holly struggled to regain her composure and to stand up straight. "It's just that I'm in trouble here."

"Hey, hey, I can help you. I'll do stuff for you around here. And I make a good pot of pasta. That's fifty cents and will feed two people. You'll be alright. And you've got a little money saved up, right?"

"I've got a dollar and fifty three cents in my checking account. How far can I stretch that, do you think?"

242

Paul did not answer the question but remained positive. "You're going to be okay. Rent is not much. Food is cheap. I'll help any way I can."

Holly stepped back and looked at him. She wiped her hand across her nose. Not the most attractive look, not as cute as the tongue thing, but still Paul did not care. "Thank you. You're sweet." She situated herself on her crutches. "Oh, sorry. I know you hate that." Paul smiled at the remark.

She collected herself as she looked across the parking lot to her apartment door. She knew it would be a struggle to make it. "Where's Mr. Money Bags when I need him, you know? He leaves me and now this happens. I called him from the hospital last night. He was drunk somewhere. Probably back on his couch with what's her name. I couldn't understand a word he said and he didn't care about a word I said."

Paul smiled at her comment. He did not know where Oliver had been the night before but he most assuredly knew on what couch he had not been.

Holly went a few feet on the crutches and Paul noted how laborious it was for her and imagined how hard her life was going to be over the next few days. "What am I going to do if I can't work?"

He could not leave her until he saw her smile even if only a little. "You could put together a wheelchair act. Go to old folks homes and strip for the old men. They'd love it. Of course they'd tip you with pills rather than bills but still, close enough."

And she did. She smiled even if slightly. "You're the

strangest person I've met in a long time. You know that, don't you?"

Paul shrugged.

Together they walked across the parking lot to her apartment door. Paul kept his hand on her elbow while she maneuvered with the crutches. She looked at Paul holding her bag but did not say anything. He was confused and uneasy not knowing what her look meant. Was it affection for him? "My keys."

"What?"

Holly pointed to his side. "My keys are in the bag." Paul realized she was referring to the bag in his hand. He fished around in the bag and pulled the keys from the bottom of it and handed them to her.

"Thanks." Holly put the key in the door but did not unlock it. She turned to Paul and pushed a strand of hair behind her ear as she had the day before. "You know, I was thinking about what we talked about yesterday in the cafeteria. Then the way Oliver ignored me when I needed him this morning. It's like it all came together. I realized you were right. He may not be the great guy I made him out to be. I can do better."

Paul put his hands in front of him and shook them to distance himself from the comment he had made. "No, no, I shouldn't have said that. I mean, you deserve the best, you're right about that but really, it's none of my business. You're having fun for now and there's nothing wrong with that."

"Yeah, I'll have a lot of fun with this thing on my

foot for the next four weeks."

Paul knew he was going to be late for work and thought of Fletcher. He took a step back from the door and looked at his car. Holly stood in front of her open door. "Hey, do you want to come in for a while? Help me get to my room." And with a playful look that Paul took as sarcasm, "Maybe help me into the tub."

Paul was caught off guard by the questions. "Uh, I've got to um, I've got to uh go to uh work." He stammered and made Holly laugh again but not intentionally.

"I'm kidding. You go to work. I'd hate for you to get fired and both of us be unemployed. We won't have fifty cents between us if that happens."

Paul turned to her again to show his commitment to helping her. "Okay. I'll check in on you when I get home, okay?"

Holly nodded and smiled. "Okay." Holly walked into her apartment and closed the door. A few seconds later Paul was closing the door of his car and began backing out of his parking space. He did not see Holly at the window of her apartment with the curtain pulled back watching him leave, just as he had watched her so many times before.

22

For the second time in a week Paul arrived for work later than he ever had before. Ten minutes, occasionally fifteen minutes late, would warrant reprimands and threats from Fletcher. He walked in to City Hall knowing he was thirty minutes late. As usual there was Fletcher waiting for him in the atrium. He panicked knowing Fletcher would likely carry through on previous threats and fire him as he had promised to do so many times in the past. Instead Fletcher approached him and got close enough to hug him as he had a few days before but he kept his hands at his sides.

"You're late, Self. Where you been?"

Paul looked straight ahead. "I had to help a friend with something. I'm sorry I am so late."

Fletcher walked a circle around him and then to Paul's surprise walked to the stairwell door. "Don't let it happen again." And that was it. Paul did not take time to wonder what the encounter meant but knew that he would spend the day avoiding his boss to be safe.

Paul went to the sixth floor reciting to himself his justification for going as he ascended the stairs. Paul felt that Oliver at the very least should know what Holly was going through and he was curious, but doubted, if her former lover would be inclined to help her in anyway.

Paul got to the frosted glass window and walked through the door without hesitation, intent on having the conversation with Oliver about Holly.

"Can I help you?" Lane slid a magazine to one side of her keyboard. Paul did not know who this person was. In each previous time he had been in Oliver's office the desk was either vacant or Ms. Connors was there.

Paul felt an instant connection to the person behind the desk. She was cute, with a short pixie haircut and wore glasses with thick black frames that seemed to magnify her eyes. She had freckles and nice teeth. She did not bare her cleavage or have on excessive amounts of eye liner and make up. Her jaw line was well defined and her eyes were wide and dark brown. Nothing drew his attention from those eyes. She was smiling but seemed to have an underlying sense of sadness about her. Paul felt he could get to know this person. He was taken aback and the intimidation he had one time felt for the office returned instantly.

"I'm here to see the Oliver. I mean the Gartrell, I mean Mr. Gartrell, the mayor."

Lane put her hand to her mouth to prevent any laugh from escaping. She was not sure if this person was being sincere or playing with her. "Okay, who can I say is asking for him?"

"Oh," for a second Paul forgot the answer to the question, "Paul Self."

"Okay Mr. Self, one minute." Lane picked up the

phone as Paul swayed from side to side shifting his weight between feet. She took the phone away from her ear and looked up before punching the button to call Oliver. "Paul Self? Where do I know that name from....oh, wait a second. You're the guy from the ledge. The nutso guy who was going to jump."

Paul's face got hot with anger and embarrassment in equal measure. "No." He took a breath realizing how loudly he had said it. "I mean, yes, I am the guy from the ledge, nutso, maybe, but no I was not going to jump. It's a long story."

Lane shrugged and placed the phone on her shoulder. She did not go back to hitting the button on the phone to call her boss. "So are you and the Oliver friends?"

Paul caught the extra word thrown in and found it clever rather than insulting. He shook his head deciding how to answer the question. Without knowing the dynamic of Oliver's relationship with his receptionist, or more aptly, her feelings for her boss he did not want to say too much. "I don't know if I would say that we are 'friends'. Just more casual acquaintances than anything else."

Before he could finish his thought the oak door to the mayor's office opened and Oliver stumbled out from the darkened room. Paul noticed how horrible he looked, unshaven, his hair a mess, his tie was loose and hung at an odd angle and one shirt tail was out of his pants. Without a word Oliver walked to his visitor and put both of his hands on the sides of Paul's face.

He leaned over to kiss both of his cheeks. He stepped back while Paul stood stunned and motionless.

With a solemn expression Oliver looked Paul in the eye. "It's good to see you, Paul. My friend. My only friend." Paul felt as if he was standing graveside at a funeral.

Oliver continued past Paul and opened the door with the frosted glass and walked out into the hallway. He turned back to Paul before the door closed behind him and said, "I love you, Paul." The door closed and Paul was left to explain himself to Lane who sat behind her desk with her mouth agape.

Lane pointed at the door. "He just kissed you."

Paul shook his head. His face still red. He raised a finger to emphasize his point. "That is the first time he has ever kissed me." He wanted desperately to change the subject while also giving an explanation for the behavior. "Did he smell like alcohol to you?"

Lane dismissed his question to ask her own. "Of course he did. He always does. Is there something I should know about my boss man? I could come in here naked and he wouldn't give me a second look but you, wow, he's got it bad for you." She put her hand beside her mouth and whispered as if gossiping. "What's your secret?"

Paul shook his head to show his bewilderment. "I'm sure he would notice if you were naked." Paul swallowed not sure where that conversation would lead. He shifted it back to Oliver. "He's had a rough few days. He's obviously not thinking too clearly. How long have you been working with, um," Paul was having difficulty maintaining his composure.

"The Oliver? About six months. What about you? How long have you two been dating?" She realized that playing with him in that way would be too easy so she changed the subject. "Aren't you a maintenance man or something in the building?"

Paul shrugged and decided to be open and honest with his new acquaintance. "I'm more of a janitor really. Scrubbing toilets, mopping floors, picking up trash. But I don't like to brag. I expect to get fired every day I come to work. I get here ten minutes late just about every day."

With an excited tone Lane said, "Me too," as if they had just found out they were from the same hometown. "I thought the Oliver was going to fire me last week I was late so much but he is so preoccupied with other things now he doesn't even know when I come or go."

"He has been dealing with some things that's for sure." Paul agreed.

"Oh, did he tell you about it over breakfast?" She did not mean to go back there but it was just so easy.

Paul shook his head and changed the subject. "Where do you think he was going?"

Lane turned back to her computer. "To pee is my guess. Or throw up. He's been to the bathroom this morning I bet four times already since I've been here and that was just twenty minutes ago."

"Is he sick or something?" Before she could answer,

the door with the frosted glass opened and Oliver reentered the room. He looked at his shoes and then to the window. He was a man beaten down and despondent.

"Ah Paul, I'm glad you came by to see me. Step in my office for a second, will you?"

Paul shrugged at Lane to show he was not sure what the man wanted as he followed Oliver into the office. Before Oliver could close the door Paul turned back to the desk and caught Lane's eye. She gave him two thumbs up as if encouraging him. They smiled at each other as the door closed between them.

"How have you been, Oliver?"

Oliver was already at the desk in the corner pouring himself a drink. "Never better." He sipped it and repeated, "Never better."

"So you're hanging in there after the election and all?"

"I'm not ready to climb out of my window again if that's what you're asking."

Paul felt different in the office. In the past the hierarchy of their power was well established but now that was in disarray.

"Have you talked to your wife? She's got to be worried about you. She may think you've done something, you know..." Paul made the familiar arc with his finger. "She knows you didn't go out on the ledge to save me. She's probably hysterical thinking about it."

Oliver threw his hand in the air and Paul saw some of the drink splash out onto the carpet. Paul thought Oliver was oblivious to the spilled drink until he licked the back of his hand to retain what he could. "Sheryl never gets hysterical, unless I break something or forget to do something. Concern for my well-being would not so much as register as a blip on her radar screen. Not after twenty years of a horrible marriage and especially not after the other night."

"Well, I know Holly's worried about you. We ate in the cafeteria yesterday and she told me she's been looking for you."

Oliver smiled but only half-heartedly. The bags under his eyes and slumped shoulders indicated how tired he was. The sting of defeat had taken its toll. "Ah, so you had a meal together, huh? My work here is done. You've gotten everything you wanted." It was a half-smile he offered to Paul as he raised his glass slightly in a toast. Paul thought he looked as though he could cry.

Paul remembered why he came to the office. "I saw Holly this morning. She said she tried to call you last night and couldn't get you. I thought you may want to know that she broke her foot. She's in bad shape. She can't work. Worried about bills and food. Being homeless. She's in trouble."

Oliver looked at Paul and did not speak for a few seconds while measuring the news and determining what his involvement would be. In his downtrodden state he had no sympathy to give. "Yeah? Tell her to join the club."

Oliver walked across the room and fell back onto his couch still with the drink in his hand.   He leaned forward and looked at the floor in front of him lost in thought.

Paul was disappointed but not surprised by the mayor's response. That confirmed all of the thoughts he had about the selflessness of Oliver Gartrell.

A question had been on his mind over the past several days and now Paul had no fear to ask it. "Hey, why didn't you just say 'no' to the whole dinner thing if Holly was your girlfriend? I mean I just clean toilets for a living but inviting your mistress to dinner at your house with your wife and a guy you're asking to pretend to take part in a charade saying that you saved his life to win an election, there's got to be some rule against that."

Oliver put the empty glass down beside him on the couch and dug his fingers into his eyes trying to wake up. "Yeah, in hindsight not the best plan in the world. I've been wrong on so many things. I am going to make some changes in my life that's for sure. Regardless of what happens. I haven't been the best husband the past few years."

Paul was befuddled by the statement spoken as if it was a revelation. Paul could only shake his head. "No kidding."

Oliver spun on the couch and laid his head down on the arm rest. With his leg he pushed the glass off on to the floor. Paul expected it to break when it landed but it only hit the carpet with a thud. Paul took the position of therapist. "You know, she has never really respected me. I know that's no excuse for what I did but it is part of it. I'm the mayor of this city. The man in charge. The man responsible for the well-being of every person in Weatherton. And I would get home at night and be made to feel like a failure because I couldn't fix the dishwasher. I had enough money to go buy ten dishwashers but she didn't see it that way. 'My husband, not much of a handyman, huh?' Well no, but what does a handyman make per hour? So then some young woman comes along who thinks I'm the greatest thing in the world. She wants me and thinks I'm a king. So I jump into bed with her. If I can make her happy I think that will make me happy."

Paul was listening to every word and felt suddenly as if he was older than Oliver. He was listening to the admission of a teenager. "Holly?"

"Yeah, she's one of them. You know in the last few weeks I thought she was cheating on me."

"Who, Holly?"

Oliver's voice grew louder, agitated. "No, Sheryl. Can you believe that? You met her the other night at my house. You heard what she said. She would never cheat on me. She's always been faithful. That's one thing I can say for her." He rubbed his face again. "Of course, that appears to have been entirely a business decision on her part. A divorce lawyer would have a field day with me."

Oliver was still deep in thought. "I can't believe she

beat me, Paul. I'm still a little shell shocked over that. She had to have some kind of help. It was some kind of conspiracy. The way I was attacked at that debate Monday. Everything just fell apart right at the end. And the money she spent. My God, the money. She spent a fortune to win this thing. And then all of the other factors. Ann Strickland on her witch hunt."

Oliver stopped talking for a moment thinking about the women who had ruined his life.

"They were out to get me. And you know, of course they wanted to ruin me. I'm a chauvinistic pig in their eyes. They hate me, Paul. I tried to win them over in the beginning. I really did. Ann being in finance for the city. I figured if she was in my back pocket I'd have my way and no worries. And then that Myers woman. She's crazy, Paul. And all of her anti-drug stuff. I ignored her in the beginning but she picked up steam. I should have recognized that sooner I guess. And then they teamed up to bring me down and found things to question and make me look bad. I should have known they were in this together."

Paul was curious and feeling superior in the room. He could not ask a wrong question he decided. "Why didn't you defend yourself more? If you didn't steal any money why didn't you just come out and say that?"

Oliver looked at Paul with a stern expression. "Oh, I stole it. I'm a politician. That's what we do." After his admission he looked away, through the window, thinking and then looked back at Paul. "Why else would we put ourselves through all of this other than to be first in line at the cash register when the lights go off? But for her to care so much. Mayors have been stealing in this city for a hundred years but it never mattered before. It was to be expected. But with her and Ann teaming up, that changed everything."

Oliver looked out of the window again and sighed deeply letting go of his thoughts knowing they would do him no good. "I'm finished, Paul."

Paul saw the clock on the office wall above the couch. Fletcher was likely on the prowl. "Nah, you're not finished. You just have to move on is all. You'll be alright."

Oliver leaned back and fixed his eyes on the ceiling again. Paul thought the man was still on the verge of tears which he did not want to suffer through. Paul tried to be positive and have hope for the future. "Maybe you can start all over. Do all of those things you've neglected over the years. You could take your son camping or something."

Oliver snorted. "Yeah, a little father-son bonding. I don't think that would happen. We haven't said, oh, I bet five sentences to each other in a year and a half. He's gotten all mixed up with other stuff."

Paul raised his eyebrows and decided to make his point. "Mixed up with people he shouldn't be mixed up with?"

"Yeah."

"Just like dear old dad, huh?"

Oliver looked at him but did not get angry at the

point Paul had made. "I guess so. I guess so."

Oliver had come to the end of this maelstrom that was the election. He could do nothing now but sulk. Paul considered his exit but wanted to leave on a positive note.

"Oh, hey, I was thinking about it. I saw your son the other night at your house and I've realized where I have seen him before. It has been driving me crazy since the dinner party at your house."

"Oh yeah, you recognize Derrick? A freak show maybe."

Paul thought about Sheryl's similar comment. They both had that belief in common, that their son was in a bad place but neither took initiative to solve it.

"When he walked through your living room before you arrived, there was something about the way he walked and oddly enough, his nose. He didn't say anything but I knew I knew him. And that's one of my talents. Placing people. Like if someone comes on television and nobody else knows where they've seen him,"

"Yeah, yeah, yeah," Oliver was growing impatient. "So where did you know him from?"

"Of course, he looks different now than he did when I used to see him. Before City Hall I worked at the golf course out on Rivers. I was in the pro shop mainly but occasionally would do some of the ground crew stuff. There was this trail through the woods on the 18th hole and kids, teenagers, were always going up and down that path. They would come hang out in the pro shop and I never had the nerve to kick them out although the manager did not put up with it very much. He probably thought they were stealing stuff but I knew these kids didn't care a thing about golf. There was nothing there they would want to steal. Your kid Derrick was one of the usual ones."

Oliver seemed more interested in Paul's rambling than Paul would have assumed he would be. "Is that right? Derrick at the golf course? Interesting. How many other kids would he hang around do you think?"

"Oh, I would say there were probably three other ones that were there as much as he was. I didn't know any of their names. I just assumed their parents were golfers and they were being dragged to the course for me to babysit. But that path through the woods, I don't know if any of them lived out there or what."

Oliver was thinking now about what he was hearing. "Melanie Myers lives out there on Rivers. Her land backs up to the golf course and she was always complaining about the golfers and the traffic. That's the first time I heard her name. She was never happy about all of those people intruding on her privacy when the course was built. When there is talk about the country club expanding she's at City Hall more than I am. Maybe that's why she ran for mayor." Oliver got absorbed into his thoughts while Paul looked at the clock hanging above Oliver's desk and walked to the door. As he reached for the doorknob Oliver asked him a question. "These kids, were all of them strange like Derrick?"

"Your son seemed to be the most normal one of them all. At the time." Paul hated insulting the man's son but he realized he could not avoid it. Oliver was not defensive about his son but had seemed to accept the hopelessness of him getting any better.

Oliver stood up and stepped over the discarded glass on the floor beside the couch. He stood looking out of his window and put his hand on his chin, stroking it as if he had a beard rather than the two days of stubble that was there. "That is very interesting. Very interesting. Derrick and the Myer's kid? Huh?"

For a minute Oliver seemed as if he was in another world. He walked to his desk but then back to the window and looked out of it for a few seconds more. His hand still on his chin, pinching his lip. Then as if coming to from a trance he turned to Paul.

"Hey listen, I appreciate you coming by. I feel like I need to get some rest. If you'll excuse me I think I'll take a little nap."

Paul was glad to be given his pardon and welcomed the chance to leave. Rather than walking him to the door as he usually did, Oliver instead walked to his desk and picked up the phone. He hit a single button and put the phone to his ear. As the door closed Paul heard Oliver say, "This is Mayor Gartrell. I need to talk to Chief Mullins."

Paul closed the oak door behind him and again was facing Lane.

23

Lane looked up from her magazine. "Wow. That was no quickie. You two must have really had some fun."

Paul shook his head. "Have you been waiting to say that the whole time I was in there?"

Lane seemed appalled at the question but in a sarcastic, mocking way. "No, I've been filing. Typing memos. Working on this report here….Okay, you got me. I was either going to go with that, the quickie thing, or, 'Hey, make sure your zipper is up'. I thought the quickie one was better though."

Paul nodded to confirm. "It was." He smiled. He wanted to say something else. He wanted to initiate a conversation. He thought back to being at Oliver's house that night and the premeditated questions he had come up with to keep his conversation with Holly moving along, interesting, and to impress her. He realized how silly the list had been but now he thought to remember what some of those more enlightened questions were. It did not matter though. A second later something caught his eye on Lane's desk. Half covered by some papers, Paul saw the corner of a red tattered notebook. As many times as he had held that notebook in his hands he was able to identify it though it was half hidden. Embarrassed and partly out of self-preservation Paul reached for the notebook to reclaim what was his before anyone could judge him.

Lane's hand met his on her desk and she stopped him. "Um, can I help you?" It was said in a playful but also defensive way. Paul realized how his impetuous gesture had appeared rude. He stood upright again and pointed. "Yeah, I think that notebook there, that's mine. I lost it about a week ago."

Lane squinted at him and cocked her head. She brushed aside the papers that concealed it and pointed to it without touching it. "That notebook there?"

"Yes."

"That belongs to you? That is your notebook?"

"Yes. How did you get it?"

"The Oliver gave it to me. He said it was sticking out from under his couch and he nearly tripped over it the other day. On his way to the bathroom one day he tossed it on my desk and said, 'Here. Do something with this.' So I did. I read it."

Paul was alarmed now and nervous. "You read it? No, no, no, don't read it. I have to have it back."

Lane placed her hand on top of the notebook and looked at Paul. "No, you can't have it back."

Paul was taken aback by the declaration and thought she was joking and being playful but in her face he could see she was serious.

"What do you mean I can't have it? Why not?"

Lane shrugged and kept her hand on top of the book. "Because I'm not done with it."

Panic overcame Paul. He could feel a person's judgment on him like he had never felt before. As exposed as he had been at Oliver's house, in the spotlight of Sheryl and Holly and Oliver, and inviting only scorn and scrutiny on himself, this was much worse. In that mansion he was merely out of his element and uneasy. But this was someone who had been given the opportunity to see his deepest thoughts and feelings. This was much more dangerous. This person had the ability to judge him for who he truly was, not who he merely appeared to be. Certainly he would want someone to read them he supposed, some day, but in his time, under his rules, his choice. He felt tricked somehow and became defensive.

"You've been reading it?" His face was hot again as it usually got when conversations became solely about him with no source of deflecting and hiding.

"Yes."

Only because it was the natural question to ask, Paul did so while biting the inside of his cheek hoping to make the redness in his face go away. "And you hated it? You're looking at me like I'm some kind of freak, I guess."

"I think it is one of the most fascinating things I have ever read. Fascinating in a good way. Not like I'm looking into the mind of a serial killer or disturbed person but fascinated in that I'm reading the handwritten words of some famous person. Not many people get to do that. Your handwriting sucks by the way."

Now Paul knew he was being tricked. His first

inclination was to feel that she was making fun of him. "You don't have to be mean."

Lane looked at him with a strange expression. "Oh, what? You think I'm being sarcastic. I guess that is a fair assumption. I am a very sarcastic person. But it's good. Very good. And I mean that. Really."

"Well, when can I have it back?"

Lane turned her lips into her mouth and looked up at the ceiling to think. Her facial expression told Paul she was calculating an answer. "I'll give it back to you on Monday. That will give me a chance to read it one more time."

"You're going to read it again?"

"Yes, I've read it once already. But I want to go back through it one more time. So be patient. You're the one who left it in Oliver's office. If you were so careless with it why do you care when you get it back?"

Paul did not have an answer to that. "Uh, with everything that has happened in the past week I haven't really thought about the notebook being lost. I don't even know how..." He snapped his fingers. "I bet it fell out of my pants when Oliver and I landed on the floor." He immediately regretted the comment.

Lane shook her head with a wide smile but refrained from making the obvious joke.

Paul felt the need to explain. "It was the day we came in from the ledge. Everything has been crazy since then."

"You know, this actually makes me feel so much better. For a week now I have been thinking it was Oliver's notebook. I would read it while he was in his office and I'm out here bored out of my head. I couldn't believe he had written all of this and I have to say I've been turned on every time I saw him. But I also kind of knew it wasn't his. I halfway suspected that because of the handwriting. His is impeccable. Yours sucks."

"Yeah, you mentioned that already."

"So come back Monday. I'll give it back to you, Paul."

Paul had to get back to work but he did not want to leave. "I'll come back each day and check. And I expect to have a very detailed conversation with you about it and you can tell me all of your thoughts on it. You owe me that."

"I would love it."

Paul pulled the frosted glass door to him and looked back at her one more time to see her working on her computer. She was instead staring at him just as intently. He walked through the door smiling. Fletcher was not on his mind.

24

When Fletcher saw Paul again later that morning he assigned him the first floor bathrooms. The condition of the bathrooms were always deplorable and Paul did his best to avoid being assigned that duty. It was the worst job in the building by far, with public bathrooms and unscrupulous people coming in off of the street for no other reason than to use them. Though Fletcher had not reprimanded him for being late or even mentioned his long absence that morning, Paul knew this was pay back for not being to work on time again.

While he mopped around the toilet in the last stall of the men's room, the most disgusting place on the planet, he could not help but think about Lane. He tried to remember all that he had written in the notebook so that their conversation about it would be that much more in depth. Despite the horrible condition of the bathroom he was cleaning he could not help but smile.

After exiting the bathroom and returning the rolling cart to the maintenance room on the ground level closet Paul walked through the atrium toward the front door of City Hall. Seeking fresh air on the front steps of the building would give him a much needed break. From the elevator he saw Oliver walk quickly toward the door with his cell phone up to his ear. His demeanor was completely different from how Paul had left him a few hours before. Paul could hear in his voice an excitement as he spoke loudly and with his free hand he made wide, animated circles in the air to help make his point to whoever he was talking to.

Made curious by the mayor's excitement Paul stopped in the hallway as Oliver passed. Covering the phone with his free hand Oliver said, "Paul, great news. Unbelievable news. I'm headed out but will be back in about thirty minutes. Come up to my office in an about an hour." The mayor did not wait for a response but turned his attention back to his cell phone and turned his back to the front door of the building in order to push it open with his backside. Paul was pretty sure the mayor winked at him as he stepped out into the sunlight. Paul could only shrug his shoulders and wonder what Oliver had to tell him.

An hour later Paul stood outside the mayor's office and pushed his hair down with his hands. He cupped his hands in front of his mouth and exhaled heavily worried that he would not like the smell of his breath. Not noticing any issue he opened the door to see Lane at the desk.

"It's you again. You're here as much as I am." Lane sat at her desk with a magazine in front of her. She did not hide the fact that she was on her own time.

Paul pointed at the door. "Oliver passed me in the hallway and told me to come meet him. He didn't say why but acted like it was Christmas morning. What happened in the last few hours?"

Lane was not nearly as interested. "I don't know what to tell you. When the guy has his mind made up on something nothing can keep him from it. I don't know what he's doing but he's on a mission of some kind. He didn't give me a glance when he walked through here either time. He's been on his cell phone since you left."

The oak door opened and Oliver stuck his head out. "Lane could you set up a," he stopped when he saw Paul standing there. He opened the door wide and walked through it with both of his hands in the air.

"Paul, Paul, Paul," he walked to him and put both hands on either side of Paul's face. As before he leaned forward and kissed Paul on both sides of his cheeks. "Step into my office. I have some exciting news to share."

Oliver turned and walked back to his desk. Red faced Paul turned to Lane who was staring at him, shaking her head and smiling.

"Okay, dude, that was weird. Both times I've seen you talk to him today he has kissed you. And you're telling me nothing is going on between you two? Yeah, right. Get a room you two. Or at least keep it on the couch in his office."

Paul did not know what to say. All he could do was blush. "I, really, I have no idea, what he's,"

"Paul come in here." Oliver called to him from the office.

"You better hurry. Don't keep him waiting. The moment may pass." Lane was enjoying this spectacle.

267

Paul walked into the office and closed the door behind him just to avoid further embarrassment with Lane. Oliver was back on the phone now but standing behind his desk. "Okay, okay, yes, okay. Thank you." He placed the phone back in the receiver and looked at his only friend in the world. "Paul, you are not going to believe this."

The animation with which Oliver said it reminded Paul of the day they had come in from the ledge. The look Oliver had in his eye was the same as when he tried to convince Paul to accept his deal. "I have made a few phone calls and apparently this Melanie Myers is not the woman we thought she was. Or at least not the woman everybody else in this town took her for. I knew it." Still he was excited and clapped his hands together. "I knew she was up to something. She had to be. There is no way a woman comes in here with as much money as she had and buys herself the mayorship." Paul was certain that was not a word. Paul saw through the charade of who Oliver was. Acting scholarly and informed, it was in these times of great emotional swings for Oliver that his supposed erudition proved untrue. "She has been up to something Paul." He walked over to his visitor and put his arms around Paul's shoulders and pulled him close. "And I owe it all to you."

"What are you talking about, Oliver?"

Oliver stepped back but kept his hands on Paul's shoulders. "Drugs my boy. Drugs." Oliver screamed it loud enough for the person in the office below to hear him. "That was her motivation. Drugs."

"Earlier when you said Derrick used to hang around the club house at the golf course that got me thinking. Melanie Myers' house is just through those woods and for years has raised a big stink about the golf course and any thoughts or talk of it expanding. She had her own little private land back there and she did not want anything to intrude on that."

Paul shrugged his shoulders to show that was understandable and to make the mayor take his hands off of him.

Oliver was getting more excited as he talked. He took a step back and again threw his hands up in the air. His eyes were huge and his hands did not stop moving. "But after what you told me I was curious about the other kids Derrick was with. One of them was probably the Myers kid who has been busted for pot on more than one occasion. I considered bringing that up in my campaign but that would have gotten ugly and opened the door to all kinds of problems, things with Derrick that I don't want to go into. But still I had never put two and two together. Melanie Myers' staunch campaign for drug control, her kid being a pot head, and that land back there behind the golf course. I called Chief Mullins and got someone to go check it out and apparently," Oliver lowered his voice to a whisper as if anyone else was around to hear what he had to say, "Melanie Myers is quite the farmer if you know what I mean."

Paul was not sure that he did. "Farmer?"

"She's growing pot back there. Most people have rows of tomatoes and okra growing in the Georgia heat, she has marijuana. The deputy didn't want to go check it out but I told him to just go to the golf course and take a peek. He did and went back to the station and got a search warrant. He just told me it's the biggest bust ever in Weatherton. Ever."

Paul had a confused expression on his face. "But that doesn't make any sense. Why would she be so against it if she grew it?"

Oliver was shocked by the naïve question though he really did not have an answer for it. His speculation was all he needed. "Don't you see? Don't you see? She didn't want to end the drug problem in our city. She wanted to monopolize it."

As soon as the words came from his mouth he snapped his fingers and talked to himself. "Oh, oh, that's good. Wanted to monopolize it. I'm going to write that down. That's good." He walked to his desk and searched for a pen. He turned an envelope over and wrote down the word, 'Monopolize'.

His voice expanded and filled the rooms as his arms flew out beside him. "At least that's the way I see it. And soon, that's going to be the way everybody in this town sees it."

Paul watched the mayor pace back and forth. Thinking. And smiling. Paul had never seen him this animated. "This is huge, Paul. Huge. The shake up, the story, the punishment to her. I've done some bad things, you and me and the Lord knows I have but this,

I can't touch this, not in a million years."

Paul could not believe what he was hearing. He was not appalled because of the actions of Melanie Myers or for the audacity of her mission and the inferior character that she possessed but for the simple fact that Oliver Gartrell had once again come out on top. It seemed to Paul that Oliver's implacable quest for power would never end. Karma would be kept at bay once again. The man just could not lose.

"So what does that mean..." Paul shook his head, incredulous at the realization, "you stay mayor?"

Oliver laughed but in an excited way. "No, it's not that simple. This isn't Miss America. Politics is not a pageant. The runner up doesn't just inherit the crown." But then his assuredness seemed to fade. "You know, I'm not exactly sure how it happens. Another election? I don't know. But I'll be finding out. You can count on that."

"So what, is she being arrested and then tomorrow you're a hero again? Front page of the paper and all that?"

"No, not yet. I'm not going to move that fast on it. I'm going to take it slow, give it a few days to evolve. And give this city a few days to forget about the election. They need to forget I lost. Three days from now everything will be quiet again, and then BAM!" he screamed it at the top of voice, Paul could only wonder what Lane was thinking at her desk, "spring it on them. Drop the bomb. Oh, this is going to be fantastic."

Paul could only shake his head as he walked back to

the oak door. "Congratulations." Oliver had already picked up the phone and waved as Paul walked through the door.

Paul was again face to face with Lane. She saw him and hung up the phone making Paul wonder if she was just pretending to be talking to someone. "So how was it? Did you smoke a cigarette afterwards or is that later?"

Paul smiled smugly but did not have a response.

Lane remembered something. "Oh, here, I have something for you." Lane leaned over and pulled out the bottom drawer of her desk. From it she pulled the notebook. "I decided to give it back to you. It's not mine. It's yours and it was wrong of me to read it."

Lane looked at him for several uncomfortable seconds while Paul assumed she was trying desperately to think of something nice to say. Finally she said, "Can I ask you a question?"

Paul shrugged. "Sure, I guess."

"Why the hell are you a janitor?" Paul was caught off guard by the blunt question. "You should be teaching English and writing books or something. Not changing toilet paper rolls and mopping floors."

He smiled to acknowledge her compliment. "Thank you. That means a lot to me." He was proud of himself for not gushing or acting foolish at her compliment but instead remaining serious and sincere. "Maybe one day something will wake me up and get me out of here. I'm just figuring it all out right now, I guess."

Lane did not accept that as a sufficient response. "So cleaning toilets, that's your gig, huh? Have you ever thought about pursuing this talent of yours? Major in it? Or hey, at least offer to write other kid's term papers or something."

Paul laughed. He was never comfortable talking about himself so he remained vague in his response. "It's been a rough road for me these last few years. I went to college and dropped out. No, change that. I'll be honest. Flunked out. Just a lot of dumb decisions. Chasing shiny objects. But I'm getting better. Refocusing." He held up his hand in front of his face and closed one eye as if taking aim.

"You've got to do something with it. At least write up the procedures for mopping floors around here or dumping trash cans."

Paul nodded. "Yeah, I may do that." He walked the three steps to the door and paused with the frosted glass at his back. "Hey, listen," but he could not bring himself to do it. "I'll see you around, okay."

She smiled and turned back to her computer. Paul saw that as confirmation that his hesitation was correct. But still he felt a connection to someone and the feeling was nice.

As Paul walked down the hallway with his notebook in his hand he could not help but feel different. There was hope in the future and joy ahead of him. He did not fear Fletcher turning the corner in front of him and berating him or Sullivan insulting him. For the first time Paul acknowledged that his time in City Hall was limited and there were opportunities out there he needed to pursue and discover. He could do so much more with his life. Oliver had gotten a reprieve on his life. He had once again come out on top but Paul did not care. At that moment no one was higher than him. He chuckled as he thought, "Unless of course, it's that Myer's kid."

25

The air was cold on Oliver's back. He wished he had on his jacket but it was somewhere buried in the pile of clothes he held in his arms. He had picked the pile of clothes up off of the hardwood floor of his foyer. When he had returned home for the first time, three days after the election, clothes were scattered everywhere after having been dropped over the second floor balcony. In her anger Sheryl had pulled them from his closet and dresser drawers and disposed of them that way.

Sheryl stood in the doorway of the kitchen with her arms folded across her chest. Despite Oliver's pleas to reconsider this permanent separation of husband from house, ties from closets, boxer shorts from dresser drawers, she kept her jaw locked, her arms folded in front of her chest and her eye on the door. Even though she had her moments of weakness, his absence over the previous three days had given her animosity towards him time to set and dry and harden to not be undone.

As he had a few minutes before on his first trip to the car with an armful of clothes, Oliver spoke to Sheryl again. "Please don't do this."

Sheryl tried to speak as little as possible. "This is the

way it is going to be."

"But what about your heart?" Sheryl only rolled her eyes. She would not be drawn into Oliver's rebuttals and closing remarks. "Come on Sheryl, let's make this a new beginning. Life is going to be better for both of us from here on out. I'm going to be different. This whole week, everything that has happened, it has made me realize what I want in life. I want to be here, with you. These last few days, being out on my own, with no one and nowhere to go, I've changed, and I want you to see that." He had not yet told her the news about Melanie Myers. Her allegiance to the new mayor had seemed too great and he did not want to be the bad guy in her eyes yet again. He wanted to play on her sympathy and his desperation. She could not resent anything about him and the way it all had worked out. Oliver had learned of all the emotions a person could feel towards him, be it hate, envy, greed, jealousy, it was resentment that he nor anyone could overcome. If they hated him, that could change. Jealous of him, good fortune for them would make that dissipate. But if another person resented him, the battle was lost, and he would never win them back.

Sheryl turned to the kitchen and looked at the stove to avoid looking at her husband. She breathed deeply. "No, I can't keep doing this. Not anymore." In truth, what he had said that night at the table with the stripper and the crazy man looking on had continued coming back to her. He had made the point that she was quick to point out his flaws in the past. That accusation was one she could not deny. And she went back and forth with it. She would tell herself, 'Of course I pointed out his flaws. What else was there?' But she had that little voice inside of her, moving her, softening her heart. The voice was the rebuttal to her justification. Perhaps she had been too harsh in the past. Perhaps it was her cold, unforgiving nature that had driven him away and not his unfaithfulness that had made her cold and unforgiving. It was a thought that she would be unable to consider with him there in front of her. She would need time. Time would allow her to consider all aspects of their relationship and give her the emotional capacity to think clearly. She wanted him to leave quickly.

Oliver took a step toward her still holding the clothes. He sensed that maybe he was causing her to respond emotionally and needed to influence that. He knew with logic he would be alone and homeless but if he could appeal to her emotional side there was a chance for reconciliation. "Come on, Sheryl. I need you. Please. Give me a second chance."

That was the wrong phrase to use and Oliver knew it as soon as he said it. Perhaps he was slipping. The comment snapped closed the door that Sheryl had cracked just a bit as he begged. "I've given you your second chance already. I've given you your second chance more than once, three times, even four. But no. I'm through. I can't do it anymore. I can't keep living this way."

The coldness in her tone of voice conveyed her lack

of caring which turned Oliver's softness to aggravation. "What way, Sheryl? In a mansion? In a mansion with a seventy thousand dollar car in the driveway? With a maid that comes in and cleans everything so we don't have to? Letting you go and be in all of your little clubs. I've worked very hard to give you all of this. Too hard."

Sheryl was not repulsed by his change in attitude but felt herself drawn to him in an unexpected way. It was this side of Oliver that had always pulled her to him. When he showed strength and impatience at getting what he wanted she would feel for him admiration. That was the quality about him that made him sexy to her and apparently to others as well. But still she remained firm in her stance and wanted to make it clear to her husband that she would not change her mind but she knew that if he pressed this way she could fold.

"So that's it? You're just going to throw it all away? All that I've given you?"

Sheryl decided to show her strength and speak louder than him. "What have you given me Oliver? What? Heartache? Embarrassment? Pain? What?"

Oliver dropped the clothes at his feet knowing he would bend over and pick them up again but for dramatic effect he needed his arms. He threw his hands in the air as if signaling a touchdown and spun in a circle. "This. All of this. All of this that I've worked so hard for. You know I've built this for us. Without the long hours, the weekends working, the politics, without being mayor, we wouldn't have had all of this. We would have had nothing. Nothing."

Sheryl screamed, "I would have been happy with nothing." Oliver could see the vein in her neck protruding below her ear. She was angry now because of his statement and the fact that he did not understand the depths of what he had said. She inhaled and calmed herself. "I would have been happy with nothing, Oliver. I would have had you. That's all that mattered to me. That's all that ever mattered. They can take all of this stuff. I don't care." After her emotional outburst she had to retreat. She could not say another word or be subject to his response. She walked quickly to the living room and remained with her back to the door.

What she said to him was so far beyond his comprehension that Oliver had no response. To not want all that they had? She could not be serious. Oliver felt she was lying or delusional. There could be no other explanation. Sheryl was in the doorway of the living room, her arms crossed tightly around her, her eyes on the floor. She had tears falling down her face but Oliver did not go to her. In silence, he leaned over and picked up the clothes he had just been holding. A shirt fell from the pile and landed on the floor. He put his heel in the crack between the front door and the door frame to pull it open without a free hand. He walked to his beat up Mercedes with the passenger side window still covered by a garbage bag. With the trunk already open he dropped the clothes into a messy, wrinkled heap.

Oliver turned back to his house with a choice at hand. He could go back inside and plead with Sheryl one more time while he got another armful of clothes or he could just get in his car and leave. He had made his argument. He had asked for forgiveness. He had asked for another chance. All of his attempts at reconciliation were refuted. It was his nature to never dwell in hopelessness but retreat from it to find other opportunities. It was hard for him to do it but he reached into his pocket and pulled out his car keys. He looked at the house one more time, with the door still open he hoped Sheryl may come to him but she did not. He walked to the driver side door of his car and placed his forearms on the roof and stood there. How could things have gotten so messed up, come so undone? A week before he was fine. He was worried but he had hope. Now his worry was gone but so was everything else. He was defeated, down, despondent. He feared what he may go and do.

He stepped back from his car and opened the door. As he did so headlights shined in his eyes from his driveway. He put a hand up in front of his face to protect his eyes from the bright lights but was curious who would be coming to his house in the dark. He thought about the mystery car that had been in his driveway for so many days in the previous weeks. The supposed private investigator may be coming to the house to pay Sheryl a visit, Oliver thought. The car pulled up beside his in the circular driveway. It was an older model, maroon Jaguar that Oliver had seen before. The door opened and when he could only see the hat emerge from the far side of the car Oliver called to him.

"Albert? What brings you by tonight?" Oliver stepped from behind his car to see Albert stepping out of his.

Oliver had not seen Albert in almost a week. He remembered their conversation and how it was a catalyst to him going out on the ledge and everything that had transpired since. Oliver did not want to see Albert. He did not want to, at that moment, confront the ramifications of his loss in the election and the effect on the larger scheme of the deal he and Albert had worked out. But he knew he would be held accountable for it eventually and it seemed natural for the conversation to take place here, in this place, on his driveway while he had just been kicked out of his house. Oliver was going from one crisis to another it seemed and he needed relief.

Oliver noticed Albert's shaking hands. The night time air had a nip to it but it was not too cold, not enough to cause a person to shiver, no matter how old and feeble. Oliver could sense the anger in Albert. Six months before he had convinced the older man to take a big risk, an illegal one, that would pay him back tenfold in Oliver's second term. But it was for naught. Oliver would be angry too. He understood. Oliver knew times were going to be tough for both of them when he was no longer in the mayor's office. Without the person in place as mayor that Albert had depended on to make the deal work and hide the information that no one else should see, Oliver and Albert had every reason to be worried.

"Are you alright, Albert? You seem a little unstable." Oliver squinted to see Albert who stood in the shadow of the cherry tree next to Oliver's garage. Oliver wanted to give Albert a reason to leave but not under bad terms. "Listen, this is not the best time but I'm glad you stopped by. I've been thinking about how we can fix this problem we have."

Albert seemed distant and unwilling to hear anything Oliver could say. "Is that right? Another one of your perfect solutions."

Oliver noted the sarcasm but believed it to be true. He did not yet want to break the news of Melanie Myer's pending arrest but also did not want to forebode suffering for the old man either. "Yeah, I've been thinking on it some. I feel bad, I feel terrible. I can't believe she beat me. It has taken me a few days to come to terms with that but now my mind is more focused. I'm not looking on what happened but what do we need to do to fix it. But I'm glad to know that we are still in this together. This will be good, we can collaborate and figure something out."

Albert's voice rose to a yell. His anger overcame him. He shook more. "You should feel terrible. You and your big talking and promises and telling me what was going to happen. You had no idea what was going to happen. You lied, Oliver. Admit it. I want to hear you say that to me."

Oliver was feeling attacked and as usual his first response was to laugh. He laughed at the accusation to show his differing opinion and to nullify it. "I did not lie to you, Albert. I do not do that. It's just like in insurance, all we can do is make the best judgment based on what we know but no one can know the future. It was a calculated risk that we took and we lost. But I tell you, if given the same circumstances, the same situation, I would do it again. Exactly as we did."

"But you still have your house. You still have your money, your cars. With this deal sideways, I could lose it all. Everything I've built in my life. You got me to gamble with my chips while you kept yours in your pocket. That's what infuriates me. That's why I'm here."

In the dark and standing behind his car Albert was still trembling. He was concentrating on something at his waist and Oliver could tell he held something in his hand. "What's that you got there, Albert? Huh?" The look on Albert's face, his demeanor, his movements were different. He could not explain it but Oliver was concerned with the abrupt end to the conversation. "What is it, Albert?" Oliver thought that maybe something was at Albert's feet, attacking him. Maybe a snake had come from the grass threatening him. Oliver walked towards the old man's car. "What is it?"

Then Albert raised his arm. The light from the house reflected off of the object in Albert's hand for a split second making Oliver blink. "Albert, is that," Oliver squinted not wanting to say what he thought it was and be wrong, but then he was sure. "Is that a pistol?"

The two loud cracks sounded as if they came from behind Oliver, the noise echoing off of his house and the tall pines surrounding him. But the pain Oliver felt was in front of him. In his stomach and hip. His body was on fire. He saw only red as he looked into the night sky. As if his feet had been pulled out from under him his full weight crashed to the ground. The impact of his body hitting the pea gravel below him rocked him again and the pain was everywhere. He heard the car door close. In his peripheral vision Oliver could see the tires of the car begin to roll forward. Then the car backed up, then forward again. Albert had to turn his car around to exit the scene. A flaw in his plan.

Oliver could not hold his head up any longer. Once the sound of car tires rolling on the pea gravel was gone he could hear only the crickets in the trees. With his head back Oliver looked up at the tops of the trees around him. He saw their silhouettes against the night sky. He knew it was in that spot he would die.

The front door of the house was still open. A cool breeze blew through the foyer into the kitchen where Sheryl leaned against the stove holding a full glass of sherry that she had not sipped in an hour. She looked at the remaining clothes piled up on the floor in the foyer. She told herself not to cry but could not help it.

The end of something always upset her.

The loud noise from the driveway shook her. She did not know what it was but knew it sounded sinister in a way. Her first inclination was that Oliver had done something, something vicious as a way of revenge but she knew that was not the case. Oliver was not a vicious or violent person. He would never hurt anyone or anything intentionally. He wanted to love and be loved. She knew that.

She sat the glass down on the stove and walked to the piles of clothes. She looked through the front door out onto the lighted driveway. "Oliver?" She saw his car. She could hear the dinging in his car alerting anyone near it that the door was open and the keys were in the ignition.

"Oliver?" She called his name again as she stepped outside, her bare feet set on the cold concrete of their front porch. She heard a noise. A voice. A meager, 'Help'. She lost her fear at that moment. Her timidity gone she walked quickly to his car. She walked around the trunk and saw his feet first laying on the driveway. She saw her husband struggling to sit up with a weak arm trying to push his body off of the ground. The other arm lay across this chest holding his stomach. She thought he was having a heart attack in that first second but then the blood. She saw the blood soaking the pea gravel beneath Oliver's legs. The interior light of his car made the liquid look black but she knew what it was. The loud firecracker noise she heard while inside came back to her. "Have you been shot?"

She said it in an accusing way that made Oliver close his eyes and shake his head. Even in his pain he thought she could not be warm. But then, in the next instant, everything changed. Hysterical, she cried out and went to him. The panic set in. The fear, the confusion, the potential loss of her husband, the permanent loss, it overtook her and he recognized it. "What have they done to you? Oh my God, what have they done?"

She fell beside him and brought his head to her chest. She wanted to stop the life from leaving him. Finally Oliver spoke and at least some of the panic left her. "Ow, that hurts." He said it in such a deadpan way, typical of Oliver that she knew his life was not in immediate danger but she had to get him help. Always needing to know everything before acting she asked, "Who did this to you?"

Oliver did not want to get into that part of it until the blood had stopped oozing from his body. "I don't know. It was dark. Maybe one of Melanie Myers' freaks." She held him tighter. "Ow, no, don't touch me."

"What should I do? What, what, what do you want me to do? Should I raise your feet or lower your head or maybe I shouldn't move you at all. I don't know." As she was hysterical, Oliver kept a level head and contributed the voice of reason.

"Babe, babe, how about this? How about going inside and calling an ambulance? They'll put my feet up or my head down or whatever they do. Okay?"

Sheryl stood up. In the well-lit driveway of his house, under the clear night sky with the stars like pin holes poked in black cloth above him, Oliver saw the blood on her clothes. His blood. He could not take his eyes from it. Her blouse had blood on the sleeves and just below her neck. Her pants were covered as she had knelt on the ground close to him in the red liquid that pooled below him. She did not notice or care, still too frantic to give it a thought. The sight moved Oliver in a way he had never experienced before. He thought of his mother's reaction to that phone call when he was a boy, finding out his dad was gone. He stared at the blood on her clothes.   The blood, his blood, dripped from her fingers without her acknowledgment. She only screamed and gasped for air in her panicked state.

"Okay, okay." She began to run to the front door but stopped on the porch. "I love you, Oliver. I really do."

Oliver's voice was weak but in the stillness of the night, over the crickets, she could hear him. "Babe, if you love me you'll keep me from bleeding to death on the driveway. Go inside, call the ambulance. Spill your guts to me later but first, let's stop me from spilling mine." He grimaced in pain.

Oliver could only lay on his back and look at a star above him. The cool breeze blew. He lost sense of time. How long had he been laying in his driveway? Had it been a second since Sheryl left or two hours? He was uncertain. The stars were all he focused on. "I should take more walks." He thought to himself. "This is nice out here."

Sheryl came back from the house with the phone in her hand. "You're going to be okay, Oliver. Oh God, I hope you're going to be okay. The ambulance is on its way. Just hold on, Oliver."

She knelt beside him and ran her fingers through his hair over his ear. Being touched and moved in any way still caused him pain but he did not object this time. Oliver moved his eyes to her. "It's been a wild week, hasn't it? A lot of highs and a lot of lows. Good and bad."

"Shhhhhhh, don't talk dear. Just rest. Just rest."

Oliver looked down at his feet and saw the large amount of blood on his clothes. He looked back up and saw his wife's chin above him. He closed his eyes and felt a warmth surround him. A calmness like he had never felt before. With his eyes closed he could hear the faint cry of a siren in the distance. His voice was leaving him and he could only mouth a single word. "Unbelievable."

Friday, November 10

26

Paul stood in the hallway looking at the door with the frosted glass. He was nervous. Conversations with Oliver had not made him so but this day was different as his motivation for being there had changed.

For the first time in many months his thoughts had not been focused solely on Holly. This Lane person, in the mayor's office, had held his thoughts and ponderings for the last twenty four hours. He took a deep breath and now had his nose only inches away from the window. Exhaling he placed his hand on the door knob, turned, pushed and walked across the threshold.

He was dismayed and maybe somewhat relieved to not see anyone behind the desk. He looked around the room and was somewhat disheartened when he saw the older lady, Ms. Connors standing beside the copy machine and staring out of the window. One hand was placed in the nook of her arm while the other was beside her face holding a tissue. She turned and looked at the source of the intrusion to her sadness.

"Can I help you?" Ms. Connors asked but did not smile or seem pleasant which came as no surprise to Paul. But something in her voice, in her stance, the handkerchief next to her face told Paul something was wrong.

"Um, yes, I'm here to see Mr. Gartrell." Paul lied knowing that was the better excuse to have been imposing on her in her current state.

"Of course he is not here. How on earth could he be here?" She looked him in the eye when she said it, short and curt. Paul sensed the rudeness and did not understand what she meant. But he had come on a mission and did not want to abandon it so quickly.

"What about Lane? Is she here?" Just saying her name to another person filled him with excitement.

"No, she will be in this afternoon. I took the morning shift and she'll be here after lunch."

Paul was confused. "The morning shift?"

Ms. Connors picked up a few sheets of paper from the tray of the copy machine. She held them upright and let them smack against the machine to get the pages in line. "Yes, I am filling in this morning while Lane is at the hospital with Mayor Gartrell."

"The hospital? What are they doing at the hospital?"

Ms. Connors kept her head tilted back at an odd angle appearing to look over Paul's head. He realized now on this day that her rudeness was to hide her worry. She was attempting to be strong by being mean. "Do you not read the paper at all? What is it with you young people today? Lane gets here and she doesn't know anything about it. And now you get here and you're just as clueless."

That did not answer Paul's question. "I have not seen the paper but what happened?"

"It's on the front page. Biggest headline Oliver's ever gotten I would think." She smiled her sad smile and looked out of the window. Her handkerchief again wiped quickly across her face. "Certainly bigger than that Melanie Myers got after she won the other day."

Paul was growing impatient. The woman was not making sense and seemed delusional. "But what happened?"

"Oliver got shot. Last night. In his driveway. By some deranged lunatic." Paul imagined her words coming off of a telegraph from years ago. Short, simple phrases. She pulled both of her lips inward and closed her mouth and eyes. Her chest expanded as she took a deep breath gathering her composure and clenching her fists to try and maintain it. "Crazy people are everywhere these days. They're just everywhere."

"Oh my God." Paul was shocked and worry overtook him. "How is he? Is he going to...die?"

Paul had to lean against the doorframe. His legs seemed to shake just slightly. It was hard for Paul to believe that it had been only a week and a day since he had met the man on the ledge outside of his office window. So much had transpired between them and now this, this grand culmination of what had been a bizarre few days.

Ms. Connors crossed the room to Lane's desk and sat down. She gave the statement she had no doubt been told to give and had done so already countless times that morning. "Details are not forthcoming at this time. I will keep you posted as I hear anything else."

Ms. Connors turned from him and swiveled in the chair to face the credenza behind her. She put her head in her hands. She shielded her face from Paul's view. She lifted her head and spoke through her tissue. "It is still just such a shock."

Paul realized then the extent of feelings this older lady had for Oliver. Oliver was a man of charm and charisma. Of course the woman who worked with him every day would become infatuated with the man and perhaps fall in love. If Holly felt it, surely Ms. Connors did too.

Paul was at a loss for anything to say. "I'm sorry that happened. I'm sure he will be fine." He was not. "Oliver is a tough person." He was not. "If anybody can come out of this okay, it is him." On that point he would stand firm. Ms. Connors did not acknowledge anything he said. She had become lost again in her thoughts and though standing just feet away from her he was no longer in her presence.

Paul left the office and closed the door with the frosted glass. He closed it gently not wanting to disturb Ms. Connors any more than necessary. He turned down the hallway and thought of Oliver. He stopped suddenly in the hallway and looked up at the ceiling biting his lip. Without warning he too felt the need to move his hand to his eyes just as Ms. Connors had done.

"Surely he'll be okay. Won't he?" A woman walking

past him in the hall stopped as she thought he was speaking to her. Paul did not look at her but with a quick pace walked to the stairwell not sure where he was going.

27

In a daze Paul stood in the stairwell for several minutes. He wondered if what Ms. Connors had said was even true. "Maybe it's just another scheme of Oliver's to get something he wants." Paul nodded confident that was the case and knowing he had to believe that in order to get it out of his head and concentrate for the rest of the day. He walked down to the fourth floor where not much was ever happening. The floor was only about fifty percent occupied with government offices and served largely as a storage facility for the entire city. He felt he could escape there for a while and not be bothered.

He walked to the end of the hallway and heard the last voice he wanted to hear at the moment.

"Well, well, well, lookie who it is. Good old Paul with all the women and all of the prospects. Hey, I've been meaning to tell you something buddy boy." With that Sullivan was only an arm's length away from Paul and with a quick extension of his arm backhanded Paul across the shoulder. Paul found it peculiar for in all the time they had interacted rarely had Sullivan touched him. Paul could sense the aggression in his coworker and stood up a little straighter. He decided it best to walk past Sullivan and go back to the stairs.

Sullivan reached out and grabbed Paul's shoulder and spun him back around. "Hey, don't be rude, buddy boy. Don't you wanna know what I gotta tell you?"

"No, not particularly. I've got to head downstairs." He took another step and Sullivan grabbed his arm.

"No, you're gonna listen. I realized where I had seen that broad that came in here looking for you the other day. It has been driving me nuts. I knew I knew her from somewhere and then it hit me. I was picturing her naked and like that," Sullivan held his hand up in front of Paul's face, only an inch from his nose and snapped, "I remembered."

"Oh yeah," Paul said it with a disengaged air about him but his curiosity was peaked. He knew what Sullivan was going to say.

"Yeah, down at old Club 21. Your girl spends a lot of time there. Up on the stage, showing it all to everybody, selling it to the highest bidder. Now it all makes sense. I know what you've been doing with your measly paychecks I guess, huh?"

Paul's urge to walk away now waned. It was the first time in any conversation he had ever had with Sullivan that Paul chose to stand facing this pathetic man with his slicked back hair and cigarette breath.

He wished he could deny everything Sullivan said but unfortunately had to accept that it was partly true. "She doesn't sell anything to anybody, Sullivan."

"Ah, I don't think so. She came in here looking for you the other day. Did your check bounce or something. She should know to only accept cold, hard cash from you."

296

Paul looked him in the eye. The petulance Paul felt for Sullivan suddenly became much deeper. "I'm just going to say this one time. Shut up. Don't say it again. You got me?" Paul was direct and loud, stern in his conviction that his coworker should stop talking.

Sullivan shrugged his shoulders with a nonchalant attitude. Paul began walking back to the stairwell. The voice, again, stopped him.

"So just one more question. How much is she? Huh? Payday is coming up. I'll have a few bucks to burn. Will she give me any kind of discount, seeing as how we've got a mutual friend? How much does she charge you? Huh? Surely, she'll give me a better deal since I'll make it worth her while."

28

Paul had only been in one fight his entire life. Third grade. Stanley Barnes. The issue was a trivial one that made Stanley confront him. Paul never really knew or understood what caused the other boy's anger on the playground that day. It seemed to have something to do with a missing pencil and someone saying Paul had told everyone Stanley was the thief. It was not a good day at school for Paul. His dog had died the night before. When the larger boy pushed Paul's shoulder and dared him to fight back Paul reacted without thinking of consequences. He swung and caught Stanley half on the shoulder and half on his chin. Paul could still remember how much more it hurt his knuckles than it hurt Stanley Barnes' face.

The only effect his impetuous aggression had was that it made Stanley Barnes mad. In a second Paul was on the ground with Stanley Barnes on top of him. A few boys gathered around and watched Stanley place his hand on Paul's cheek and push it into the dirt. Ms. Barnes, the third grade reading teacher and Stanley's mother made her son stand up and release the weaker boy from his punishment for swinging at her son. Paul dusted himself off and nothing was ever said about the incident from that day forward. No principal was involved. No detention was given. The only ramification was Stanley Barnes' icy stare when they passed each other from that day until the end of the school year. Over the summer Stanley Barnes moved to Atlanta and Paul never saw him again.

On this day, the day after Oliver Gartrell had been shot, Paul entered the second fracas of his life. Perhaps he could see the anger in Paul's eyes and it was not aggression but fear that made Sullivan reach out and push Paul away from him. He even followed the push with a slight slap to Paul's chin. That was the initiation that Paul needed.

Paul threw a quick punch that landed on Sullivan's cheek bone and nose. Immediate recollection of that day on the playground came back to him as the pain shot through his knuckles and he shook his fingers as if his hand had just been pinched. Sullivan was now coming back at him with a punch of his own. With watered filled eyes Sullivan missed the mark and Paul easily slipped to one side of the oncoming fist. Not wanting to hurt his other hand Paul stepped into Sullivan. He held the smaller man's shoulders and placed his leg behind Sullivan's. With surprising ease he swept Sullivan's legs out from under him and guided him to the ground as more of a restraint maneuver than aggression. With Sullivan now on the ground beneath him, Paul had his attention.

"Never, and I mean never, say anything about any friend of mine again or I'll take you out." In the adrenaline fused moment he could think of nothing better to say. Sullivan did not respond but squirmed trying to shake his shoulders free of Paul's weight.

Blood oozed from Sullivan's nose and the more he jostled his head back and forth the more of a mess he made on the already stained and worn carpet of the fourth floor. Paul considered slapping him one time for good measure but instead decided that amount of blood gave him enough satisfaction. Paul stood up and left Sullivan on the ground. He walked backwards away from the other maintenance man not wanting to turn his back. When he made it to the stairwell door Sullivan sat up and touched his nose and examined the blood covered fingers when he pulled his hand away. Still breathing heavily, Sullivan wrapped his arms around his knees like he had just finished a race.

Paul felt the need to justify his actions before leaving the bleeding man in the hallway but was breathing heavy and used few words. "I did not like what you said. It made me angry. Don't do that again." And with that Paul pushed the stairwell door open and walked up the stairs. He could feel his heart beat in his ears. Pounding. He knew that if ever there was a reason he would be fired this would be the day.

29

The next seconds were a blur to Paul. He found himself in the little enclave of the sixth floor. He had not been there since the day he had met Oliver on the ledge. He stepped out onto the ledge and sat down on the overturned bucket. The bucket seemed familiar but distant as if he was visiting a room he had not been in for years. He watched the sky and the people down below for a few minutes and then closed his eyes. He thought of Oliver and all that had transpired in the last week. He had been to his house, met his wife, seen him in the depths of despair and been called his last friend. Now the man was possibly dying in a hospital a few miles away. Paul closed his eyes and said a little prayer on the mayor's behalf. He remained silent, his eyes closed with the November sun shining down on him. He breathed deeply.

Again, just like the last time he had been in that place, on that bucket, on that ledge, his peace was disturbed by a noise, a voice. He opened his eyes and tried to regain his bearings while wondering what was happening.

He heard the voice again. "Self, get in here."

He was being summoned. He walked slowly, cautiously back to the window and stepped inside. He could see Fletcher at the end of the enclave standing on the marble floor waiting for him.

"My office. Five minutes." That was all he said and disappeared from view. Paul heard the stairwell door open with the thud of someone shoving it. His hiding spot had been discovered or perhaps was known all along. Fletcher it seemed, was always a step ahead of him.

A few minutes later, on the ground floor of City Hall, Paul cautiously approached the half closed door marked 'Maintenance'. He knocked quietly on the door but pushed it open slightly to see Fletcher at his desk.

Fletcher looked up and pulled his reading glasses from his face and dropped them on the book that was open in front of him. "Have a seat."

Paul sat down. He had only been in the office one other time that he could remember, the day he was hired and brought in there to sign some paperwork. Other than that the office in the corner of the maintenance room was nonexistent to Paul. He tried to avoid it. He looked at the various stages of clutter all around him. Some things in the room had been there less than a day, a mop in one corner, a rag on top of the lone filing cabinet in the room. Other things were dusty and old. Pictures on the shelf behind Fletcher had not been wiped off in a long time and Paul could see the faces of a group of soldiers looking out at him through a thick layer of dust.

Fletcher stood up and paced back and forth behind his desk, only able to walk four steps in either direction before turning around and walking the other way. He did not speak but looked at the floor.

Paul decided to speak first. "I'm sorry about what happened. I did not plan on doing anything to him but then he said some things and I....I couldn't ignore them."

Fletcher stopped pacing and looked at him. "What's wrong with you, Self?"

Paul could only shrug his shoulders and show his palms face up expressing confusion and contemplation. He had no answer to the question but yet had so many answers to the question at the same time. None though he assumed that Fletcher wanted to hear. "Um, well, nothing really that I can think of."

"I'll tell you what's wrong with you. You are always focused on the bad. On the faults and missteps and mistakes of your past. You walk around here all the time, late, stressed out I'm going to fire you. Never smiling. Just wandering around. Hiding here and there. Oh I know about all of your little hiding places. I'm not dumb, Self."

Paul shifted his weight in his chair.

"You're sleep walking through life, Self. Wasting it. Are you confused? That's alright. Everybody is confused at times in their life. Regret? Yeah I'm sure you got that in spades. Most of us do. But lazy, man." He shook his finger as he spoke. "That's the part I don't like. That's what drives me crazy. Either do something or don't do something but don't just go halfway looking back over your shoulder all the time. You gotta figure some stuff out, Paul. Figure out what you want to do with your life."

"Yes, sir."

Fletcher squinted at him.

"Listen, I know you've had a tough couple of years. That's why I hired you. I knew you needed a chance, a reason to get up in the morning, something you could accomplish without drinking yourself to death. Getting kicked out of school and going through what you did, it had to be tough. I get that. And you've stopped drinking. I pay attention to that Self. That's why I meet you at the door every time you're late. I want to be near you, smell your breath, know you haven't fallen off and done something stupid. And you haven't. Oh trust me. I would know. I'm proud of you for that."

Paul looked at his lap. He bit his lip and shook his head. Fletcher was the only person that knew his secret. He was the only one that knew because he had to know. When he interviewed, Paul told him the whole story. Getting kicked out of school. The public drunkenness. The arrests. He was open and honest. And he was surprised when Fletcher stood up and shook his hand and told him to come back the next day, ready to work. He had never asked his boss for a reason and was not sure he wanted to know.

Fletcher stared at him for a few seconds sizing him up. "You're like an old buddy of mine back in the Corp. You remind me a lot of him. I almost call you Stephens somedays you remind me so much of him. Even look like him. Stephens, man, smart, funny, decent looking, but lazy. Just plain lazy. And confused. He hated civilian life so he joined the Corp. He hated the Corp and counted the days before he could go back to being a civilian. He couldn't decide what he wanted. Just wandered around. Hiding. Sleep walking. Does that sound familiar?"

Paul nodded.

"My old sergeant used to say him, Stephens, you gotta charge in a hundred percent or stay out a hundred but fifty percent of either will get you killed. And he was right. It will get you killed, Paul. You understand?"

Paul nodded again this time looking up at the ceiling while Fletcher's focus never left Paul's face.

"I'm gonna help you, Paul. I'm going to help you if you let me?"

Paul sat in the maintenance man's office with all of the paraphernalia around him and he could not help but ask the question to break the tension. "Are you going to teach me karate or something? So I can beat up the bullies?"

Fletcher smiled and shook his head. "Man, just like Stephens. Never serious. No, I'm going to do something better for you. I should have done this months ago but today is your lucky day, Paul. You're fired."

Paul's mouth fell open. "But Fletcher, I need this job. I've got to pay rent and buy food."

His boss held up his hand. "Let me finish. January fifteenth, you're fired. You got two months to make some kind of change. Do something that you want to do. Now if you're in school or working on something and want to stay on, okay then. But if you're doing the same thing then that you're doing now," his finger no longer shook at his employee but was pointed down at his desk, "coming in here giving half the effort you need to, showing up late, hiding from me, you're finished. I'll can your ass. And you'll thank me for doing it." He paused before adding, "Someday."

Paul nodded and looked down at his hands, rubbing his fingers together. Thinking. He knew he needed to go back to school and learn something new, find a new direction with his life. Find his purpose.

"My sergeant told Stephens to get out of the Corp. He couldn't handle it. His head wasn't in it. He got out just in time. Going nuts. Like you up on that ledge."

Paul smiled. "I have to confess something. I go up there sometimes and sit for a while where no one can see me."

Fletcher gave him a look of surprise and shock. "No? You don't say."

Paul could tell by the tone he was being sarcastic. "Did you know I would hide up there?"

"Hide up there? Your damn feet stick out over the ledge for God's sake. Of course I knew you were up there. You're lazy, Self. You're just plain lazy. But maybe you can find that thing that will wake you up. Get you moving. Don't waste your life. It's going to be over before you know it. You're chasing this mayor guy all over the place. Probably taking notes. Wanting to be just like him I bet. Don't waste your time. The man tries to make everybody think he's got it all figured out but he's so far gone you don't even know."

Paul considered what Fletcher had said. But he wanted to challenge his boss to make him elaborate. "He has been pretty successful in life it seems, up to this point. But it is unraveling on him. I know that for sure."

"And do you know why? He's not disciplined. He runs off desire. He sees something shiny and takes it. Steals it if he has to. Hedonism will only get you so far."

Despite his confused feelings for Oliver, Paul felt it was his duty to defend him. He was after all possibly dead at that moment. "He has issues for sure but there is some good there too. I went to his house a few days ago. He lives in Hillside Estates. The place is huge. Like an expensive hotel."

Fletcher shrugged his shoulders dismissing the example of the mayor's success. "That's not as impressive as you may think. I could live in a house like that if I wanted to."

Paul shook his head and smiled. "With all due respect sir, Hillside Estates. Mansions. I would say the house is easily a million. At least. I don't think there is any way you or I could live in a house like his."

Fletcher was being challenged. And he loved it. "Why? Why do you say that? Because I'm a black man? A black man who cleans City Hall for a living?"

"No, you being black doesn't have anything to do

with it. But a loan for a house like that...I've been to the bank. I know how hard it is to get a loan for a car. I'll never get a house like that."

Fletcher smiled but with a wry look on his face. "What if I told you I wouldn't need the bank to get a house in Hillside Estates? I could pay cash for it. Guaranteed.   I've got more than enough in investments, savings, equity. No problem. And do you know why? Discipline. Not desire. I can afford a house like that because I don't have a house like that. Does that make sense to you, Self? See, you got a lot to learn. Oliver Gartrell, he can't teach you. He can't teach anybody. This more, more, more attitude is not the way to be. See. He's gone all in but he's holding bad cards. Eventually that catches up to you. Figure out what a good hand is before you start going all in."

Paul sat there in silence. He realized Fletcher may be the smartest guy he had known but he had never realized it before. "You know what, take the rest of the day off. Cool off. Breathe. Beating up on a coworker is about the most energy you've ever expended here I believe. You must be worn out. You have some thinking to do, Self. The next day, the next month, the next year of your life is going to be the most important day, month, year you'll ever have. Trust me on that. Even the next hour of your life could change everything. But not like this." He moved his hand up and down, pointing at Paul. "You have some things you need to figure out. But no more sleep walking. Wake up. WAKE UP!" He screamed it the

308

second time and made Paul jump. That made Fletcher chuckle to himself. "You know what, go check on your boy in the hospital. He probably wants to see you since you two became buddies." He added, "If he's still alive."

As he got to the door Paul turned back to his boss who was once again looking down at the book. "Hey, you didn't even ask me why I got in a fight with Sullivan in the first place?"

Fletcher shook his head and shrugged. "I know why. I've been wanting to knock that guy out since the day I hired him. I'm glad somebody finally took him down." He put his reading glasses back on and looked down to the book that was in front of him. Paul stood there for a few seconds looking at the older man. He appreciated his wisdom. He put his hand on the door frame trying to think of something else to say rather than just a simple 'Thank you.'

Fletcher pointed a finger at him without looking up from his book. "Pull that door closed will you. I need some quiet around here." Paul knew it was Fletcher's way of saying, 'You're welcome.' He left the room and shut the door behind him.

30

Paul stepped onto the shining linoleum with hesitation. Down the hallway the fluorescent lights reflected off of the buffed floor making the end of the hallway feel like death to him, walking into the bright light. Navigating the sterile maze of elevators and hallways knowing some floors were free from communicable diseases but others were not and one wrong turn could put him in the middle of it, he hated the pressure. He liked the filth of City Hall and preferred it over the cleanliness of a hospital. In City Hall filth may disgust people, may let them go away with a bad opinion of their government but it would not, most likely, be fatal. There was no pressure in City Hall like in a hospital.

He stepped off the elevator and knew he was in the right place when he saw Lane across from him looking at a vending machine.

"Hey."

She turned to him calmly, "Oh hey." She turned to face him and the vending machine was forgotten.

Paul pointed down the hallway to no one in particular. "Is he alive?"

Lane looked down the hallway. "He was a few minutes ago but his wife is in there with him now so, who knows."

Lane walked to the bench beside the vending machine and sat down. Paul sat beside her. She pushed hair behind her ear and looked at him. "So how did you find out about it?"

"That old lady in your office, Ms. Connors, is that her name? She is a very mean old lady that just seems to hate the world."

"Oh, you mean my mother?"

Paul was suddenly red faced and stumbling. "Oh, no, I just meant, no that,"

Lane laughed. "I'm just kidding. She's not my mother."

Paul laughed and was relieved. "Oh good."

"She's my sister. I'm sixty three years old."

Paul liked that this girl did not take herself so seriously. Her self- deprecating wit was in line with his own. Maybe it was because of their environment. Hospitals made him uncomfortable and caused him to talk too much but with her he was relaxed and laughing. In all of his other experiences, while standing in hospital rooms with loved ones in the bed surrounded by worried onlookers he was ill at ease.

Paul sat on the bench beside her looking up and down the hallway. From the elevator a purple haired boy emerged. He was dressed in all black as he had been on Sunday night. His hair was shaved off one side of his head now, a look he did not have when Paul had seen him days ago. For a topic of conversation Paul pointed to the boy discreetly and leaned over to Lane's ear. She smelled nice. "Hey, do you know who that is?"

Lane looked at the person. "Yeah, that's my brother." But she smiled.

Paul whispered to her, "That is Oliver's son. Don't you see the resemblance? I saw him at Oliver's house the other night."

"You went to Oliver's house? Was it a sleepover?"

"I was there for a quick visit. It was no big deal. But his son looked so familiar to me. It had been driving me crazy. When I realized how I knew him and told Oliver, that's what changed everything yesterday and got Oliver so excited."

Lane changed the subject away from Oliver and took the opportunity to ask something that obviously had been on her mind. "Speaking of you being crazy, tell me about the ledge. Why were you two really out there?"

Paul smiled. He knew for the first time a person was asking about the events of that day out of concern for him and not for entertainment. Perhaps it was concern for herself too and for that reason while sitting there on a bench in the hospital Paul told the entire story of the ledge to another person. And she believed him.

"That makes sense, I guess, in some kind of weird bizarre world. So this girl that you were going on a date with, what happened to her?"

Paul smiled and realized he had been put on the spot but did not shy away from telling the truth. "We have become friends, I guess. But that's all that we'll ever be I think."

312

The door of the hospital room across from them opened. Sheryl and Derrick walked out. As Derrick walked by them with his head down and looking at his shoes, Sheryl stopped in the doorway and told her husband she would be back soon. She closed the door and saw a person she knew on the bench.

"Hi, Paul. How nice of you to come check on your friend." As always Paul did not know how to take her comment. She was smiling but her tone had a harsh judgement underneath.

"Yes, ma'am. I just wondered how he was and thought I would come over and see if there was anything I could do." Paul clarified. "To help."

"Maybe you can tidy up in there a bit. The bathroom is in need of a little attention." And with that she laughed and patted him on his arm. Paul only smiled. Her unkind remark was her way of telling him the circumstances of their last encounter was to never be spoken of again. Being only a janitor, no one would believe him if he ever did tell anyone that she had come on to him in her vinous state.

"Okay, thank you." Sheryl walked down the hall to where Derrick was waiting at the elevator doors. His purple hair had an illuminated quality under the fluorescent lights and white of the hospital.

Paul turned to Lane. "Are you going in or...?"

"No, no, you go in. I'll stay out here for a while."

He waited for the joke to follow but she refrained from making one.

Paul tapped lightly on the door and let his knuckle

push it open.

"Oliver?"

He walked into the room. Oliver was in his bed looking out of the window.

"Oh look who it is. It's Paul, everybody."

Paul was reminded of Banquet Room Number Two and his mood on that night. Now his melancholy seemed to be the same only with the accompaniment of beeping machines and a smell of disinfectant.

"How are you, Oliver?"

"Never better. Never better. Great to be alive." He held up his hands to prove his convivial state but dropped his hands quickly onto the many blankets that covered him knowing it was pointless to fake it. "Don't this beat all? I mean, don't it? Shot. In my own damn driveway."

Paul made conversation. "Any idea who did it or why?"

Oliver tossed his hand in the air to dismiss the question but said, "Ah, it doesn't really matter who it may have been. My list of enemies is far longer than my list of friends these days. I know that. I doubt anybody will ever be able to figure out who did it. I'm alive and I guess that's all that matters, huh?"

Oliver turned his head and continued looking at the window.

"Look at me, Paul. Look at me." Oliver was emotional. His previous comment about feeling alive was no longer who he was. "What is wrong with me?"

Oliver shook his head and was looking at his feet covered with the many blankets. He was looking so intently at the foot of the bed Paul looked at his feet also.

"You know what Paul, I was thinking about it today. I've never been happy. Ever. Not in my entire life. But really, what is that? What does that even mean? Me, all my rich friends, with our cars, our houses, our influence, but what is it for, Paul? What?"

Paul stood motionless watching Oliver and wondering where this thought was going to go.

"It's all been wasted time. Wasted. I'm so....stupid."

Paul tried to console the patient. "Listen, you've had a traumatic experience. You're hooked up on all of these machines, meds running through you. You are not stupid."

"No, don't try to make me feel better, Paul. Come on. Let me have it. You're weak that way, Paul. Say what you think. Tell me. Don't worry about repercussions."

Typical Oliver. In Paul's attempt to console him he is criticized instead. Paul decided to be firm with him despite his current condition. "Okay, well, I stand by it. You're not stupid. But you are the dumbest person I've ever met. Ever. In my whole life. Very dumb. You make decisions that an orangutan wouldn't make."

"Fair enough, Paul. Fair enough. You're right. I've made some foolish decisions in my life. I think about what I did as mayor, stealing from the city. I had to know I was going to get caught. But I did it anyway. And as a husband. More bad decisions. Fatherhood. My God, I've been so miserable."

Paul decided to be positive. "I saw your wife in the hallway. It is good to see her here. I guess this may be the beginning of reconciliation."

Oliver looked at Paul. "I don't know. I can hope but I wouldn't forgive me. Why should she? But this whole ordeal, it's changed me. I," again he drifted off and looked back to the window. After a long pause he looked at Paul. His eyes were moist. Quickly Oliver wiped the back of his wrist against both eyes and choked on his words. "I was laying there in my driveway last night, bleeding. The pain, it was intense, it felt like fire all over my body and there was Sheryl. I haven't told anybody else this, Paul. But she leaned down next to me. Hysterical. And when she got up, when she went to call an ambulance she stopped in front of me. Her clothes, they were red. Covered in my blood." His eyes narrowed, visualizing the scene, remembering. He looked at Paul again this time with his eyes narrowed to slits, a tear fell to his cheek that went ignored. "And Paul, when I saw my blood on her clothes, I knew," his voice became weak and his speech mumbled, Paul leaned in to make sure he would hear what Oliver said, "I knew right then that I would never cheat on that woman again. Never. Not as long as I live. I don't know if she is even going to take me back but if she does, as God is my witness, I'll be faithful until I die."

Oliver again turned to the window. His face was moist. He did not bother to wipe his eyes with his hand. He grimaced in pain as he shifted his weight in the bed. "Paul, I think I need some rest. People have been in and out all day and I need to rest."

"Oliver, are you okay?"

"I'll be fine. I just," again he looked like pain was consuming him, "need some time. I've got all of these drugs pumping through me. They make me numb. And I itch. Like crazy. All of these blankets on me. I'm in bad shape, Paul. I can't even move my toes around cause of all these drugs and blankets. My leg is itching like crazy but they won't let me scratch it. Treating me like I'm a crazy person, strapped down to the bed like this."

Paul had not realized it before but a strap went across Oliver's chest that prevented him from leaning forward. His hands were free to touch his face but without being able to pull himself up from the bed that was all he could do. He could not help but wonder why. And the blankets. There had to have been five blankets piled up on the man's legs.

"Have they told you what is wrong? Something with your legs?"

Oliver moved his hand to his hair. "They say I lost a lot of blood. My legs, something is wrong with them. I'll need rehab they told me. Something about a cane. Can you see me with a cane, Paul? I don't think so."

Paul tried his best to remain positive. "There's nothing wrong with a cane. It could give you a distinguished look. Like Churchill."

Oliver remained solemn and spoke softly. "I guess I could be worse. I could have ended up in a wheelchair."

Paul shrugged his shoulders. "Or a casket."

Oliver nodded considering the comment. "Yeah. I guess so."

Paul walked to the door and turned the knob slowly, quietly. The bright light from the hallway charged into the room and landed on Oliver's face. Paul stepped quickly through the door but was stopped by Oliver's voice.

"Paul," Oliver paused, thinking, "thank you. Thanks, for whatever, and all that."

Paul smiled again. "Sure. Thank you too. It's been an unusual week. The craziest of my life and that's because of you. I'll come back sometime in the next day or two and check on you."

He closed the door behind him and turned. There she was. A magazine sat on her lap but Lane was looking up at him as he stepped into the hallway.

Thoughts were running through Paul's mind. He focused on Lane. "Are you going to hang out here all day?"

Lane looked at an imaginary clock on the wall. "Just until noon. Then I'm going back and someone else is coming up here. I don't know why I'm even here really but I don't mind."

Paul paused. He thought. Too much thinking.

"Well, have fun here in germ central."

Lane looked at him with a surprised expression. "What? This place is immaculate. I've seen a guy with a mop go by six times already. Have you seen City Hall? That place is disgusting. Nobody cleans that place." She looked down and flipped the page of the magazine with a flick of her wrist making the paper snap for emphasis on what she said.

Paul acted as if he was offended but then saw her smile and he laughed. "Okay, I'll see you around, okay?"

Lane was looking back at her magazine and flipped the next page loudly. "Yep, see ya."

Paul turned and walked to the elevator. He hit the button and waited.

He looked back down the hallway in Lane's direction. He did not want to leave but felt he should. He looked down to the other end of the hallway and something held his attention. Sheryl was standing in front of the window with her arms crossed. She was alone. Her son must have found his escape from the prison of the hospital waiting rooms and would return only when forced Paul assumed.

The elevator door opened but Paul did not pass over the threshold. Instead he walked toward the window, toward the woman in distress.

He walked up to her slowly and considered what he should say to not startle her. Her arms were crossed in front of her, her thumb was at her mouth, her teeth pinching the nail.

"Hey." The woman turned around but did not move her arms. Either she was not surprised to see him approach her or did not care. She seemed as if he had just returned from the bathroom.

Paul bit his lip before speaking. "So, I guess he's going to make it. I couldn't believe the news when I got to work today. It's just so," he searched for the word, "shocking."

In her same even keel tone she spoke with at dinner a few days before she said only, "Is it? Is it really shocking? The man has been messed up with the wrong people for years now. The whole mayor thing has completely ruined him. It all went to his head and he's tried to be something he's not."

"So I guess this is kind of a wakeup call to him then. He just told me he's changed. He said that this...incident has given him perspective." Paul knew Oliver had not said those words but felt it was okay to paraphrase a man heavily medicated.

"Our life together has been hard, Paul. It has been so much searching and wishing and trying to find something that is just not there. For as long as I can remember we both have always had this attitude of, 'Okay, now it is going to be better. Now we'll find that thing we need. We'll find our peace. Happiness. But it has never been there. We just keep moving, thinking joy is just ahead. But it's not." She turned back to the window and put her palms together in front of her rubbing them together. "It just gets worse."

"When he recovers from this there is nothing

stopping you two from being better. I know he loves you. He told me he does. And you, so distraught the other night, worried about him. You love him. So build on that. You can't worry about what may go wrong."

Sheryl closed her eyes for several seconds before speaking but she did not acknowledge Paul's optimism. "Did he tell you about his leg?"

"He said the doctors were worried that he may need rehab. But that's okay. Could be worse."

"They're talking about amputation. His left leg. Something about blood loss and clots and tissue damage. I don't understand it all. But if he takes a turn for the worse that is likely to happen. He doesn't know it yet. Just me. And you."

Paul put his hand to his mouth trying to process the news quickly to respond in the best way possible. "Oh no, that's, that's not good."

Paul regretted the lack of substance in what he said.

"No, no it's not good at all." She inhaled deeply and raised her shoulders before blowing out a calming breath. "But we'll get through it, I suppose. Somehow."

"Yes, you will. Let me know if there is anything I can do." He thought to hug her but decided against it when she nodded in silence and turned back to the window and crossed her arms again.

Paul walked back to the elevator trying to comprehend what he had heard. He pushed the button again and waited.

When he heard the ding that the elevator had arrived he turned and walked back down the hallway. "Come on, Paul." He clenched his fists as he walked. "No more sleepwalking."

He approached the bench and Lane still looked down not knowing he was there. "Hey," she looked up as Paul sat down beside her and spoke quickly. "Do you want to go out sometime? Go eat or whatever."

Lane leaned back in her chair as if to consider the offer and fell back into her sarcastic wit. "Ooooh, whatever. I like the sound of that. Yes. I'll put 'whatever' right here in my calendar." She picked up the bag and sat it next to her on the bench. From it she pulled a small scrap piece of paper and wrote her phone number. Paul nodded his acknowledgement and accepted the paper, a gum wrapper. He leaned back on the bench and put the wrapper in his pocket.

"So, you're staying here another hour or so, huh?"

Lane nodded. "Yeah, why not?"

"I'll wait with you, if that's okay. Watch some people go by." The news of Oliver was weighing heavily on his mind and he did not want to be alone. He needed to talk to someone about anything and felt fortunate to be sitting there with her.

Lane closed her magazine and put it down. "Okay. So tell me Paul Self, where are you from? Where are you going?"

Paul was caught off guard and felt put on the spot. Lane laughed and reached out and put her hand on his shoulder. "Relax. I'm messing with you. You wrote that in your notebook. And you went on for a couple of pages I might add. But I am curious. Who you are? What makes you tick?"

And for an hour they talked. And they laughed. Paul's heavy heart subsided. He embraced the joy of his company.   It was the best afternoon Paul remembered having in a long time and certainly the best he had ever had in a hospital.

31

Paul walked to his apartment door in the late afternoon. The air had gotten cold again as the warm front that had begun the mild winter was now gone. The afternoon felt more like a November in Georgia should. He looked down the breezeway in the direction of Holly's door.

She had asked him for help the day before but in his back and forth way, going from confidence to self-doubt he wondered now if her request for help had been made in her weakened state. She did not need his help. Surely, she had friends whose company she desired more than her strange next door neighbor. Or maybe not. Paul thought of Oliver's loneliness. The mayor of the city calling him his only friend.

As Paul walked up to his apartment door to unlock it he took his time and looked in her direction again hoping to see the door of Apartment 7 open. He would run into her on happenstance. All Paul had spent his life doing was linger and hope while considering that which may go wrong. He made the other person's opinion more important than his own. That, he had come to realize, was the biggest difference in who he and Oliver was. But in the past days Paul had grown. With Lane on his mind he was excited and invigorated.

He walked into his apartment and looked at the wall

separating his apartment from Holly while Daisy sat on the bed staring up at him in her usual complacent way. He pulled the contents of his pockets from his jacket and pants and dropped them on the table. There was the thing that gave him hope and made him smile. The gum wrapper with Lane's phone number sat among the change and keys he had placed on the table. Paul picked up the paper and stared at the number written in the girl's handwriting. She made her sixes in an odd way he thought. Odd but cute.

He stared at the phone. He spoke to Daisy. "Oliver has never cared what people think of him. He does what he wants. Period. If people like him for it great. If they judge him negatively, he convinces himself that the opinion is wrong or at least irrelevant. But he always does what he wants!" Paul said the last part with a raised voice loud enough to garner Daisy's attention. Daisy raised her head and looked at him before laying back gently on her paws. Paul looked at the phone and then at the door.

"I will call her but first I'm going to go check on Holly." Daisy licked her paw and rubbed her head. That was not the answer Paul needed.

He pulled back on the coat he had just taken off and walked quickly to his door and closed it behind him.

He walked along the breezeway with fast, long strides to Holly's door and stood before it. He raised his hand, took a breath and knocked on the door. There was no response but the cold, steel door on the back of his knuckles stung and he perhaps had not knocked loudly enough. He looked in the direction of his apartment door and contemplated returning to the comfort of his space. She had likely not heard his knock. He could retreat and she would never know. No. No more sleep walking. He knocked one more time, louder and called her name.

"It's open." He heard the muffled response from the other side of the door and found the statement to be true when he turned the knob and pushed the door into her apartment.

Her apartment was much darker than his with only a single lamp on in the back, near the kitchen. He closed the door behind him to keep the cold air from entering. Without the outside light his eyes had to adjust to the dark interior of the room. The physical space was the mirror image of his own with the kitchenette on the opposite side and the built in shelves to his left. The apartment smelled of ointment and alcohol.

"Holly? Are you here?" A stupid question he regretted but said only to have something to say while his eyes came into focus.

"I'm here." He saw her in the corner of the room at a chair next to the table. Her elbows were on the table and her head was in her hands with her fingers spread through her hair. A beer bottle stood in front of her.

"Are you okay?" Paul took a step into the apartment alarmed somewhat by her appearance. As he walked closer to her he saw that her foot in its cast was on the chair facing her. She lifted her head and moved her hands to the table.

"Oh yeah, I'm great. Fantastic. How are you?" Paul noted the sarcasm. He thought of Oliver earlier that day in the hospital. He waited to get more evidence of her demeanor.

"I uh, just wanted to come see how you are, with the foot and all or leg or knee. Whatever it is." The dark, musty room with the distinct odor had him breathing in a shallow way and swallowing hard. He stumbled to find words.

"Oh, yeah, I'm good. Yeah, just hanging out. Passing the time."

Paul shifted his weight. "Oh, okay then. I just thought I would check. And um, tell you that if you need anything to let me know if you need anything okay." He was talking the way she looked. Incoherent and babbling.

Holly said nothing but looked at the wall in front of her. She put her hands at the base of her beer and spun the bottle around carelessly, mindlessly. Paul was stuck, halfway in her apartment unsure whether to walk to the door or to the table.

He spoke from where he was. "I guess you heard about Oliver."

She did not move her gaze from the base of her beer bottle but said in a playful but forced way, "I didn't have anything to do with it. I swear. I've got my alibi right here." She nodded to her foot.

"Oh, okay then. I assumed you were innocent. If he had been maimed by a golf club then, you know I would have had to go to the police." His attempt to make her laugh failed. She was lost again in thought.

"I loved him, Paul. I really did." He saw this as an invitation to sit down and he did so on the corner of the bed nearest the table. She shrugged as she said it again. He had found himself in yet another awkward situation with an inebriated woman regarding Oliver.

"But," Paul paused to show that his question was to be sincere and that he did not know the answer. "Was there very much to love? Is there very much to love?" He shrugged to emphasize his innocent perspective of the situation but did not know if she would even see him in the dim room. "He's not a great person. He may have great wealth. He may have a great house, a great car. He may even have a great personality, one that draws people in, gets people to vote for him but," he paused again before repeating his question, "is there very much to love?" He waited in the silence of the darkened room and finally continued. "He's like a lure. You know, when you go fishing?" Paul raised his voice to ask the question and wondered if she would follow what he said but knew it was too late to stop with the analogy. "He looks like the thing we want, as a politician, a boyfriend, a contact, a friend, but how happy are the people who bite. He's got hooks and trust me, I've learned, he is in it for him. He doesn't care a thing about the people he catches." He thought of Oliver's soul searching in the hospital and felt bad saying what he did but Paul felt that judgment was warranted with the selfishness Oliver had shown.

Holly looked Paul in the eye, considering what he had said. "He cared about me. I believe he did. On some level. Maybe not the level I thought but he cared about me, I'm sure of it. He cared about what he gave to me." She looked at the wilted, dried flowers around her.

"And not what he got from you?" Paul was testing her mind and feelings. "See it has occurred to me, recently, that there are some people in our lives who give to us and there are other people who primarily take from us. If you had to say which one Oliver is what would you choose? Which of those two things is he?" He did not want to be too forward because of her emotional state and the fact he was in her apartment. He did not have the right to do that but he hoped he could make her see.

"In the beginning he gave. He brought me flowers," Holly raised her arm and Paul looked around the apartment for the first time. It was as unkempt like his but he saw the dead flowers lining the bookshelf and knew she had him beat in that regard. He realized in that moment that he had imagined her apartment to be flowers and sunlight and pink and pretty in all those times he thought about her right next door. His apartment was cluttered but hers in his mind was something else. Something perfect and pure. Now the reality faced him. She was not perfect as he had thought. She was a mess. Her apartment proved that. It was as discombobulated as her mind. Being in love with Oliver and the unsanitary condition of her living space were one in the same, he thought. For some odd reason he had the urge to begin cleaning the apartment next door though he rarely cleaned his own.

Paul turned his attention from her dresser and back to the conversation. "You know I spoke to him earlier today. At the hospital. Shot in his own driveway. That can change a person. He seemed different. Not just being in a hospital gown, laid up in bed but different emotionally, physically. I think his life may be very different after what happened." Paul alluded to Oliver's leg but left it at that giving Holly the chance to ask for more details.

Holly did not say anything but continued spinning her beer in circles on the table in front of her. Paul continued, "I guess he is back with his wife now. It seems that way at least, for now. That, in a way, is a good thing, right?"

Holly looked away from him. "That crazy woman. Oliver was miserable with her. Just miserable. He was not a happy person when I met him."

Paul shrugged. He did not want to offend Holly but she had to hear the truth. "He didn't seem very happy these last few days that I've known him either. He has issues. More issues than anybody I've met in a long time."

Holly looked at him again. "We all do. Oliver just expresses his more than others when he finds someone who will listen. It's got to be tough, being in the public eye. Being in charge of everything. It's a tough life. But I helped him with that. I would always help him. He needed me." She looked down at the table. "Or I thought he did." She continued to spin the bottle on the table. "I'm in love with him, Paul. That's all it is."

"Are you? Are you in love with him?" She looked at him, offended. "Are you in love with him or," Paul paused to find the words, "or do you just not want him to be happy with someone else?" Holly looked angry. She had leaned forward as they spoke but now she fell back in her chair. She looked at the wall and Paul knew she was hurt by the comment. "Because, if you love him, if you really love him you would be happy if he was happy. Whether with you or with her or with anyone. If you love him, you would want the best for him. And, I know it's hard to admit it or see it or want it, but his wife is the best person for him."

Holly considered what he said. She looked down for a long time at her foot in its big cast. Then, in a swift movement that made Paul jump slightly, she swung her foot down from the chair and began to stand up. "Do you want anything? Beer, water, whatever food I have?"

Paul raised his hand and shook his head. "No, but you stay there. I'll get you anything you want." He walked toward the refrigerator and she forced herself up placing her weight on the table and stopped him.

"No, I'm good. I just, I just hate this cast. I hate it." She fell into the table and her arms held her up. Tears came. "This damn cast, I hate it. It's unfair." She sobbed for only a few seconds and then used her arm to wipe her nose and stand up straight again.

Paul knew she was not talking about her foot.

"Does it hurt?"

Holly held up a bottle of pills that had been sitting near the center of the table. "Not with these. With these the pain goes away."

"How many of those do you take?" Paul realized he had said it with an accusatory tone. It made him nervous seeing Holly celebrate the fact she had pills.

Holly looked at the bottle and squinted in the dimmed light. "I don't know. As many as I want I guess."

Paul took the opportunity to walk towards her and held her elbow as she fell back into her chair. Touching her he could tell she was shaking, not drastically, not enough to even see in the dim light but in his hand her elbow shivered just slightly in an unnatural way. He felt the tremors through her body that registered as only a small but consistent movement. With those he was familiar.

Holly pushed her hair out of her face. "Do you think they'll always be together? One of those miserable marriages that go on until they die."

"She was at the hospital with him. I don't think he's in the best shape right now and he needs her. But long term, I don't know. He has a lot of recovering to do."

Holly nodded and drank from the beer bottle. "Yeah, we all do then I guess, huh?"

"Now apparently that woman, the new mayor, she's

in some kind of trouble. She may be out before she ever gets in. Oliver may end up being mayor again."

Holly shrugged again. "Not surprised." Paul realized in all of their conversations and at the dinner that night, Holly never cared one bit about Oliver's political career.

Paul turned the conversation back to Oliver's marriage. "So whether they will always be together. Yeah, I think so. I really do. I know it is hard to accept but they must love each other."

"No, that's crap. She may love him, I'm sure she does, but him? No, no way. The stuff we did in this apartment, the phone calls, the trips we took out of town, no, he was a man in prison just looking for an escape. Nobody goes back to the prison willingly."

"But there may be another side to him, one that you have never been shown. The side of him that married her, that had a child with her. He was not going to show that to you." Paul thought back to the conversation on the ledge and how distraught Oliver was at the thought of his wife cheating on him. "I think you have to step back, move on, and let what happens between them happen."

Holly stood and hobbled to the kitchen. The grimace with each painful step made her look angry and old. She opened the refrigerator and closed it without removing anything. She put her hands on the countertop and leaned into it. She was caged and restless.

"You can do better, Holly. You can find a better

situation. You said it yourself in the cafeteria. You have to move on from this. Go be that teacher or whatever it is you want to be. But don't just wallow in misery. You have to move on."

The advice he gave her struck him as ironic. He was telling her what Fletcher had told him. He watched her. Her back was to him as she cried. Paul had the courage to go toward her and put his arms around her. "I'm sorry. I'm sorry for everything and how it all happened. But you are going to be okay." She accepted his embrace and put her face on his shoulder. "You've got a friend next door if you need anything. You're going to be fine."

She backed away from him and pushed her hair out of her face. "You're beautiful and smart. You can have anything you want. You just have to figure out what that is." She nodded. Her nose had mucus now running from it and she used her sleeve to wipe it away. From that one movement alone, he knew she would never have any feelings for him other than that of a friend. And he was fine with that.

"Ha, beautiful and smart? You sound like Oliver now. Is this when you take off my shirt?" Holly looked at him as he took a step back. She had embarrassed him. "Sorry. I know you're not like that." She hobbled to the nearest chair and placed her hands on the kitchen table. She cocked her head to one side and studied him. "Why aren't you like that? I'm curious."

Paul was uncomfortable by the question. He had never been asked that before. "I, uh, I'm just not. I

334

mean I think about things but I don't know if I should or if the other person," he was stumbling now.

Holly nodded. "And you know what, that makes you a good guy. But sometimes you gotta not worry about what the other person thinks or wants. What do you want? Go for that. And hey, if it comes back and bites you, like it has me, you live and learn. But maybe sometimes, good things come from it. Maybe we're both due for some good."

Paul smiled and nodded. Without meaning to she had given him the final injection of motivation he needed. Holly sipped the beer bottle that was on the table.

He made the decision to open up to her. "I met somebody yesterday. I think I'm going to call her."

Holly seemed interested in the news. "Oh, well see, good things are happening for one of us already."

Paul appreciated the comment. "And you know what, you're the reason. You've given me confidence these past few days. You really have. Getting to know you, being your friend. It has helped me. Right now you don't see it but you're capable of great things, Holly. You really are."

He walked backwards to the door but knew when he left it would not be the last time he would see the inside of her apartment. "Hey, if you need anything let me know, okay. I'm right next door. Apartment 8. Right there." He pointed to the wall being foolish in an attempt to make her smile. He opened the door and began to walk outside. "You're going to be okay, Holly.

Get some rest."

Holly nodded. She stopped him again. "Hey, Paul, could you do me a favor?"

"Sure, anything."

Holly picked up the bottle of pills sitting on the table. With surprising dexterity she threw them across the apartment. Paul held up his hand to catch them but misjudged the trajectory and they whizzed by his hand and smacked into the wall behind him.

"Oh, my bad. Catching is not my forte." This time Holly laughed and he could hear her as he leaned over to pick up the bottle of pills. He would swear he had missed the pill bottle on purpose for that reason if asked but he would be lying.

"We'll have to work on that. But for now I was wondering, could you hold on to those for me? Don't let me take too many of them or anything. Sometimes I lose track."

Paul looked at the pills and understood what she was asking. "Sure. I can do that. Just bang on the wall or something and I'll come over."

"Yeah, or just come over every couple of hours and check on me."

Paul nodded. "I'll do it." He opened the door and stepped out onto the breezeway.

Holly called out to him from her dark corner, "And go call that girl." Paul smiled as he closed the door. He walked back to his apartment door twenty feet away looking at the pills. He looked back at her door before opening his. He knew in a little while he would go back and check on her but in that moment he was anxious to get back to his apartment.

He opened the unlocked door. Daisy was still on the bed. "Okay girl, this is it. Why not, right?"

Paul walked to the table and picked up the slip of paper with the cute sixes on it. He reached for his phone and dialed without hesitation.

Daisy watched him walk back and forth from his door to his bathroom while the phone rang. On the fifth ring there was an answer and a familiar voice.

"Hey, hey, Lane? Hey, it's Paul. Paul Self. Yeah, I met you yesterday. I talked to you at the hospital today...for an hour straight. Yeah, yeah, that's right, that Paul." He smiled as he played along.

He sat down on the edge of his bed to talk. "I'm good. I'm very good. How are you?"

As he talked, Daisy watched him but soon lost interest and closed her eyes. Paul did not notice as he was absorbed in the conversation. Paul was happy.

About the Author

W. Brunson Snipes lives near Athens, Georgia, with his wife and three children. He graduated from the University of Georgia and in the years since has spent his days working on spreadsheets and talking to customers while in his spare time thinking of stories and writing them down. This is his first book.

Made in the USA
Columbia, SC
18 May 2019